The Intern

Sometimes the best medicine is love

Peter Hogenkamp

Relax. Read. Repeat.

THE INTERN
By Peter Hogenkamp
Published by TouchPoint Press
Brookland, AR 72417
www.touchpointpress.com

ISBN-13: 978-1-946920-66-9

Editor: Kimberly Coghlan
Cover Design: Colbie Myles
Cover illustration: Peter Huntoon

Visit the author's website at https://www.peterhogenkampbooks.com/

First Edition

Printed in the United States of America.

For Lisa
And in loving memory of Bill Hogenkamp

Without love, our earth is a tomb.

—Robert Browning

Unless you love someone, nothing else makes any sense.

—E.E. Cummings

Chapter One

Maggie Johnson pushed open the back door of the hospital and trudged across the empty parking lot. Our Lady of Perpetual Mercy Hospital stood on the corner of 112th and 2nd for over one hundred years, and yet, everyone referred to the hospital as Our Lady of the Golden Arches ever since the McDonald's restaurant was built next to it in 1974. And that included the few remaining Sisters of Perpetual Mercy who ran the place, all the residents of the local neighborhood—which New Yorkers referred to as *El Barrio*—and Roger Johnson, Maggie's father, who'd done his own internship here in the early eighties. (That Maggie might have chosen a different hospital for her internship had been out of the question since the time her father bought her a toy doctor's kit for her third birthday.)

She cut through the spruce trees some previous administrator had planted in a failed attempt to shed the hospital's moniker and passed inside the restaurant. In the eight months of her internship at Our Lady of the Golden Arches, she'd frequented McDonald's every day and had never ordered anything other than black coffee.

"You again?"

"'Fraid so."

The tall, almost gaunt woman set two cups of coffee on the counter. "I saw you coming."

"Thanks, Cindy."

Cindy nodded her head in acknowledgement. "You want something to eat?"

Maggie shook her head. "No, thanks."

"You ain't some kind of anorexic, are you?"

"If you're taking a history on me, Cindy, your bedside manner could use a little work."

"This ain't no hospital, and I ain't no doctor, Sweetheart, so I could care less about my bedside manner."

"In that case, isn't that the pot calling the kettle black."

Cindy splayed her arms and spun around, causing her black apron to flutter. "What's the matter with me? You sayin' I'm too thin?"

Maggie took a sip of her coffee. "No, not at all. I think you look good."

"Is this some kind of half-assed come on, Sweetie? Because I don't go that way, no matter what bullshit my ex keeps spreading around."

Maggie moved to the back of the restaurant and sat down at her usual table, in between the twosome of elderly gentleman playing dominos and the larger than life statue of Ronald McDonald someone had stashed in the far corner. At half past seven, exactly on time, her father strode in through the side door. He gave her a peck on the cheek as he sat down across from her and accepted the coffee she handed him.

"Ready for your big night?" he asked.

She shrugged and they just sat there, listening to the click of dominos and the hum of traffic on 2nd Avenue.

"How was your case?" Maggie asked.

Although Roger Johnson did the bulk of his surgery at Columbia/Presbyterian, the hospital where he was Chief of Orthopedic Surgery, he still did cases at Golden Arches on a weekly basis. He started into a detailed description of the total hip arthroplasty he'd just finished with such enthusiasm it would be easy to assume this was the first hip he'd ever replaced, not the two-thousandth.

"How's Mom?"

Interrupting Roger Johnson was a risky proposition; do it wrong, and you faced the unwelcome prospect of him starting over, from the very beginning.

"Mom?" he asked.

"You know, the woman you've been married to for thirty years?"

"Oh, she's good, I guess."

"You guess?"

"We've both been so busy lately, our paths have barely crossed."

This was 'dadspeak,' of which Maggie was an accomplished interpreter. In plain English, this meant that *he* had been busy lately—as always—and that he had no idea what his wife had been doing.

"What's Mom been up to?"

"Oh, you know, Mom things…"

Mary Johnson had been a wonderful mother to Maggie and her brothers and sister—for which Maggie was devoted to her—but with the youngest of her four children gone to preparatory school, she'd been struggling of late to fill her time. She'd dabbled at oil painting, joined a tennis team, and taken up cross-word puzzles, but nothing seemed to be filling the void left by her children's absence.

"You should've gone straight home after your case," Maggie told him.

"And miss a date with my best girl?" He winked at Maggie. "Not a chance. Besides, I wanted to show you some cool films."

He extracted a tablet from the side pocket of his tweed blazer and sat next to her on the bench. The last thing she wanted to do after a long day on the Pediatric Ward and before a long night of call was to look at X-rays, but she wasn't going to disappoint her father.

"See that little crack in the cortex there?" He was pointing to a long bone of some kind. She supposed it was the femur. "The radiologist at the hospital missed it, but it was pretty easy to see on our new high-resolution viewing software."

He'd just spent hundreds of thousands of dollars to update the X-ray equipment at Gotham Orthopedics, the medical practice he'd founded twenty years ago, in anticipation of Maggie taking over the radiologic duties there when she finished her residency. The fact that Maggie had never really shown any interest in this plan had never seemed to lessen his enthusiasm for it.

"Check out this awesome Bone Scan!" A cartoon of a skeleton appeared on the screen. "Fifteen-year-old boy complaining of leg pain." He pointed to the skeleton's knee, which glowed dark in contrast to the whitish hue of the bones. "See how the knee lights up?"

It seemed like an odd term to use in this circumstance, but she knew better than to point that out—not unless she wanted a fifteen-minute dissertation on the history of medical jargon, one of his favorite topics.

"Look at the corresponding plain films." Another long bone popped up. "See this big goomba here?"

She nodded, as thoughts of all the work she had to do danced like sugarplums in her head.

"Know what it is?" he asked.

It was an obvious osteosarcoma, a malignant tumor found most commonly in young men. Maggie looked at the upper right corner of the screen. The osteosarcoma belonged to David Barnard. As her father stared at the tablet, Maggie wondered who David Barnard was and how he was feeling about having an aggressive cancer in his leg.

"It's an osteosarcoma, right? You knew that, didn't you?"

She nodded.

"See this crack. This is where a fracture..."

He droned on, but she wasn't paying attention. She had endured enough of his lectures to know how to not listen without being caught. A smile here and a knowing nod there and it would be over before too long. He finished his presentation and stowed the tablet back in his jacket, a grey Harris Tweed that was indistinguishable from any of the two-dozen others in his closet.

"I'm glad you came in though, Dad... I want to talk to you about something."

"What's that?"

"I'm thinking about changing to pediatrics."

"Changing what, dear?"

"My residency."

He sipped his coffee and set it down on the table. "You're thinking about changing your residency to pediatrics... Seriously?"

"I talked to Dr. Clarke. She's the pediatrics residency director at Golden Arches."

"I know who she is." He said the word *she* without inflection, but the lightning strike in his deep blue eyes betrayed his dislike of her. "What did she say?"

"There's an opening." He accepted this comment without response other than the narrowing of his bushy eyebrows, so she continued. "One of the pediatric interns is pregnant, and she wants to take a year off. Dr. Clarke said I could have the spot."

"Let me get this straight. You want to swap your residency in radiology at Colombia/Presbyterian for a pediatrics residency at a hospital named after a McDonald's restaurant?"

Ronald McDonald smiled broadly despite Dr. Johnson's derisive comment about his franchise.

"I said I was thinking about it," Maggie said.

"A radiologist makes three times as much as a pediatrician. You realize that, don't you?"

"Money isn't everything, Dad."

"That's easy to say when I'm paying your rent."

"I didn't ask you to do that."

"Did you think I want my daughter living in some rat-infested shack in *El Barrio?*"

"No, I don't. And I appreciate your generosity, but..."

"Promise me you won't make any quick decisions, Maggie."

"There are two months left in my transitional internship, both electives. I'm supposed to be spending them in radiology to get prepared for my residency, but if I change them to pediatrics, I can start catching up with the other pediatric residents."

Roger Johnson went quiet for a minute, but Maggie could hear the conversation underneath his thick crop of salt and pepper hair, the argument between the Roger Johnson that loved his daughter and the Roger Johnson that wanted her to follow the blueprint for her future, of which he was the chief architect.

"But you haven't had any radiology rotations yet," he said. "How can you switch away from radiology if you haven't even given it a chance?"

It was a good point; she hadn't had any radiology rotations yet, although the fact that she had deferred all work in radiology to the end of her internship spoke volumes about her interest in the discipline.

"No, that doesn't make any sense. You have to at least give radiology a try," he said with finality.

Her head nodded of its own accord. She tried to keep it still, but she could feel it move up and down despite her efforts.

"Let's do this. Keep the schedule as it stands, and we'll discuss this again in July," her dad said with a smile. "Sound good?"

July would be too late, and she was confident he would never broach the subject again, but she mumbled her agreement anyway.

"That's my girl."

He stood up, pecked her on the top of the head before she could think of a rebuttal, and scurried out the door, a flash of tweed in the evening twilight.

Chapter Two

Maggie awoke at midnight with a squeezing pressure in her chest; if someone had ever asked her to describe the feeling—no one ever had, and she'd never brought it up to anyone—she would say it felt like someone was smothering her with a wool blanket, stuffing it deep into her throat to staunch the flow of air. She sat up in bed, folded her legs underneath her, and drew in a series of long breaths from her diaphragm. After a while, air returned to her lungs, and the pounding of her heart subsided, but she remained anxious and unsettled. Her books were lying on the desk next to the bed, and she flipped the lights on and opened the first volume, *The Sanford Guide to Antibiotic Therapy.*

Having read it before, she knew that doxycycline was first-line treatment for Lyme disease, babesiosis was best managed by a synergistic combination of atavaquone and azithromycin, and *Plasmodium falciparum*—the parasite that caused malaria—was generally resistant to quinine. The combination of small font, long names with too many vowels and the dry subject material usually carried her off to sleep, but not this time.

She placed *Sanford* back on the desk in its usual position next to the crack in the laminate some unknown intern had made—so the story went—by slamming her fist repeatedly against the desk. It had seemed an unlikely story when she first heard it, but that had been before the

Emergency Department had called her six times in one hour on her first night of pediatrics call. Awake, she folded her hands on her lap and listened to the tinkling of the antiquated air-con system, the hum of the fluorescent lighting, and the tread of footsteps as the security guard made his rounds.

Her plastic clogs beckoned to her from their customary spot on either side of the longitudinal crack in the floor tiles; she swung her long legs off the bed and inserted her feet. The white coat her father had used when he was an intern hung from the hook on the door; she slipped it on and went out. She eyeballed the kidney infection in Room 2 and the appendectomy in Room 4 as she walked past, noting that both patients were resting comfortably. Passing Room 6, she was pleased to hear nothing other than the hiss of oxygen, indicating that the wheezer she had admitted yesterday was responding to the treatments she had ordered.

Room 12 was at the west end of the Pediatrics Ward and to the right, at the far side of an alcove few patients ever entered—and none left. Maggie paused at the corner, reaching into the recess where the nurses stowed the food cart, and tucked away a couple packages of graham crackers into the pocket of her coat. She had never cared for graham crackers, but Bobby loved them, and there were few things—none actually—she wouldn't do to see a smile on his pale, drawn face.

Room 12 was dark save for the reading light she had fixed to the headboard of Bobby's bed so he could read the latest edition of the *Uncanny X-Men* for the hundredth time. Bobby was curled up in a ball underneath the light, clutching the beaten comic book in his outstretched right hand.

"Hey, Maggie."

"Hey." She sat down on the hard plastic chair next to the bed, on which she had sat for so many hours the seat had become molded to the contours of her backside.

"Couldn't sleep?" he asked.

She shook her head.

"You alright?" he asked.

"Sure, why?"

Bobby shrugged his shoulders, which didn't come off quite right because his left arm had been amputated three years ago. "You're the doctor; you tell me."

"I'm fine."

She deposited the crackers on the table, in between the plastic pitcher of water he never drank and the pile of *X-Men* comic books he never stopped reading. The knot in her neck ached, and she massaged it, squeezing the tension out of the muscle using a technique an elderly Chinese patient had taught her.

"Don't you have your boards tomorrow?" he asked.

"Yes."

Bobby swatted the magazine against the pocket of her coat, which was stuffed full of notebooks overflowing with her precise script. "Why aren't you studying then?"

It was a question to which her only answers— 'Because I'm sick and tired of studying,' and, 'I couldn't care less about the boards'—seemed better left unsaid.

"I can't get any studying done when I'm on call," Maggie said.

"I thought Melendez was on call tonight?"

Caid Melendez was also a transitional intern, a first-year resident doing a year of general practice internship before transitioning to a specialty residency at a different hospital, rotating through pediatrics this month.

"He volunteered to split the night with me so I could get some sleep."

A rare grin crossed his narrow face. "Oooooohhhhh, Maggie, I think he likes you."

Maggie's face flushed red; her brow warmed.

"Hey, you're blushing," Bobby said.

"No, I'm not."

"Yes, you are."

"You better pipe down, or I'll go back to my call room."

"See if I care."

She feigned getting up, and he dropped the comic book and reached out to stop her with the shriveled hand of his right arm. Bobby weighed only 50 pounds soaking wet and stood only four-and-a-half feet high—when he had the strength to stand—living proof that mustard gas and rat poison should never be given to growing boys.

Maggie closed her eyes and tried to conjure up the sheet of formulas Yoda had given her, but all she could see was a page full of insensible smudges superimposed on Bobby's face. At the moment, with the tepid warmth of Bobby's hand on her forearm, the formulas didn't seem all that important anyway. She knew Yoda—the diminutive chief resident—would disagree, but making Bobby happy seemed far more worthwhile than going over the best way to calculate the glomerular filtration rate, which, according to Yoda, was the best way to measure kidney function.

"What's today's date, Maggie?" Bobby asked.

Maggie shrugged. "Twentieth? Twenty-first? How should I know?"

"You could try looking at your fancy watch."

She glanced at her wrist and spotted the Tag Heuer Maggie's father had bought her for her twenty-seventh birthday. "It's the twenty-second, what difference does it make?"

"How many days are there in April?"

She was vaguely aware there was some sort of mnemonic for this, but when she tried to click on the mnemonic file in her brain, the one for the twelve cranial nerves popped up instead: *Oh, Oh, Oh, To Touch and Feel a Virgin Girl's Vagina and Hymen.* "Thirty or thirty-one? Why do you care?"

"Why do I care?" Bobby raised his hairless eyebrows. "Because a new month means a change of service. What if I get another dork like I had last month?"

She leaned forward and tickled his armpit, causing him to drop the comic book and squeal and flail his arm in the air. The oldest of four children, Maggie was an accomplished tickler, and one of Bobby's previous chemotherapy drugs had ravaged his nervous system, making him especially sensitive.

He could only take a few seconds. With compromised lungs and a weak heart, it took no longer than that for Bobby's wind to be used up, resulting in the accelerated heaving of his tiny chest. He would have been able to last longer if he wore the oxygen she ordered for him, but he stubbornly refused to wear it, and the nasal cannula that administered it remained looped over the bedpost.

Bobby retrieved the comic book and resumed reading. She closed her eyes and listened to his rapid inspirations and the beat of his enlarged heart against the enclosing wall of his thorax. Somewhere close to his usual respiratory rate, oblivion overwhelmed her and she nodded off to sleep.

Her cell phone vibrated on her waist, waking her after an indefinite amount of time. It was Dr. Foster, the attending physician on pediatrics this month, notifying her that there was an admission in the Emergency Department. She extracted herself from the chair.

"Wait, you can't go. You just got here," Bobby said.

"That was Dr. Foster; he doesn't like to be kept waiting."

"You're leaving me to see that dog with fleas."

"What's the matter with Dr. Foster?" Maggie asked.

Bobby's face grew narrower, and his button nose wrinkled. "What's the matter with Dr. Foster? Are you kiddin' me? He's an arrogant cock."

"I think you're jealous."

11

"I'm jealous of people who buy green tomatoes. Stop changing the subject."

"I don't see anything wrong with Dr. Foster; I think he's nice."

"He's just trying to get down your pants, you know."

It was one of the things she loved about Bobby, his bluntness. As he had told her many times before, "When you don't have long to live, there isn't time not to get right to the point."

In disregard for almost every regulation she could think of—medical and otherwise—she leaned down and kissed him on the forehead. The way she looked at it, medical regulations should not apply to twelve-year-old boys who were dying without anyone in the entire world to care about them. Bobby continued to complain about Foster, but she slipped out the door and stood at the basin, washing her hands of the microorganisms his body was too weak to defeat. She ran her hands through the microwave drier and walked past the elevator on her way to the Emergency Department using the staircase at the back of the ward.

"*Rule #1 of being an intern,*" Yoda had told her on the first day of her internship, a thousand years ago, "*Never take the elevator.*"

"*Why not?*" one of the other interns had asked.

"*There is no why or why not, Intern. There is only do.*"

Maggie reached her destination without seeing anyone and found Melendez at the nurses' station, holding court with a small group of people—nurses, orderlies, and residents—all of them female. Melendez saw Maggie and disengaged from the throng, joining Maggie by the big board, the list of all the patients currently being tended to in the department.

"Did you get any sleep?" he asked.

"Yeah, thanks. Were you busy?"

He shrugged. "You know, the usual shit." Melendez

never went into detail about anything, with the exception of his love life, about which he filled Maggie's ear whenever he could. "There's an overdose in Room 13. I was going to do it, but another opportunity has come up." He nodded his shaved head in the direction of the nurses' station, where Maggie's friend Rachel was staring down a drunk and jabbing her finger repeatedly into his chest. "She's not as cute as you, but damn, does she have some chutzpah. I love girls with chutzpah."

"Rachel Woods isn't the slightest bit interested in you, Caid," Maggie said.

His large brown eyes twinkled with confidence, and his lips curled into a devilish grin. "We'll see about that."

"Anything you want to tell me about the kids you admitted?"

He gave her a terse summary of the two admissions he'd done, a twelve-year-old boy who had contracted viral hepatitis after eating at a restaurant on 156th–at which Maggie had eaten a few weeks ago—and a fifteen-year-old girl whose Crohn's disease was flaring, resulting in a bloody diarrhea that Melendez described as 'lava flowing from her ass.' He handed her an index card choked with illegible scrawl and sauntered off in Rachel's direction.

Room 13 was a depression in the old back wall of the hospital against which the orderlies parked a gurney when space was tight. She fought her way back through the chaos of darting bodies, flashing lights, and the banshee wail of a dozen alarm bells and slipped between the two dividers put there to offer the illusion of privacy.

A girl of sixteen or seventeen lay prone on a rolling stretcher, dozing peacefully despite the noise. Maggie called up her chart on the laptop; the word 'overdose' was all that was written under the 'History' tab. She scrolled down and found the ambulance report, in the hope of finding out what the patient had taken, but all she saw were the times of dispatch and arrival. She was tempted to click on the toxicology report and satisfy her curiosity, but she put the computer aside and grabbed her stethoscope.

"Rule #1 of internship. Take any opportunity to learn, no matter how busy or tired you are because most of your time will be spent doing my scutwork."

"What's scutwork?"

"Scutwork is anything I don't want to do, like measuring the amount of foul-smelling pus that's collected in a drain, or unplugging a rectal tube that's jammed with shit, or picking lice out of someone's hair. Got the drift?"

There was nothing remarkable about the patient's exam, other than her tachycardia, and few patients didn't have a racing heart in the Emergency Department, a place Yoda referred to as *"the asshole of the hospital,"* as well as dozens of horizontal cuts on her arms in various states of healing, none very fresh.

She scooped up her laptop and found the urine toxicity screen. As was often the case in these teenage overdoses, the patient's urine looked a lot like a medicine cabinet: there was Tylenol, of course, Advil, aspirin, Benadryl and a smattering of Xanax for good measure— all washed down with a half-pint of cheap vodka. The mixture was a tough go for anyone's stomach and— fortunately—she had vomited up most of it. The Emergency Department had done the rest. By the time they had stuffed the biggest tube they could find down her nose, vacuumed her out and then stuffed her full of charcoal to absorb the rest, there was only enough sedative in her system to knock her out and buy her a night on the Pediatrics ward.

She typed the History and Physical and then wrote the orders, deciding on a dilute salt solution for the patient's intravenous fluids, and went back to the nurses' station to find the attending. Rachel was alone at the desk; Melendez was nowhere to be seen.

"Rach, have you seen Foster?" Maggie asked.

"Dr. Delicious?"

"Yes, him."

"I think he's in the cafeteria," Rachel replied.

"Thirteen's family show up yet?"

Rachel shook her head.

"Send them up to Pediatrics when they come in," Maggie said.

Chapter Three

The cafeteria was usually quiet around this time, and tonight was no exception. Maggie walked past the plastic-wrapped sandwiches and the basket filled with sad-looking fruit and located Foster in the back of the cafeteria, sipping a cup of coffee and reading a battered copy of *People*. He looked up as she approached and nodded for her to sit down. She would have preferred to stand, but Yoda had been clear about the issue: "*You don't have to be a suck-up, but don't be a pain in the ass either. No one likes a pain in the ass.*"

Foster set the magazine down and regarded her with his eyes the color of the spruce trees that were planted in between McDonald's and the hospital. "How's the overdose doing?"

She reached for the notes in her pocket but decided against using them, fearful of being accused of 'bad form,' and launched into her presentation of the case, using the same formula interns had been using for all of eternity.

Foster nodded when she was done, smoothing down the cowlick of loose curly hair that had a habit of spiking up from his forehead. "Plan?"

"Admit her to Pediatrics for observation."

"Why are we admitting her?" he asked.

"Monitoring status post overdose."

"If we're going to monitor her, why not admit her to the Pediatric Intensive Care Unit?"

Attending physicians, who the interns referred to simply as attendings, had been shouting rapid-fire questions at interns—a process the interns called 'pimping'—for over one hundred years. When she knew the correct answers, Maggie enjoyed being pimped; when she didn't, it was a unique form of torture.

"She doesn't need heart monitoring," Maggie said. "The cardiac strips in the Emergency Department didn't show any rhythm disturbances, her EKG was normal, and her blood pressure and pulse are stable. I'll place an oximeter on her finger; if her oxygen saturation drops, the alarm will sound."

Foster sat back in his chair and clasped his hands together behind his head. Maggie got the feeling this wasn't going to be a quick-hitter. "Meds?"

"She doesn't take any regular medications, and there's nothing we need to give her."

"Shouldn't you reverse the Xanax?" A hint of a smile appeared on his rugged, athletic face; Foster appeared to be enjoying his role as inquisitor.

"I don't see the point. The Xanax has a short half-life; it will be gone soon enough on its own."

"Good answer, Maggie. Don't do things just for the sake of doing them."

And the pimping went on. He asked her about the diet she ordered, the flow rate of oxygen being administered, what lab tests she wanted, how often she thought vital signs should be taken. Yoda had said that Foster was a laid-back attending, which meant he generally let the interns manage the patients on their own without micromanaging them, but this morning he was full of questions. Perhaps he didn't trust her yet, which, this late in the month, wasn't a good sign.

"Fluids?' he asked.

"Half-normal saline at 250cc/hour.'

He rubbed his pronounced chin—the one with the

central dimple that mesmerized most of the nursing staff. "No potassium?"

"It was normal when the Emergency Department checked it."

"Yes, you mentioned that, but that was three hours ago. Check it again—you said the patient had been vomiting. Vomiting wastes potassium, and it usually takes a while for the potassium debt to show up in the blood work."

She nodded, vaguely remembering she had heard Yoda say that before.

"Did you place a catheter in her bladder?" he asked.

"The Emergency Department did, yes, but I was going to take it out."

"Leave it in, it's the only good way to measure urine output. And measuring urine output—regardless of what Yoda told you—is the best way to monitor her kidney function."

She jotted this down in her notebook and looked up expectantly. "Anything else?"

"I don't think so. You had most of it covered," Foster said.

She guessed it was meant as a compliment, but Bobby had made her too wary of Foster to be happy about it: "*He's a dog with fleas, just trying to get down your pants.*"

"Any questions for me, Maggie?"

"I don't think so, Dr. Foster."

He smiled at her, the smile that induced a Ketamine-like paralysis in Garcia, one of the other interns on Pediatrics this month. (*Don't you just think he's absolutely the cutest, Maggie?*) "I thought I asked you to call me Jack?"

He had, in fact, asked all the interns to call him by his first name, but only Garcia had complied.

"Don't forget rounds are at five tomorrow," he said. She nodded.

"Are you sure you don't want me to take call for the rest of the night? You've got the boards this morning. I'm sure a little rest would be helpful."

"That's okay. I probably wouldn't be able to sleep anyway."

He slid a card across to her as he stood. "I'll be in house all night. Here's my beeper number and cell if you need me."

Foster left, and she opened up her laptop and added the potassium to the intravenous bag, annoyed with herself she had missed something. Foster had left the copy of *People* on the table, and she flipped through it by way of distraction, wondering as she leafed through the worn pages what she might have done with her life besides doctoring—not that her father would have allowed any other choice. She flipped to a book review and thought about her ambitions to be a writer, which her father had squelched when she was about Bobby's age. *"No money in it,"* he had said. *"Maybe as a sideline."*

She tossed the magazine down and headed back to the pediatrics floor. The night shift was well underway, and she saw Babe—the charge nurse on nights' for over a score of years—shuffling back to the break room behind the nurses' station. Maggie followed her in and took the seat beside her. It wasn't mandatory to touch base with the charge nurse, but Maggie had made a practice of it. (What else was there to do anyway?) Getting some rest was just the fantasy of a tired mind, and she couldn't even stomach the *idea* of studying for the boards; she was either going to pass, or she wasn't. At this moment in time, she had no preference.

"Damn, am I glad to see you, Maggie." Babe clapped her on the back with her thick hand. "That damn fool Melendez nearly killed half the damn ward. That boy has got less damn sense than hair, and he's got none of *that*."

Babe said *damn* a lot, pronouncing it like the word had

three syllables instead of one: *"DddAAAAAmmmmmnn."*

Melendez had needed just only a few days to catch ire from Babe. One of the other nurses gave her an encouraging look, and Babe launched into an embellished tale of his incompetence, highlighted by his failure to administer racemic epinephrine to the crouper in respiratory distress. Babe didn't like Melendez—or any of the other interns for that matter—and therefore didn't mention the patient in question had a history of supraventricular tachycardia, an episodic racing of the heart that contraindicated the use of the adrenaline.

"You got to give them *daaaammmmnnnnn* croupers the epinephrine. *Evvvveeeeryybbbbooooody* knows that."

Babe looked at her to see if she was going to challenge her story, but Maggie said nothing. There was no point in seeking out Babe's ire; it would come soon enough anyway. Maggie was just about to nod off when the shrill wail of the code beeper whipped her eyes open.

Shit.

She ran out of the room and followed a pair of nurses pushing the crash cart, heading toward the alcove where Bobby's room was.

Please. No. Not Bobby.

They rounded the corner and plunged straight into Room 12, liberating the flyers Infection Control had posted there. Maggie followed them in and saw him, pale and lifeless on the bed with his fingers still clutching his comic book. She ran to his side and opened his mouth to check his airway, but there was no obstruction. She auscultated his lungs, hoping to be rewarded with the hiss of his breath sounds, but all was quiet. A quick check of his carotid revealed no pulse.

Damn. Damn.

She grabbed the defibrillator and placed the pads on Bobby's tiny chest as Babe shuffled in, huffing and puffing like an old freight train. One of the nurses switched the machine to the diagnostic mode, and a rapid wave appeared on the screen, which the intern recognized to be ventricular fibrillation, a lethal disruption of the heart's normal conduction.

"Twenty-five joules," Maggie said.

Babe walked over to her and stood with her powerful hands at her side next to the crash cart. "*What* are you doing, Intern?" Maggie tried to ignore her, but Babe wouldn't be ignored: "This is a mistake, and you know it."

Maggie yelled 'clear,' and checked the bed to make sure no one was touching the patient. Her thumbs found the triggers and she depressed them, arcing twenty-five joules of energy through Bobby's body, which caused it to leap off the bed.

"Diagnostic," Maggie ordered.

One of the nurses switched the mode to diagnostic, and the dancing line reappeared, even more chaotic than before.

"Charge," Maggie said.

She felt Babe brush up against her. "I'm going to ask you one more *Dddammmmmnnnn* time, *Intern*. What are *you* doing?"

"He's a full code, Babe."

"Only because his state-appointed guardian doesn't have a lick of sense."

"He's a full code. We have to run a code," Maggie said.

"So run it slow...and let this poor boy go," Babe said.

Maggie hesitated for a minute until she heard it— Yoda's hoarse voice whispering in her ear: *The nurses are smart and experienced, Intern, but they are not in charge. You are in charge. Always remember that. When things go bad—and they will go bad—the nurse isn't going to have to answer to the attending. You are.*

Babe looked at her expectantly, and Maggie leaned

21

her shoulder into her and pushed hard with her legs, driving the charge nurse away from the bed.

She yelled *CLEEEAAAARRRR* and shocked him again, filling the air with the smell of ozone and scorched flesh. This time the chaos went away, yielding to a nice clean rhythm.

"He's got a pulse," a nurse announced.

"Blood pressure?" Maggie asked.

"80 over palpable."

Maggie took one last look at the neat, organized complexes on the LED screen—she had never seen anything so beautiful in her life—and risked a glance at his face. His cheeks were stained pink, and his eyes were open and locked on hers.

Somewhere behind her she heard the sound of Babe stomping back to report, muttering loudly under her breath: "Don't you ever cross me again, *Innnternnnn*."

Chapter Four

If there was one thing Maggie liked about internship—and that was a big *if*—it was pre-rounds. It was true pre-rounding robbed her of yet another hour of her time, but it was the only one she didn't begrudge. She knocked on the door of Room 20 as she entered and sat down next to the young girl who was sleeping on a cot beside her baby.

She put her hand on her shoulder, gently rousing her from a light sleep. "Good morning, Carla."

Carla blinked a greeting to her with her long, thick lashes.

"How's Diego this morning?"

She nodded her head, and they both stared at her three-day-old baby, who looked ghastly in the blue wash of the lights Maggie had ordered to lower his bilirubin count. Diego was a tiny thing—his mother's diet had consisted of cigarettes, crack cocaine, and Mountain Dew—but Diego was spirited, and Maggie had always admired spirit.

She washed her hands and reached inside the plastic incubator to listen to Diego's heart and lungs and to probe his soft belly with her fingers. Diego kicked his scrawny legs in protest and then settled back to his fetal position. She made sure his foam blinders—used to protect the baby's eyes from the ultraviolet light—were in good position, and then she sat next to Carla again.

"How are you?" Maggie asked.

"Good."

It was the only response Maggie had ever received from her, including the time she had showed up at the maternity ward to deliver in the grips of full-on cocaine withdrawal.

"The bilirubin was down this morning, Carla. I'm going to turn off the lights and see how he does," Maggie told her.

Carla brushed her long dark hair away from her face, which was pretty in a sort of overly made-up way. "Okay."

Bilirubin was a breakdown product of red blood cell metabolism. It was usually broken down by the liver, but often built up in newborns, especially those—like Diego—born prematurely. Ever since an astute ward sister in Essex, England had noticed that the jaundiced infants on the sunny side of the nursery got better faster, doctors had been using ultraviolet light to help infants excrete bilirubin, which could have a toxic effect on the developing brain if left untreated.

"If the bilirubin stays down this afternoon, Diego will be ready for discharge."

Carla nodded.

"Are you ready to take him home?"

Another nod.

Maggie glanced at her laptop and saw that the nurses had indeed gone through the checklist:

Car Seat: √

Bath Instruction: √

Bottle Feeding Video: √

Medical Social Work Consult: √

One-week Supply of Pre-Mixed Formula: √

For a brief second Maggie wondered if there were more to successful parenting than getting all five checks—her best friend from college and her husband were infertile and wanted a baby desperately—but this was dangerous train of thought and she disembarked immediately. Her iPhone beeped the alarm for 5 a.m., and Maggie patted Carla on the shoulder and headed off for rounds.

The rest of the interns were gathered by the coffee pot—the traditional starting line for rounds—waiting for Dr. Foster to arrive. She noticed that Garcia, a local girl who had been born three streets away, had already filled Foster's favorite cup, a stainless-steel travel mug with 'The Doctor Is In' written on it in black marker.

Perhaps Garcia had never heard Yoda's admonition against being a suck-up.

Maggie grabbed her own mug and poured herself her third cup of the day. She knew she had been drinking *way* too much coffee, but she couldn't remember the last time she had a decent night of sleep.

Mike Williams, another one of the pediatric interns, sidled up to her from her left. "How was your night?"

"Not too bad. Three admissions."

"Three admissions, that's all?" Mike asked.

"I only did half the night; Caid offered to split it with me since we have boards this morning."

"That was really nice of him."

"Oooooohhhhh, Maggie, I think he likes you."

"Yes, it was," Maggie replied.

"What were the admissions?" Mike asked.

"A nine-year-old with pneumonia, a Sickler, and another OD."

"What was it this time?"

"Oh, you know, the usual cocktail of everything she could find in the medicine cabinet and a fifth of cheap vodka to chase it down."

"She going to be okay?"

Maggie thought she detected a hint of compassion in Williams' voice, and she was impressed that eight months of hell hadn't killed all of it.

"Yeah, she's going to be fine."

She wanted to add 'till the next time' but they were both thinking it anyway, and a burst of laughter from the nurses' station indicated Foster had arrived and rounds were beginning. They started off in queue: Foster first, Aaron Schwartz, the senior pediatrics resident next, and the four interns after that, parading down the ward. The hierarchical procession stopped in front on Room 1, a gunshot wound that had been transferred down from the surgical floor because he had a traumatic brain injury—and because surgery didn't want him anymore. (Surgery carried a lot of weight, being the only profitable department in the entire house.) The GSW was Melendez's patient, and so he passed to the front of the interns, taking position in between Foster and Schwartz.

"Sixteen-year-old black male. Post-op day 12, status post an exploratory laparotomy for gunshots. The wounds are healing well, and the surgery resident has signed off."

Melendez stopped for a second to allow everyone to mutter under his or her collective breath about the departure of the surgical resident: *of course, he did; why wouldn't he; and leave all the paperwork for us*?

"Current medical problems include a TBI, which therapy is seeing him for, and a small little left lobe pneumonia. He's taking fluids and solids, moving his bowels, walking around as much as the cops will let him, he's off all intravenous medications, he's not wearing oxygen, and respiratory therapy has signed off. But I can't get him off my service because nobody wants him. I've been riding social services like a rented mule, and still they can't place him."

"Who's his social worker, Caid?" Schwartz asked.

"Tammy Hunter."

Ms. Hunter was one of those weepy-eyed, big-hearted social workers who held a lot of hands but did little else. It was rumored she slept with a few of the suits in the cube farm—which was the only logical explanation why she still had her job.

"Get on the horn and find someone a home for this kid yourself..." Schwartz told him.

"That's not my job, Aaron. I didn't sign up to be a social worker."

"Sure you did, Caid, when you became an intern. And just in case you want to know, you're also a phlebotomist, nurse, x-ray tech, and whatever-the-hell-else you need to be to get this patient off your service. Find him a home. I don't care where; just get him off your service."

They processed toward Room 3, as one of Yoda's fifty-plus '*Number One Rules of Internship*' rattled through Maggie's head: "*The Number One Rule of Internship, Interns, is to get the patient off your service. Let me repeat, for those of you who are a little slow: Get-The-Patient-Off-Your-Fucking-Service.*"

Someone—Garcia or one of the other suck-ups who always stood in front—had the audacity to question why. "*I already told you that there is no why, Intern, but to make sure this gets through your thick skulls, I am going to make an exception.*

"*Because there's a shitstorm blowing at you, Intern, and you never know when it's going to cover you knee deep in foul-smelling crap. So, you take any chance you get to Get-The-Patient-Off-Your-Fucking-Service. Got it?*"

Room 3 was the overdose Maggie had admitted last night, so she went to the head of the line: "Sixteen-year-old white female, previously healthy, admitted last night status post multi-drug OD including Xanax, alcohol, and Tylenol. She got the usual treatment in the Emergency Department, and her levels are all low, her vitals are stable, and she's awake and alert this morning."

Garcia raised her hand, even though Schwartz had asked her a hundred times not to. "Usual treatment? Do you mean nasogastric lavage followed by the administration of activated charcoal?"

Everyone knew what the usual treatment was, but

Garcia just couldn't stop herself from making sure the attending and the senior resident knew how smart she was.

"Yes, that's what I meant." Maggie looked around to see if anyone else had any questions. No one did. Schwartz twirled his index finger, indicating he wanted her to wrap things up and keep moving. "Labs this morning show her potassium is back up from a low of 3.0 last night, and I am cutting back on the intravenous and ordering clear fluids."

"Plan?" Schwartz asked.

"Keep her today on observational status, psychiatry consult...that's about it."

"Psychiatry is never going to see her in time for discharge—they are so backed up, an enema the size of an anaconda couldn't get them unplugged. Get social work to see her, and call them yourself; don't wait for the nurses to do it. And make sure you call her primary care provider to arrange a follow up."

Maggie nodded.

"Better yet, see her yourself in the clinic—doubt she has an actual primary care, and the coverage for the unassigned patients is a joke."

The procession moved on: a wheezer in 5; another gang member in 7, suffering from a flail chest after being beaten with a tire iron; another wheezer in 11 (East Harlem had the highest rate for asthma admissions in the country, a whopping five times the national average); and on and on until they arrived at 12, which, due to the geometric configuration of the pediatric floor, came after 36. Bobby had been here for so long that the queue usually just paraded on by, but today, Foster stopped in front of the door and nodded at Maggie.

"Twelve-year-old white male with Acute Myeloblastic Leukemia, status post two failed bone marrow transplants. His most recent round of chemotherapy caused pancytopenia, and all cell lines, red blood, white blood, and platelets, remain severely depressed."

She thought it was a gross dereliction of duty to reduce this courageous boy into a pile of terms and abbreviations, but she continued on: "Status post witnessed cardiac arrest...successfully defibrillated on second dose of 25 joules..."

She could see the other interns perking up at the discovery she had run a code— an intern's fantasy—and stopped as a chorus of congratulations came her way.

When the tide of *attagirls* ebbed, Schwartz asked, "What's he still doing here?"

Protocol demanded that any pediatric patient who survived a cardiac arrest be immediately transferred to the Pediatric Intensive Care Unit on the 5th floor, but Foster had vetoed the transfer. In the meantime, a heart monitor had been wheeled down from the PICU.

"That was my decision. I've asked for an ethics consult—there's no good reason this poor boy is still a full code. We'll keep him here on the monitor until the ethics team can meet to determine his disposition," Foster said.

Garcia raised her hand again; Schwartz groaned audibly. "Can the ethics team change his code status? I mean, isn't that his guardian's decision?"

"It is, yes, but the guardian will meet with the team, and they can guide her," Foster answered.

Foster nodded at Schwartz, and the queue began its way towards the coffee pot for the customary post-rounds interrogation. Maggie started to follow, but Foster reached out and placed his hand on her shoulder and held her there until the others had disappeared around the corner. "I'm not saying you did the wrong thing last night. You did a good job not letting the nurses bully you into running a slow code, but that boy has been through enough."

She nodded and started off to catch up with the other interns like a stray goose, but his hand was still in place on her shoulder. "There's something else I wanted to discuss."

"Okay, what's that?"

His hand dropped off her shoulder, brushing lightly against her arm as it fell. "I, uh…"

His spruce green eyes regarded her as his lips curled into a bashful grin; his hand strayed unconsciously to the loose curl of hair that spiked up from his forehead.

"Yes?"

He seemed to have lost his train of thought. He stroked the stubble on his chin.

"You were going to ask me something?"

He nodded in recognition, his eyes flashing green. She heard Melendez at the coffee pot, going after Garcia for being a suck-up and a know-it-all—the two things interns hated the most.

"I've requested that you be on the ethics team," Foster finally said. "Are you alright with that?"

"Sure, thanks."

"Good."

"Is that all?" Maggie asked.

The bashful grin faded; the green glow emanating from his eyes dimmed. "Yes, that's all."

Chapter Five

In 1992, the National Board of Medical Examiners changed the name of its iconic exam to the United States Medical Licensing Examination, but no one seemed to have listened; everyone still referred to it as 'the boards.' Taken in three parts, Part 1 as a second-year medical student and Part 2 as a fourth year, Part 3 of the boards was never far from Maggie's mind for the simple fact that her medical licensure was dependent upon a passing grade. Horror stories abounded: the high-school valedictorian who had spent her whole life preparing to be a doctor, endless hours of studying, volunteering at the local hospital, a spring break trip to bring medical care to the impoverished island of Haiti, only to throw herself off a bridge upon failing the last part; the foreign medical grad who had practiced medicine for ten years in Pakistan and failed Part 3 on four occasions; the former electrical engineer turned medical intern who wanted to become a cardiologist but fizzled out on the final leg.

Maggie had heard all the stories, and although she was sure most were either greatly embellished or fabricated entirely, she had spread some of them around to pass the time on a lonely night of call or a slow afternoon in clinic. She tapped her finger nervously on the desk (where was her No. 2 pencil when she needed it?) waiting for the proctor to signal that the last part of the exam was about to begin.

"Computers open. You have ninety minutes to finish this section."

She flipped open the laptop and typed in her code word. A medical scenario popped up on the screen:

A seventeen-year-old white male presents to your office with a ten-day history of rhinorrhea progressing to a non-productive, episodic cough. Vitals signs indicate a temp of 37.5 and a respiratory rate of 18...

She could see Bobby lying in his bed, clutching the comic book with his only hand. He was coughing hard enough to break a pair of ribs despite the cough medicine she had ordered, and the intravenous antibiotics dripped uselessly into his veins from a silver pole in the background.

Check all the following that apply:
__1. Order a pertussis swab and treat with ciprofloxacin, 20mg/kg by mouth twice daily.
__2. Treat with azithromycin, 10mg/kg daily
__3. Order a Complete Blood Count, Blood Cultures and a Urine Legionella Antigen.
__4. Order a TdaP
__5. Treat all members of the family with azithromycin
__6. Quarantine the patient until the cough has resolved

Once again, a conversation with Yoda entered her mind. *'Listen, Maggie, about Bobby.'*

'What about him?' Maggie asked.

'You're too close to him. What's the No. 1 rule of internship?'

'You've given us fifty No. 1 rules of internship, Yoda. Which one are you talking about?'

'The one that applies to you and Bobby. You're too close to him, you need to back away,' she said.

'He needs me.'

'You're right. He does need you. He needs you to be objective, and you're sorely failing him,' Yoda said.

'There're plenty of doctors in this dump, Yoda. What he needs is a friend, and that's what I'm going to be.'

'What he needs? Are you sure it isn't what you need?' Yoda asked.

A seventy-five-year-old woman presents to the Emergency Department with a four-hour history of shortness of breath without chest pain or cough. Vitals signs include temperature of 36°, pulse 120, and respirations 26. Her initial EKG shows sinus tachycardia and her Chemistry panel is as follows: BUN 51 (12-20mcg/dl); Cr 1.9 (0.5-1.0mcg/dl); Hemoglobin 8.2 (12.5-14.0mg/dl); troponin 0.20 (0.04mg/dl-0.15mg/dl).

Check all that apply in regards to her initial care:

__1. Order Aspirin, Nitroglycerin, and Metoprolol, Oxygen by nasal cannula and continuous cardiac monitoring.

__2. Order 2 units of O Negative Packed Red Blood Cells, Type and Cross, Normal Saline IV at 500cc/hour

__3. Place a Nasogastric tube to Low wall suction and...

"Computers closed. The exam is concluded," the proctor said.

Maggie closed her computer and rubbed her sleepy eyes. She wasn't sure how long she had nodded off but doubted it was long—she certainly didn't feel rested. She closed her eyes again and rested her forehead against the desk as she waited for the room to clear out. But it didn't clear out, and the sound of nervous chatter replaced the tense silence.

"I've never heard of lactobacillus."

"What drug do you treat high altitude sickness with?"

"It's a urinary tract colinant; you don't treat it."

"Are we still using bicarbonate to treat acidosis?"

The collage of questions and answers continued, but she wasn't interested enough to listen; she only wanted to go back to her little flat on Murray Hill and sleep. It was possible she'd have more interest tomorrow, but it was also possible she wouldn't. In some ways, she admired them—their constant desire to get every question right, to win top marks on every exam, to be in the front of every line—but in most ways, she did not. Bobby referred to them as cutthroats.

'Why do you call them that?' Maggie asked him.

'Because they would cut your throat for an extra point, and don't think I'm kidding.'

'You read too many comic books.'

'And you don't read enough.'

When the hubbub died down, she extricated herself from her cubicle and tried to slip out the back entrance, but she hadn't given them enough time, and many of them were still standing there, arguing about the merits of using colloid infusions to treat liver failure.

Melendez tapped her on the shoulder. "Want to get something to eat? I'm going over to Ray's."

"No, thanks."

"Why don't you join me? You need to get some food before you go to bed anyway," he said.

"I have some leftovers in my refrigerator."

"Come on, Maggie. Don't be such a sissy."

He wrapped a powerful arm around her shoulder and escorted her outside. It was a damp and rainy evening in East Harlem, but no one seemed to notice: the bodegas were full, the streets were congested, and the sidewalks spilled over with every race, color and creed of people on the face of the earth.

Ray's was crowded, but Melendez managed to find a table in back. They sat down, savoring the aroma of oregano and freshly-baked dough. A young woman from behind the counter materialized, bringing Melendez a large cola with lots of ice.

"Haven't seen you in a while, Caid," the waitress said.

"They're killing me at Golden Arches, Rosa. I barely get the time to eat."

Rosa snapped her gum and rolled her lips into a snarl. "That's not what I hear." She looked at Maggie without encouragement. "You want something?"

Maggie was hungry, and, despite what she had told Melendez, there was nothing in her refrigerator except a couple bottles of Snapple and a carton of moldy Chinese take-out; she ordered a small cheese pizza.

The waitress left without taking Melendez's order but returned a few minutes later with a large pizza smothered with meat, which he started into without preamble. Maggie's pizza came ten minutes later, by which time Melendez's was almost gone.

"Come here a lot?" Maggie asked him.

"I used to. Not so much recently." He wiped a small speck of tomato sauce that despoiled the dark shadow perennially adorning his chin. "Man, do I miss the pizza."

"Rosa, she's an old flame of yours?" she asked.

"Old? Yes. Flame? No." He swallowed half of his last slice in one bite. "More of a flicker, really."

Rosa came back with another large cola, which she set in front of Melendez. "You want something else?"

He shook his head.

"Other than her," Rosa said.

"She's just a friend," Melendez replied.

Rosa glanced at Maggie out of the corner of her eye, her gaze trolling lazily over Maggie from head to toe. "Sure she is."

"It's not like that," Maggie told her.

Rosa snorted and disappeared behind the counter. Melendez washed the last of his pizza down with a swallow of soda.

"I don't think she likes me," Maggie said.

"She doesn't like anybody; I wouldn't worry about it."

One of the other customers asked Melendez how he was doing, launching him into a diatribe about the injustices of being an intern. Maggie started into her pizza and listened to him harangue: interns were slaves; attendings were obnoxious pricks who got off on abusing them; Golden Arches was a pathetic excuse for a hospital.

He finished up, as always, by counting the days until he could 'crawl out of this fucking rat hole,' threw three crumpled twenties onto the table, and stood up to leave. Maggie slid the last two slices of her pizza into a paper bag, and they left, turning up the street toward Golden Arches, and entered the back staircase through the service entrance. Maggie fumbled for the small purse in the breast pocket of her lab coat.

"What do I owe you for the pizza?" she asked.

"My treat, Maggie."

Interns at all hospitals were underpaid; interns at Golden Arches notoriously so. It was rumored that an intern a few years back had applied for Welfare benefits and had started receiving them, only to be cut off after the administration had discovered the issue and raised the intern's salary to one dollar above the eligibility income. As a consequence, none of the interns had any extra cash, and Caid Melendez, who had worked his way through college, was no exception. It was an unwritten rule that all meals shared between interns were self-pay.

"Come on, Caid, let me pay," Maggie said.

She dug a twenty out of her purse and tried to hand it to him, but he just clapped her on the shoulder and disappeared into the basement. Maggie returned the money to her purse and started up the staircase leading to

Bobby's room. The sound of a man's voice echoed inside Room 12 as she approached, and she wondered if someone other than her was attending to the poor kid. A middle-aged man with Harry Potter glasses and thinning hair pulled back into a ponytail looked up at her as she walked in and set the pizza down on the bedside table. She introduced herself and went to fetch another chair from the hallway.

"Don't bother to get another chair, he was just leaving," Bobby said.

Maggie retrieved the chair despite Bobby's protestations and sat down next to the man. Bobby tore at the bag and started in to the pizza as she eyed his visitor. Forty-five or so—and not a good forty-five—with nicotine stained teeth and bloodshot sclera, he looked like a heavy metal rocker twenty years after his prime.

"How do you know Bobby?" Maggie asked.

"I don't," the man replied.

Maggie looked over his faded plaid shirt for a nametag of some kind. There was nothing to identify him. "What are you doing here?"

He pulled out a wallet as thick as a brick and handed her a card. According to the cheap business card, he was an investigative journalist named Rex Miller. She handed the card to Bobby who gave it a glance and threw it on the table, where it landed atop the pile of comic books.

"Do you have some kind of business with Bobby?" Maggie asked.

He nodded. "I'm an investigative journalist, ma'am."

"That's what the card says. What are you investigating?"

A troop of small people paraded past—brothers and sisters of a patient perhaps, or maybe a pack of Cub Scouts trying to earn a merit badge.

"I'm doing a story about LDK369, the experimental chemotherapy agent that Bobby received, which failed its Phase III trial and didn't receive approval from the FDA."

The journalist pulled a thick stack of paper out from the beat-up canvas satchel at his feet. "This is the report of the failed Phase III application."

He offered it to Maggie, but she waved him off. She couldn't imagine willingly reading the tedious and sleep-inducing minutiae regarding hypothesis, methods and data. She already had to review several medical journals every week, for presentation at Journal Club—which, of all the miserable obligations of internship, was the most miserable—and she couldn't stomach another study.

"What's so interesting about a failed drug application? It happens all the time."

"What's so interesting is *why* it failed."

Maggie looked at Bobby; he was eating a second piece of pizza and reading an old *X-Men* comic as if it weren't the 100th time through. It didn't appear as though he was paying any attention.

"Bobby wasn't the only patient to lose an arm," the reporter said. "Some patients lost both of their arms."

"Are you working for a law firm?" Maggie asked.

He denied it.

"If you're not working for the law firm, whom are you working for?"

"Rex Miller. I work for myself. I specialize in investigative work regarding corruption in the FDA. That's why I am writing a story about LDK369."

"But it failed its Phase III trial. How is that corrupt?" Maggie asked.

Maggie glanced at Bobby, noticing that he hadn't turned a page in a while. The slice of pizza remained half eaten.

"It isn't." The reporter fumbled through the stack of paper and handed her a single sheet highlighted with red ink. "Read this."

She complied, reading about an eight-year-old boy who had lost his arm after receiving a loading dose of

LDK369. It was a terrible story, made worse by the hygienic and clinical wording—as if no one had actually suffered—but one that she knew well. A perfect example was lying on the bed next to them, listening to their conversation.

"How did you find out about Bobby?" Maggie asked.

Rex Miller's acne-scarred face remained impassive. "I can't say."

"What do you want from him?"

The low oxygen alarm started beeping, quiet and slow at first, then louder and faster as the oxygen saturation on the portable monitor dropped into the eighties. Two nurses busted in the room, followed by an orderly pushing the crash cart. One of the nurses pushed Rex Miller out of the room, as Maggie remained seated in her chair with her clogs off.

***

"You're a little shit, do you know that?" Maggie said.

Bobby took this as a compliment. A rare smile slipped onto his narrow face. "Did you see the look on that guy's face?"

Maggie had seen it, an odd mixture of concern about Bobby's welfare mixed with horror over the prospect of losing his story.

"Oh, come on, Maggie; don't be mad. It's not like I haven't done that before."

It was a favorite trick of Bobby's—holding his breath until his oxygen saturation dropped—one that he employed whenever he wanted his visitors to leave. He usually reserved this for the social workers who came to evaluate him for placement in foster homes and respite houses, to which Bobby had no desire to go.

"You know the nurses have to fill out a ton of paperwork every time they run a code?" Maggie asked.

"So what?" Bobby picked up the most recent copy of *Extraordinary X-Men*, which he had dropped in order to pinch the oxygen tube.

"Don't you think you should at least consider helping him?"

"Nope."

"I guess I'll be leaving then."

Extraordinary X-Men came down. Bobby's small eyes pleaded with her to stay.

"Why don't you want to?" Maggie asked him.

"Don't want to."

The stifled cry of a small child with an asthma exacerbation filtered in through the open door, which the nurses hadn't shut properly when they left.

"Yes, I know that. *Why* don't you want to?"

"Just don't."

Maggie picked at her slice of pizza. Her appetite had abandoned her. "The *X-Men*... they help people, right, Bobby?"

"Of course, they do. So, what?"

Maggie's nose wrinkled with the harsh odor of the industrial disinfectant Housekeeping used in the never-ending battle against *staphylococcal* infections. "You have a chance to help people also. The reporter is trying to make sure that no one else loses an arm from a bad medicine."

"I heard you say LDK369 never made it to the market."

"Yes, that's true. But there are hundreds of other medicines being tested. Your story will help make sure the testing is fair and not influenced by anything else other than good judgment."

Bobby stretched out his shriveled arm. His skin was so thin Maggie could make out the wasted bulk of the *Pronator Teres* muscle, which he used to point his thumb at the floor, a gesture he made often to indicate his intense disagreement.

"You live in a freaking fantasy land, Maggie, a world of never-ending, nauseating perfection. Money has always made the world go 'round, and it always will. And why are you so fired up about this anyway, what's it got to do with you?"

"It doesn't have anything to do with me, Bobby. It's just the right thing to do."

"The right thing to do! *IIhhhaaaaahh..."* Bobby thumbed his nose at her, one of the many things he had learned from watching an endless tide of gangster movies. "For once, Maggie, just for once, I'd like you to do something because you wanna, and not because it's the freaking right thing to do."

The walls vibrated, flecking off miniscule pieces of plaster, as the floor-cleaning machine rumbled past on its rounds.

"And besides, who says it's the right thing to do? Your daddy?" Bobby asked.

"What does my father have to do with this?"

"You're kidding, right?"

Maggie shook her head.

"Come on, Maggie...You don't take a dump without your father's say-so."

"What on earth are you talking about?"

"Seriously? Your whole life is just one big search for his approval." Bobby used his spindly *Supinator* muscle to turn his hand over, and he held up a skinny index finger. "He went to Brown; so, of course you went to Brown." The middle finger joined the index. "He went to Yale for medical school; so did you." The fourth finger came up, adorned by the *X-Men* Wolverine ring she had bought him at the Midtown Comics on 143rd. "You even came to this crappy excuse for a hospital just because he did... God forbid you ever had an independent thought."

Her intestines gurgled, her face twisted into the beginnings of a snarl, and her eyes narrowed. She was going to have to stop telling him so much about herself—the little shit never forgot anything. "You about done?"

"Hardly." He raised his pinky finger, which was bowed inward at a steep angle, a condition called clinodactyly. "And where will you be going in July, instead of staying here with me? Yup, that's right, that high-falluting hospital where your daddy is the Chief of the Medical Staff."

"Why aren't I going to go for Orthopedics then, if I want to be so much like him?"

"It's not that you want to be like him—it's because you want to *please* him. That's why you're going to be a stupid radiologist because your daddy's practice needs one." Bobby rolled over, an exertion that left him panting and winded, and for several minutes he was quiet as he struggled to recover his breath. "Didya ever think, Maggie, that you'd be a hell of a lot happier if you did things because you want to and not because your daddy says so?"

An ambulance wailed past. She tried to imagine what cargo it carried: an elderly lunger struggling to breathe; a middle-aged man infarcting his heart; or another teenager unconscious as a result of a bottle of pills and a fifth of cheap liquor.

"You think it's so easy being me, don't you? Well it isn't..." Maggie started.

Bobby remained silent and slumped over with his back to her.

"Imagine doing everything you were asked, and it's still not good enough. Imagine working your ass off every day to be the daughter you're supposed to be, and no one notices unless it's the one time you slipped up a little."

"That's why I wouldn't do it," Bobby said.

The lights stopped flashing in the window, indicating 'the car service'—as Bobby referred to it—had disappeared into the ambulance bay. She wondered which intern on which service would soon be getting another patient to add to his or her list.

"Anyway, that reporter just wants to sell his story, and he's lookin' for the most pathetic victim he can find." Bobby pulled up the scrubs he was wearing and pointed to his legs, which were as skinny as a chicken's. It was one of the reasons he could hardly stand up; his leg muscles had wasted away because of the nerve damage. "It's bad enough to have legs like this... You think I want them posted all over the Internet?"

Maggie said nothing. Prior to starting her internship, she had always believed every problem had a solution, every illness had a treatment, and every question had an answer, but eight months of hell and the little boy lying on this dirty stretcher were teaching her otherwise.

He ran his hand over his hairless thigh. The skin on his legs had taken on the hue of a dirty sock, consequent to the effect of a platinum-containing drug that had circulated through his body for weeks.

"I look like I haven't had a bath for months," Bobby said.

The demonstration went on, as Maggie fought back tears—God how Bobby hated tears. He showed her: the yellow glint of his eye, a sign of his failing liver; the stump of his amputated arm; the sallow glow of his bare scalp; the rotting stumps of his teeth.

"That's why he wants to use me...because I'm a bad joke of person. That's all."

She knew she shouldn't have asked him (What would Yoda say if she had overheard?) but something—the sleeplessness, the hurt from Bobby's words, the vice gripping her heart—let it slip out before she could hold it back.

"So if you don't want to help anyone else, Bobby, what is it you do want?"

She had thought about this very question for hours, as

she sat in the call room waiting for her beeper to ring, or in the conference room waiting for evening rounds to start, or in the Emergency Department waiting for a patient to come back from Diagnostic Imaging. The monotony had always provided the answers: a mother and father; no cancer; a life outside these godforsaken four walls.

Bobby's answer was none of these: "I want no one to feel sorry for me. I want no more dumb ass smiles that people think are going to make feel better about my lousy life. I want no more pity. I am so sick and tired of pity I could spit."

He rolled over and tried to spit on the floor for emphasis, but his salivary glands had been torched by five years of chemotherapy and he couldn't make any. It started slowly, just a slight tremor in his back, but it gained momentum. The sobs came, followed by great whoops of air that Maggie worried would break his brittle ribs. Perhaps it was just the emotional drain of venting his spleen to Maggie; maybe it was the fact he couldn't even spit when he wanted to; probably it was everything—the cancer that wouldn't go away, the life that was so short *and* so interminable, the unbearable boredom of his everyday existence.

She would not be able to remember making a conscious decision to lie on the bed with him, but that is where she ended up, holding him in her arms, hugging him as tightly as she dared. Just the occasional tear flowed down his face, his lacrimal glands being as shriveled up as the rest of him. She wiped these away with a tissue, ignoring the tears welling in *her* eyes, dripping down her face, and spilling—salty and warm—over her lips.

They fell asleep, locked in a three-armed embrace. Her iPhone woke her at five a.m., and she slipped out of the room and headed to her locker in the basement to start a new day.

Chapter Six

The Chapel of Perpetual Mercy was on the ground floor of the hospital, wedged in between the cafeteria and the phlebotomy station. Years ago, when the hospital had been constructed by the Sisters of Perpetual Mercy, it had stood alone as the central focus of the architecture, but times changed, technology advanced, and hospitals grew—even Our Lady of the Golden Arches.

Maggie pushed open the heavy wooden doors of the chapel and knelt down in the last row. The chapel was quiet; only one other person, a member of the cleaning staff she had seen there many times, knelt in front of the large wooden cross above the simple altar. She listened to the quiet murmuring of the woman as she prayed the rosary in Spanish—*Dios te salve, Maria; Llena eres de gracia*—and wondered what is was like to be inspired by something other than the feel of the rain on a spring morning or the smell of lemon grass from the Thai restaurant across the street from her flat.

The woman crossed herself and exited the chapel, head down in supplication, leaving Maggie alone with the wooden figure of Jesus nailed to the cross. The door opened again, and Father McDaniel stepped inside. By a contract in existence since the early part of the last century, the Jesuit priests from Fordham University provided pastoral care for the patients at Golden Arches and manned the chapel.

"Hey, Maggie."

"Hello, Father."

"Thanks for coming to see me."

"Sure."

She moved over and the priest knelt down next to her. "You must be happy to have the boards under your belt?"

"Assuming I don't have to take them again, yes."

The priest rubbed his well-clipped beard. "The law students always say the same thing about the Bar exam."

There was something about the Jesuit she liked, although perhaps she was prejudiced by his interactions with Bobby, which were characterized by humor and an absence of proselytizing.

"Dr. Foster ordered an ethics consult on one of your patients. He told me you would be the best person to fill me in."

As in all hospitals run by Roman Catholic orders, the chaplain served as the head of the ethics committee, and Maggie couldn't think of a better person than Father McDaniel to fill the role. There was fairness about him, judiciousness that flavored his comments, his actions, and—she supposed—his thoughts.

"What would you like to know?" she asked.

"Everything." He smiled, and his bright blue eyes shone despite the dim lighting in the chapel.

How many broken hearts had he left behind him on his path to the seminary?

"Well, he's twelve-years-old. You have to keep that in mind when you talk to him—he acts like he's much older."

"I remember that about him. It started with his upbringing, I'm afraid, and being in and out of hospitals hasn't made things any better. But I was thinking more in medical terms."

She went through Bobby's case in detail, encouraged by his frequent questions, from his diagnosis at age seven to the events of yesterday morning. If Father McDaniel hadn't been wearing a collar, she would have sworn he was an attending—but one with a bedside manner actually suited for medicine.

"Tell me about his code status," Father McDaniel said.

"There's not much to tell, really. His court-appointed guardian isn't around much, and she refused to sign the Do Not Resuscitate order the last time she was here."

"When was that?"

"A few months ago."

"You can't be serious."

"Sadly, I am. The OSG is strapped, and the guardians have a hard time even making their quarterly visits," Maggie said.

"OSG?"

"Office of the State Guardian. The court appoints them when there is no one else."

"And there is...no one else?"

"Hard to say. His mother gave birth to him under the Brooklyn Bridge. A couple of NYPD officers delivered him. She was dead before she got to the hospital, and she didn't have any ID. Social work made its usual anemic attempt to find any kin, and he ended up a ward of the state."

"So why do you think the guardian wouldn't sign the DNR? You said Bobby's case is terminal, correct?"

"Bobby is status post two bone marrow transplants; both failed. An experimental chemotherapy agent resulted in the amputation of his left arm. He started another round of chemo after that, but it had to be stopped because it caused a dangerous enlargement of his heart. As soon as we stopped the chemo, his leukemia snuck back, and that's where he is now, between a rock and a hard place. Pediatric Oncology won't give him any further chemo, he isn't a candidate for another bone marrow transplant, and his enlarged heart hasn't killed him yet—although it tried real hard the other day."

"A big heart isn't a good thing?" Father McDaniel asked.

She shook her head. "The structural change in his heart not only hinders its ability to pump blood, it also predisposes it to potentially lethal disruptions of its normal rhythm."

The chapel vibrated as the hospital's antiquated boiler, which was immediately underneath them, exploded into life. The hum of the flame was loud enough to drown out the soft melody of the music—one of Handel's lesser-known concertos—being played by the overhead speakers.

"Okay, so why didn't the guardian sign the order?" he asked.

"Because it requires a court order to make a ward of the state a DNR. And the OSG doesn't have the time to fill out the paperwork."

Father McDaniel sat back in the pew. "I was afraid you were going to say that."

***

Located on the other side of the McDonald's, Our Lady of Perpetual Mercy's Outpatient Care Center—a place the interns called 'the orifice'—stood as a concrete reminder that nothing should ever have been built in the 1970's. It had been scheduled for remodeling several times, demolition on at least two occasions, and repainting once, but it had rebuffed all of these attempts strictly on a monetary basis. No one—least of all Greta Oberhausen, the hospital's tight-fisted CEO—wanted to spend any money on a clinic that was always awash in red.

Maggie had none of these thoughts in mind as she weaved her way through the crack in the barbed wire fence guarding the parking lot and entered the building 'black,' a term Garcia—who read too many spy novels— used to mean not going through the waiting room. She set her coffee down on her desk, a three-foot square section of cracked linoleum countertop with a picture of her family around last year's Christmas tree.

She opened up her laptop and started scrolling through the list of triages waiting for her: a young girl who wanted to go on birth control; an elderly lunger asking for a Rx for an air conditioner; a middle-age man complaining about erectile dysfunction caused by the blood pressure medicine she had prescribed; and on and on. Midway through the list—a thorny one from a man requesting a few days off work for a 'personal issue'—the door banged open behind her, and Bertie, one of the nurses who staffed the clinic, shuffled into the room, canvas bags hanging from her outstretched arms.

"There you are, Minnie. I've got something for you."

Everyone in the Outpatient Care Center had taken to calling her 'Minnie' ever since she had stuck a picture of her favorite cartoon character over her own picture on her nametag. It was a gross violation of hospital rules, of course, but none of the administration had enforced the rule ever since one of the interns had been stalked several years back by a sexual predator.

Maggie got up and helped Bertie unload the 'food bag:' two Tupperware containers filled with home baked ginger snaps, a four-pack of Chobani Greek Yogurts, a tin of chocolate-covered almonds, and a six pack of Diet Coke, to which Bertie was hopelessly addicted. The other bag was chuck full of softball equipment—Bertie was one of the leading home run hitters in MUNY history and often practiced her swing when it was slow. Bertie tucked her athletic bag underneath her desk, levered open one of the cookie containers and grabbed a handful of cookies for her.

"You've got to try these. New recipe," Bertie said.

Maggie thanked her and tried one of the cookies—it was, as always, one of the best things she had ever tasted. She was also sure the half-dozen cookies Bertie had given her would set her back a month on the diet she was always on working, but some things couldn't be helped.

"So, Bertie, what's been going around here?"

It had only been three days since Maggie had been at the clinic, through which she rotated two afternoons per week for the whole year, but three days was an eternity at the orifice, where gossip and shit accumulated at the rate of an inch per hour each. And there was no one better to fill her in then Bertie, who—the interns loved to claim—worked at the orifice for the sole reason that it was the epicenter of gossip.

They ate their cookies and sipped their diet Cokes as Bertie gave a breathless monologue about the goings on at Our Lady of the Golden Arches: one of the senior radiologists had been caught with his pants down in the Diagnostic Imaging center; Sister Josephine, the hospital's president (and, at 56, the youngest of the Sisters of Perpetual Mercy) had been diagnosed with pancreatic cancer; one of the housekeepers had announced that he was no longer female (Bertie had suspected it all along); and so on. Bertie's gossiping always ended with what the interns called 'the short list,' the lucky ladies, who—in Bertie's estimation—were likely to be the next women to date Dr. Foster, on whom the clinic nurse had had a longstanding crush.

"How are you, doctor?" Bertie asked Maggie.

"I'm happy the boards are over."

"I bet. How did they go?"

Maggie shrugged and got up to start clinic, which began poorly; the first patient—a diabetic follow-up—came in with a list of blood sugars all over 300, and the second patient screamed at her when she wouldn't refill her Vicodin Rx early. The third patient no showed for his callous removal, which was a shame because Maggie had been looking forward to it. Things started to improve with the fourth patient, who Maggie, with the help of one of the attendings on hand, had diagnosed with Polymyalgia Rheumatica, an inflammatory condition that stiffened the hip and shoulder muscles. The patient was feeling better, and there was nothing like helping a patient to feel better to make an intern happy.

Ariel Travers—the overdose she had attended to in the hospital—was her fifth patient of the day. Maggie found her in Room 2a, a closet like room the custodians had created a few years back to add more space.

"It's good to see you, Ariel. How are you doing?" Maggie asked.

"Good."

Ariel stared down at the floor as Maggie tapped a few keys and imported the history and physical she had written into the chart note.

"You look great, Ariel."

Ariel smiled at the compliment, transforming her plain face into a pretty one.

"So, you've been home for what...three days now?"

A nod.

"You live with your mother, right?"

"Uh-huh."

"Anyone else living there?"

"My mom's boyfriend."

"You get along with him okay?" Maggie asked.

"He doesn't beat or molest me if that's what you're getting at."

The intern clicked on her H&P, and called up the Social History. According to what she had gleaned from the record—the patient hadn't been conscious on admission—Ariel lived with her mother in a single-family home on a street, the intern knew, that had undergone gentrification a few years back.

"Anyone else?" Maggie asked.

"I have a little brother, but he spends most of his time with my dad in Westchester."

She clicked on the Patient Information tab and saw that the patient's insurance—Blue Cross, no less, a rarity in the clinic—was provided by a Scott Travers, same last name as Ariel, home address in Sleepy Hollow.

"That's it?" Maggie asked.

"Why are you asking me all these questions?"

"Just trying to get to know you."

The intern smiled, and the girl blushed and softened. "No, no one else."

In truth, she should have responded, 'because I am curious and I want to know why you tried to kill yourself,' but lies of omission were allowed, at least according to Yoda:

"Keep it about the patient, Intern. It's always about the patient. I know your mother likes to brag about you in her bridge club, and I have never met a doctor who doesn't like to talk about him or herself, but don't do it. For once in your life, keep the focus on someone else."

And that's what Maggie did, finding out that Ariel had no significant medical history; had never been operated on; did not have any psychiatric problems, history of mental illness or prior suicide attempts; did not take any regular medications, Rx or otherwise; and had no family history of psychiatric illness.

"Have you been back to school yet?" Maggie asked.

A slow shake of the head, her face pointing at the floor, long brown hair hanging down over her forehead.

"Are you having problems at school?"

"No."

"Then why didn't you go back?"

"Just not ready, I guess."

The inquisition continued: no, Ariel was not sexually active; no, Ariel did not use drugs; and, no, other than the vodka she had drunk to wash down the pills, Ariel had never drank alcohol before. Teenagers usually denied these things in the company of their parents, but Maggie generally believed them when they were alone in the room. The problem was that there was—as Ariel had insisted prior to being discharged—no reason she had tried to kill herself.

"Is your mother here?" Maggie asked.

A nod.

Maggie left the room and located Ariel's mother in the waiting room. They went in to the intern's office and closed the door.

Ariel's mother was excellent evidence that social problems extended to all rungs of the socioeconomic ladder: her powder blue Nieman Marcus dress had been professionally tailored, highlighting the curvature of her breasts, which, Maggie was certain, had been surgically augmented, and her silk pashmina stank of Talbot's.

"Is there a problem, doctor?"

Of course, there's a problem, you Idiot, your daughter tried to kill herself.

"Just trying to make sure Ariel is okay. How does she seem to you?"

"Alright."

"She isn't having any problems at school?"

"Not that I know of..."

"No boyfriend issues?"

"I don't think she's seeing anyone."

"Her grades are good?"

The woman consulted her Cartier watch as if someone had hidden the answer to the question there. "Report cards don't come out for a while, so I wouldn't know."

"What does she say about her classes? Are they going well?"

"To be honest, my boyfriend moved in a few weeks ago, and with all the extra commotion, I haven't had the chance to ask."

A picture started to form in Maggie's mind—a picture of a young woman playing second fiddle to her mother's love interest. "I see."

"Will it be much longer? I'm in a bit of a hurry."

The woman smiled—the humorless smile that Botox inevitably granted. The woman didn't say what her hurry was, but Maggie was pretty sure it was a play on Broadway (this lady had *Hamilton* written all over her) or dinner at Daniel on the Upper East Side.

"Just a few more minutes," Maggie said.

Maggie excused herself and rejoined Ariel—who was busy looking at the computer she had left behind. The young girl was so absorbed by it that she almost didn't hear the *thunk* of the heavy soundproof door closing or feel the vibration as the poorly aligned edge scraped against the jam.

"Pretty cool, isn't it?" Maggie asked.

Ariel looked up. "Very cool. You don't mind, do you?"

"No, not at all." Maggie sat down next to her and spent the next fifteen minutes showing the electronic health record to the girl who had, not five days prior, tried to kill herself by swallowing every pill she could find in her mother's medicine cabinet. (After meeting the patient's mother, Maggie realized why there had been Xanax inside.) "Are you interested in medicine, Ariel?"

"I might be. Or maybe in writing medical software." Ariel reached up to tuck a strand of her hair behind her ear, allowing the long sleeve covering her forearm to drop. Several fresh cuts, beefy and red, adorned the inside of her forearm.

"I want you to see a counselor, Ariel."

Ariel pulled her sleeve down. "I already am, Maggie, some stupid lady my mother goes to. She doesn't know the first thing about me because she never shuts up long enough to listen."

"I'll find someone else."

"It's okay; I'll be alright."

It was something teenagers told her all the time, despite all objective evidence to the contrary. Maggie had told her own mother the same thing, some ten years ago when her panic attacks had first started, and consequently, nothing had ever been done about them.

"Have you ever thought about volunteering at Our Lady of Perpetual Mercy?" Maggie asked.

"Not really."

"Would you like to? I can arrange it."

Ariel lifted her head and smiled, revealing her perfect teeth. "I guess so."

"Good. Give me your cell, and I'll text you the details after I speak to the volunteer coordinator."

Room 4 was at the end of the hall, on the other side of a utility room filled with outdated medical equipment that the interns called 'the dung heap.' Maggie pushed open the door and sat on the table next to the patient, who was sobbing quietly into a crumpled tissue.

A number of opening lines presented themselves to her brain—"*What brings you in today?*" and "*What can I do for you?*" and "*How are you doing?*"—But none seemed appropriate so she just draped her long arm over Carla's back and gave her a shoulder to cry on.

"It wasn't supposed to be like this, Maggie. I just don't know what happened."

Curiosity urged her to ask what had happened, but experience insisted she remain quiet. She handed Carla a box of tissues.

"It was my fault. I should never have said anything to him." Carla lifted her head for a second, and Maggie spotted them right away, the ugly bruises on her cheeks that even Carla's heavy application of make-up couldn't hide.

A touch of anger surged through her intestines, but she ignored it, and it went away. Yoda had been insistent with them about anger: *This is Golden Arches, Interns, not some private hospital in the Hamptons. You're going to see some bad shit—real, bad shit—and you're going to see it all the time. Rule number 1? Know what it is? Never get angry. It's easy to give in to anger, interns, but don't ever let me catch you do it. Never once, not even one time. Anger is the enemy of good doctoring. Got that?*

Maggie passed over to the supply cabinet and fetched some solvent, which she used to clean all the foundation away from Carla's battered face. A half-dozen bruises greeted her, in various stages of bloom; there were a few yellowed ones—ten to fourteen days old—a pair of bluish bruises the color of the wood violets that grew in her mother's garden, and two black ones, new and fresh, just underneath her cracked cheekbones.

Opening up her laptop, Maggie ordered a series of X-Rays of her face and examined Carla's pupils with a flashlight. They were equal and reacted normally.

"He didn't mean to hurt me, Maggie. You understand that, don't you?"

She lifted the sleeves of Carla's shirt, revealing the shear injuries on her forearms, and added a skeletal survey to the X-Ray orders tab.

"You're not going to report this, are you Maggie?"

Underneath Carla's skintight blouse, Maggie noted a handful of cigarette burns on her back.

"Those were accidental," Carla said.

Selecting a tongue depressor from a—supposedly—sterile glass jar, Maggie used it to examine Carla's teeth; several were chipped, and one had been busted off at the root. She scrolled down to the orders section and clicked on the tab for a dental consult.

"Where's Diego, Carla?"

"With my mother."

Carla's mother was a slightly older version of Carla, with the same shade of lipstick and a similar penchant for wearing clothes two sizes too small. Maggie had met her briefly in the hospital, when she had dropped by to smuggle in a pack of cigarettes for Carla.

"Did he hurt Diego?" Maggie asked.

Carla dropped her head. "No."

Maggie passed to the wall and activated the intercom. "Bertie, get the social worker on call please."

"No social worker." Carla tried to get off the exam table but the intern stiff-armed her back.

"Are you still using?" Maggie asked.

The head dropped again.

"Carla, I'm not trying to take Diego away from you. But he's in danger."

"What's a social worker going to do, anyway?"

"Get the police involved; get a restraining order."

"What a joke. You have no idea what Reggie's like. A restraining order's just going to piss him off more than he already is."

"What's he so upset about?"

Carla didn't say. "Just please don't call the social worker."

"Carla, I don't have a choice."

Carla slid off the exam table, grabbed her purse, and headed to the door. The intern put a hand out to stop her, but Carla brushed past it.

"I'm still going to call the social worker, Carla."

Carla stopped at the door and turned to face her. "You were good to Diego, so I'm tellin' you. You're going to be sorry if you call the social worker, Maggie. He'll hurt me, he'll hurt Diego, and he'll hurt you."

Chapter Seven

Situated next to the morgue in the sub-basement of Our Lady of the Golden Arches Hospital, the Medical Records Department was the only department in the long history of the hospital never to have been moved. There had been talk, ten years ago when the computerized medical record had started, that 'the cave' was going to either move or be phased out, but the talk had been just that, and the cave stayed put.

Maggie pushed her way in to through the heavy door at the front and sat down at a cubicle deep in the bowels of the department. She plugged her laptop in, left her white coat on the chair to mark her territory, and went forward to the main desk. It was Saturday, and only one person was staffing the desk, a man the interns called The Bear due to his heavy black beard and ursine disposition.

"I'm Maggie Johnson. I asked for some charts to be pulled."

The Bear eyed her over, looking back and forth from her nametag—which claimed she was Minnie Mouse with Minnie's picture to prove it—to her face and back again. He vocalized some sort of acknowledgement and disappeared, returning a few minutes later with two stacks of charts that he piled on the counter. Maggie gathered them in her arms and returned to her desk.

She logged on to her computer, clicked on the Delinquent

Discharge Summary tab, and watched with dismay as the computer generated a list of twenty patients for whom a discharge summary had never been created. She collected a diet Coke from the vending machine and started pacing through the stacks, wanting to do anything but start on the list of summaries on her screen.

"Hey, Maggie."

Maggie stopped and turned to see Melendez camped out on a desk filled with charts. "What are you doing here?"

"Same thing you are...discharge summaries. The damn suits won't give me my diploma unless I do them."

At this point in her career, Maggie had rotated through a half-dozen hospitals, and in every one, there had existed a natural antipathy between the administrators, who made all the policy but did none of the work, and the interns and the other house staff, who did all of the work but made none of the policy.

"You wouldn't do them otherwise?" Maggie asked.

"Hell, no. It's total crap we have to do this bullshit. The attendings should be the ones doing 'em; they're the ones who are getting paid the big bucks."

"Look at it as a learning opportunity."

Melendez scowled, sharpening the features of his round face. "Learning opportunity? Fuck that. It's good old-fashioned slave labor, and you know it." He resumed typing, mumbling under his breath about the injustices of internship. "For Christ's sake, you sound like Yoda. You're turning into Yoda; did you know that?"

"What's the matter with Yoda?"

"Besides being a fucking dwarf, you mean?"

Melendez smoothed down the tuft of hair that had a habit of sticking out of the V-neck of his scrub top. Almost all the other interns wore T-shirts underneath their scrubs, but Melendez had stopped this practice long ago.

"Yoda can kiss my big, fat ass. She's just another administrator as far as I am concerned. If she's such a genius, why the hell doesn't she have a regular job? I heard she's been the chief resident here for ages," Melendez said.

Almost everything about Yoda was innuendo and rumor; few facts were known. Some said she had been the chief resident at Golden Arches for at least five years; others claimed she had been there almost ten. One of the nurses said that Yoda had done a short stint as a private physician in an office somewhere in Yonkers. A custodian who had done time in the Lincoln Correctional Facility reported she had been the prison's doctor, but nobody could corroborate the statement.

"Maybe she just likes what she's doing, Caid. Did you ever think of that?"

He shook his head. "There's only three motivations for doing something: money, sex, and power. And, when you think about it, people use money and power to get sex, so that means there's really only one motivation for doing anything."

"Where does helping people fit into the equation?" Maggie asked.

"Good question. I help people all the time because that agency nurse on pediatrics I've been shagging gets all crazy horny when she sees me putting a bandage on a cut finger or bringing some kid an ice cream cup."

"That's really why you became a doctor? As a way to get laid?"

"At least I'm honest with myself. I know you and Williams and all the rest of the hand-holders want to save the fucking world, but I'm just in it for the sex. And it's working like a fucking charm, you know that. This hot Dominican chick I'm dating right now...or let me say one of the hot Dominican chicks I'm dating now...she wouldn't have given me the time of fucking day before I became a doctor, and now she can't stop herself from screwing me every time we see each other. Hell, I don't even have to buy her dinner to get in her pants. Do you know why that is?"

Maggie knew why, but she gave Melendez the satisfaction of telling her.

"Because she wants to be a fucking doctor's wife, that's why. Not all of us grew up in some swank town in Westchester. She wants to fuck her way out of *El Barrio,* and I'm going to let her try. I know you think I'm horrible for saying stuff like that, but I tell it like it is. I look out for number one, Maggie. And it's time you did also."

"What does that mean?"

"Look at yourself, for Christ's sake. You're a beautiful girl and all, but you look like hell. You've got circles under your eyes, your eyes are bloodshot, and I don't know what the fuck is going on with your skin. Shit, Maggie, when you walked into this hellhole ten months ago, you had skin like a China doll."

"Geez, Caid, you really know how to make a girl feel good."

"I'm not trying to make you feel good, and—I can't believe I'm fucking sayin' this—I'm not trying to get you in the sack, either, which isn't to say you don't pop up in the occasional fantasy."

Melendez grabbed a pack of gumdrops from his lab coat and started chomping on them. He always carried a steady supply of sugar in his pockets—Twizzlers, Skittles and Chuckles were his favorites— most of which had been pilfered from the various nurses' stations throughout Golden Arches. He gulped down a mouthful and regarded Maggie without a trace of embarrassment on his face.

"I'm trying to do you a fucking favor," he said.

"You want to do me a favor?"

He nodded. "Uh-huh. That big mouth Garcia spilled it to me the other day that you're thinking of staying on here as a pediatric resident?" He looked at her, with his full lips in a pouty smile. "Are...you...out...of...your...fuckin'...mind?"

Melendez had a way of putting things such that no matter what he said he always sounded like he knew what he was talking about, even though, in most cases, he did not.

"Let me get this straight... you want to stay here at this sad excuse for a hospital because you want to help people?"

She couldn't think of one single reply; she didn't even nod.

"You can make a difference in people's lives anywhere, Maggie, doing anything. It's the way you go about it, not where you are or what you're doing."

It was great advice, and she couldn't believe she was hearing it from a man who wanted to be a doctor solely as means to get laid.

"They'll suck the life out of you if you stay here. Listen to me for once, will ya. Smile and nod until they hand you that diploma, and then get the hell outta here."

***

At times that the insanity of being an intern really got to Maggie, and this was one of those times. There was nothing worse than writing the discharge summary—as Melendez had so eloquently stated—and she had a list of twenty she needed to complete. She started to get up, to go somewhere, anywhere else, but Yoda's words rang in her ear:

"There will be a moment, Intern, when being an intern sucks to the point where you will want to throw up your hands and just walk away—and it won't be the death of a patient you were close to or making a mistake you shouldn't have made or being so tired that you don't care about anything but sleep. It will be the tedium, Intern, the monotony, the awful boredom of doing the same stupid task again and again without point. And when that happens, what do you do? You shrug your shoulders, grab a diet Coke, and keep doing what you're doing. You're

not the first intern who had to do all the scutwork, and you won't be the last—so just shut up about it, drink your damn diet Coke, and get it done."

Maggie settled back into her chair and clicked on the next patient. She liked to play a mental game with herself in an effort to make the task at hand bearable. The game was a simple one. Using only the patient's name, DOB, primary diagnosis and dates of the admission and discharge, she tried to recreate the entire hospitalization in her mind. It was a formidable task given the complexity and the volume of information generated by the modern medical machine, but one that she could usually master, except for today. Today, with the sun shining somewhere overhead and her mind swirling, she failed miserably and had to resort to the chart straightway.

By the time morning gave way to afternoon, Maggie had knocked off ten names from the list, but her momentum was waning despite the collection of diet Coke cans on the desk.

"Yoda told me I might find you here."

Maggie looked up from her misery to see her father standing there. He was wearing a nylon tee and a pair of khaki shorts that revealed way too much of his skinny legs.

"What are you doing here?" Maggie asked.

"I came to take you for a walk in Central Park. It's a gorgeous day out there."

"I can't right now, I have to finish these summaries."

"Can't you get the intern to do it?" She stared at him as his face broke out into a smile. "Oh, that's right, you are the intern."

Maggie's father was a serious man for the most part— she was sure his colleagues at Gotham Orthopedics would agree—but with a silly side that few but his children, especially his youngest children, ever saw. There was the time he'd squeezed into one of her mother's dresses and pretended to be *Mary Poppins,* singing the entire score in an excruciating falsetto; a weekend when he'd bought a puppet theatre at a garage sale and played the whole cast of *Pinocchio*; and—her favorite memory—the night he had recited every line of *Monty Python and the Holy Grail.*

He sneezed, then blew his nose into a handkerchief.

"You getting sick?"

He shook his head. "Nope, just allergic to dust, and Shady Cottage is loaded with it."

Shady Cottage was the name of their second home in the Catskills. It had been in the Johnson family for generations.

"You seem to be spending quite a lot of time there recently."

He shrugged his shoulders.

"I thought you hated the place."

Maggie could remember him stubbornly refusing to take her up there, despite her vociferous begging.

"It's growing on me." He wiped his nose again with the handkerchief, then stuffed it into his pocket. "I haven't done a discharge summary in a while; it'll be fun."

She tried to protest, but he wouldn't listen, and they went to work. A few hours later, she submitted the last delinquent summary and gave her father a big kiss on the cheek. "Do we still have time to go for a walk?

"I'm afraid not, Maggie. I've got some things to do before your mother and I see you for dinner."

Maggie's face fell; she'd forgotten all about this evening's dinner with her parents, which meant she'd lost the opportunity to create an ironclad excuse. It wasn't that it wouldn't be good to see them—her mother, in particular, who she adored—but she hadn't had a free night in weeks, and Melendez had been making some noise about organizing an intern's night out in Hell's Kitchen.

"You didn't forget, did you?"

She considered telling him she had nothing to wear, but that would have ended with an impromptu shopping spree on 5th Avenue during which cost would be the only thing not considered. As he had access to the intern's call schedule, she couldn't just tell him she was on-call, which was a pity, as being on-call was the best possible excuse for getting out of anything. If she told him she was coming down with something, he would play doctor and treat it. If she told him she had a date, he would insist she bring him.

"Of course, I didn't. Can't wait."

"That's my girl. See you at seven."

Chapter Eight

The restaurant was one of those intimate affairs that dotted Lexington Avenue between 33rd and 40th. Her parents were there when she arrived, her mother having made the trip down from Sleepy Hollow. Roger Johnson had, of course, made the reservation—it was someplace one of his buddies from Columbia/Presbyterian had insisted he try—and texted the address to her.

She gave her father a peck on the cheek and slid next to her mother on the high bench seat at the back of the room. Her father was dressed in an Oxford shirt and Harris Tweed coat—the same thing he wore every day to work—and her mother showed off her long, slender arms in a cornflower blue sundress. A bottle of Pinot Grigio was chilling on the table, and the remains of two drinks— she would have bet her modest paycheck they were Grey Goose and tonics—lay in front of her father.

"How long have you been here?" Maggie asked her mother.

"I got here a few minutes ago. Your father has been here for a while." She glanced sideways at his empty drink glasses for a brief second, then returned her gaze to Maggie. The waiter appeared, and her father ordered a plate of calamari for the table and another Grey Goose and tonic for himself.

"Your father tells me you're enjoying your Pediatrics rotation?"

Roger Johnson grimaced, started to say something but thought better of it, and took a long sip from his drink instead.

"It's alright."

"Just alright? Roger was telling me you were thinking of switching your residency training to pediatrics."

Her father's glass slapped the table, just hard enough to slosh a few of the ice cubes onto the tablecloth. "I thought we agreed not to bring that up."

"*You* agreed not to bring it up, dear; *I* think it's something we should discuss."

Her father let out his breath in a long, slow exhalation. Her mother ignored him, turning her head toward Maggie and placing her hand on Maggie's forearm. "Your father forgets you're not a little girl anymore."

"I haven't forgotten anything of the kind; I just can't sit idly around and watch…"

"Roger." Her voice was even and calm—as it always was—but firm enough to prevent a rebuttal, although Maggie was sure her mother would hear about it later. Her father spied someone he knew at a different table, and got up to go say hello.

"Now tell me about this interest in pediatrics."

She told her mother about Bobby, Diego and Carla—the baby who had a baby—and about the girl who had taken everything in the medicine cabinet trying to call for help.

"You can change to pediatrics if you want to," her mother said.

Maggie said nothing; their eyes locked.

"There's no law saying you have to do exactly as your father wants."

"There seems to be one for you," Maggie said.

Her mother lowered her head for a moment and then raised it high, tucking a loose strand of long grey hair behind her ear. "I made my choice; now I'm living with it. You're going to have to live with your own choice, so you may as well be the one to make it."

Her father returned with the waiter, who laid down a trio of Capresi salads, which they ate in tense silence broken only by the occasional burst of nervous laughter from a table in front and the false assurances of the man in the booth behind them: *'I'm going to leave her...soon. I promise.'* Things took a turn for the better with the arrival of the entrees. Her father lightened up a bit with the first few bites of his *bistecca alla Fiorentina,* and her mother's pursed lips relaxed as she started into her *Cioppino*. The dinner conversation revolved around her oldest brother's exploits on the high seas around the Cape of Good Hope—he was a Captain in the Merchant Marine—and her younger sister's successes in soccer at Taft. By the time the panna cotta showed up for dessert, the atmosphere had warmed appreciably.

Her father paid the bill, and they walked out. It was a balmy spring evening and they strolled up Lexington Avenue taking in the wares displayed in the windows. They arrived at her mother's Volvo wagon, and her mother kissed her on the cheek and slid behind the wheel.

Her father put his long arm around her shoulder. "We need to talk about this pediatrics thing."

"It's just something I'm considering, Dad. You don't have to get all upset about it."

"We had a plan, Maggie."

It had been his plan all along—it had never been hers. She'd wanted to be a pediatrician ever since she'd bandaged her little brother's skinned knee after he'd fallen off his bike.

"You've always done the right thing, Maggie; I have no doubt you'll do the right thing again."

She nodded.

"Give me a call if you want. I would be happy to talk things through with you."

Didya ever think, Maggie, that you'd be a hell of a lot happier if you stopped trying to do what's expected of you? Maybe you'd be able to sleep like a normal person if you did things because you want to and not because your daddy says so.

"Okay, Dad. Thanks."

Maggie watched them drive off and started off towards Central Park. It was a lovely night for a walk, and her favorite place in the whole world was close enough to smell the nuts being roasted by the street vendors. She walked past the horse carriages and weaved through a queue of dog walkers before settling onto a track toward the lake. Half way to the Bethesda Fountain, she stopped on a bench to slip out of her fleece and found herself next to a man tightening his sneakers.

"Maggie?"

Maggie took a second look at him. He was wearing tan chinos and a blue polo shirt and didn't look anything like his white-coated alter ago. "Hello, Dr. Foster."

"Nice night, isn't it, Maggie?"

"Beautiful."

"Out for a walk?"

She nodded.

"Mind if I join you?"

"No, not at all."

She tied the fleece around her waist and they started off side-by-side, stopping frequently to accommodate the other pedestrians on the narrow path. They took a break at the overlook and watched a pair of geese intimidate a flock of ducks, and monitored the slow progress of a dozen rowboats.

"I was going to get some dinner at the Boathouse. Want to join me?"

"I've already eaten, but thanks."

"Okay, just drinks then."

He moved along before she could respond, and she caught up with him by the rowboats turned upside down against the eastern shore of the lake. They went around a busload of Japanese tourists and ducked inside the building with the copper-covered roof. The Boathouse was crowded, and a large group of people was waiting, but he grabbed her hand and led her to a small table overlooking the lake. The waitress materialized, and he ordered a bottle of Vinho Verde, which she brought back to the table before Maggie could stretch the napkin across her lap. He poured them both a glass of wine and raised his: "To a beautiful spring night."

She clinked his glass and sipped the wine: Dr. Foster had excellent taste.

"I heard a rumor about you, Maggie."

"Oh? What's that?"

"I heard you were considering staying on with us."

"Who told you that?"

"Dr. Clarke."

Dr. Clarke was the director of the Pediatrics Residency at Golden Arches.

"Well that's not really much of a rumor, then, is it?"

"No, I guess it isn't. How serious are you about it?"

"Now you sound like my father."

"You're comparing me to the most prominent orthopedic surgeon in Manhattan?"

"You say that like it's a good thing."

The waitress came back with a plate of Beef Carpaccio and a serving of Yellowfin Tuna Sashimi. As soon as she left, a brunette in a dark pantsuit detached herself from the bar and strolled over to them. "Hello, Jack."

"Hello, Greta. How are you?"

"Not as good as you, I can see. Who's this pretty young thing?"

"This is Dr. Maggie Johnson."

Maggie extended her hand, and the woman grabbed her fingers and gave them a limp shake.

"Nice to meet you, Maggie. Don't listen to anything Jack has to say about me—he's a fearful liar." She walked away, exaggerating the sway of her wide hips but swiveled on one stiletto heel and returned. "And he's not very good at returning phone calls, either."

Dr. Foster smiled and sliced into the beef, and Greta left for good this time. Maggie gazed out the window at he ate, watching the light fade over the water. It had been a cold winter in New York, and the warm night was crawling with park-goers: boaters, walkers, street performers and the inevitable lovers, meandering around Central Park as if they had nowhere else to go.

"Who was that?" Maggie asked.

"Her name is Greta Oberhausen; she's the CEO of Golden Arches."

Maggie had heard many stories about the chief executive, all of which included the phrase 'biggest bitch in Manhattan.' "Know her well?"

"We had a few dates last fall."

Foster finished the last of the beef carpaccio. Maggie inquired about Oberhausen again, but he waived noncommittally and changed the subject. When he was finished eating, he insisted on escorting her back to her apartment, and they headed north and west to the subway stop at 77th and Lexington. The train was crowded, and they stood, pushed against one another by the throng of riders. They disembarked at 33rd Street, and he saw her to the door of her building.

"Thanks for the wine," she said.

"You're welcome."

"Good night, Jack." She reached for her wallet and placed it against the ID pad. The door clicked free, and she pulled it open, turning to watch him walk away. But he was still standing there, staring at her awkwardly. She smiled a good bye; he leaned in and gave her a kiss on the cheek, close enough to her lips to taste the tiramisu he had eaten for dessert.

***

Maggie got off the Number One train at 116th and headed south along 3rd Avenue. It was an early Sunday evening, the sun was still shining, and even *El Barrio* looked like a reasonable place in its bright glow. The Robert F. Wagner Houses, which everybody in Spanish Harlem called the Triborough Houses, occupied a swath of land bordering 106th street. Maggie wandered around until she found Carla's building, a twenty-two-story brick tenement in disrepair, and followed one of the residents inside. She considered taking the stairwell but didn't think Yoda's admonition against elevators applied to real life and rode up to the 16th floor. Carla's apartment was in the back, down the length of a dimly lit corridor that smelled of stale urine and cats. She knocked on the door, causing an outburst of Spanish to erupt from inside.

She knocked again; a parade of footsteps came to the door, which opened a fraction until the chain pulled taught. Carla's swollen eye appeared in the slot.

"What are you doing here, Maggie?"

"I just wanted to make sure you were you okay."

"I'm fine; now go before Reggie gets here." Carla tried to shut the door, but Maggie had inserted her toe into the crack.

"I'm not afraid of Reggie."

"That's because you're a fool, Maggie. Even the police are afraid of him."

Somewhere in the recesses of Maggie's brain, she wondered how a pretty girl like Carla had ever gotten involved with a guy liked Reggie.

"I'm not leaving until you let me in."

Carla glowered at her but eventually released the chain and opened the door. The apartment was a small one; a compact kitchen drowning in dirty dishes abutted the front of the main room, and a pair of narrow bedrooms with a bathroom between them let off the back.

"Why did you come here, Maggie?"

"I already told you."

"And I already said you were going to make it worse."

"Where's Diego?"

Carla pointed at one of the bedrooms. "If I show him to you, will you leave?"

Maggie nodded.

Carla opened the door to the nearest bedroom and switched on the lights. Diego was lying on stomach, fast asleep. Maggie picked him up, inhaling the stench of his full diaper. "I'll change him."

Carla tried to grab him away, but Maggie brushed past her and set him down on the changing table.

"Reggie will be here any minute now, Maggie."

"Diego shouldn't be sleeping on his stomach, Carla. You remember I told you that?"

"What difference does it make?"

Maggie put the finishing touches on a new diaper and placed Diego back in the crib on his back. "Sleeping on his back or side lowers the chance for a crib death. You don't want that, do you?"

Carla shook her head. Despite the dim lighting, a handful of bruises—some fresh—were visible on her face. A dark welt underscored her right eye.

"There's a women's shelter near the hospital, Carla."

"Please leave, Maggie.

Footsteps echoed from the hall. A key scraped against the lock, and the front door swung open. A boy in his late teens walked into the room, throwing his leather coat down onto the old denim sofa. He spied Maggie, and his light brown face twisted into a snarl. "Who the fuck are you?"

Maggie stepped forward and stuck out her hand, which he ignored. "I'm Maggie Johnson, Diego's doctor."

His thin lips pressed into a line. "What the fuck are you doing here?"

"A house call, of course." She sat down on the sofa and crossed her legs. "Are you the baby's father?"

He took off his flat-brimmed Yankees cap, revealing a shaved head, and tossed it on the couch next to Maggie. "Get the fuck outta here."

Maggie sat still. "There's no need to be like that. I just came to make sure the baby is doing okay."

"I'm not going to tell you again."

Maggie had only been in one altercation in her life, a shoving match in a field hockey game against Harvard. *Where was her Rugby stick when she needed it?* She could almost feel the hardness of the hickory in her hand. How she would have loved to bring it crashing down on this punk's head. Instead, she got to her feet, smiled at Carla, and made for the door.

"Don't never show up here again, bitch."

The hard handle of her Rugby stick slapped against her hand, but Yoda knocked it away. Maggie opened the door and slipped out without another word.

Chapter Nine

Maggie pushed open the door to the conference room and sat down on the only empty chair at the table. She poured herself a cup of coffee from the thermos in the middle of the table and looked around as she drank a long sip. She'd never been to an ethics conference before, and the prospect of something new and different piqued her curiosity. Father McDaniel sat at the head of the oval table, speaking in low tones with Dr. Foster, who sat to his right. Tammy Hunter, Bobby's social worker, held down the chair to McDaniel's right. On the other end of the table, across from Father McDaniel, the state-appointed guardian from the OSG—Saundra Mills according to her nametag—nursed a Diet Coke and what looked to Maggie like a hangover. *No wonder she had trouble making her appointments.*

"Would you mind passing me the sweetener?"

Maggie reached for the plastic cup filled with packets of sugar and a variety of artificial sweeteners and set it down in front of the woman who had just taken the seat next to her.

"Dr. Johnson, isn't it?"

Maggie nodded. "Ms. Oberhausen, right?"

Oberhausen stirred in two packets of artificial sweetener with a plastic spoon as Father McDaniel cleared his throat and opened the thin manila file in front of him. He started off with a short prayer, asking for wisdom and prudence. Maggie would normally have found this to be off-putting, but there was something about the priest that put her at ease. Father McDaniel introduced himself briefly and then nodded at Dr. Foster to do the same. The MSW and OSG followed suit, and then it was Oberhausen's turn.

"I'm Greta Oberhausen, CEO of the hospital."

Hospital by-laws required that a member of the administration be on the Ethics Committee, but Maggie hadn't expected the chief executive officer to be the one attending.

"Maggie Johnson, resident physician in charge of Bobby's care."

"Thanks for coming, Maggie. Why don't you bring us up to speed on Bobby's status?" McDaniel asked.

Maggie set her coffee down and sat upright in the hard plastic chair. Interns almost always presented standing up, and she found it a little awkward to present sitting down. She began, starting with the time-honored tradition of reducing every human being into his or her age, gender and race, *'thirteen-year-old male.'* She had almost said twelve out of sheer habit, but Bobby had celebrated his birthday just yesterday—she'd bought him *The Complete and Unabridged Dictionary of the X-Men* for his birthday.

"This morning Bobby was alert and awake, with no complaints, vital signs stable, cardiac rhythm without ectopy."

"Dr. Foster, anything to add?" the priest asked.

He shook his head.

Maggie sat back in her chair, noticing for the first time the yellow legal pad filled with flowing script that appeared on the table in front of Miss Oberhausen. "Anyone have any questions for Maggie?"

The social worker shrugged her shoulders—in such a way as to magnify the outline of her already large boobs,

over which she had pulled a white top with some effort—
and the OSG sipped her soda.

"I have a few." Oberhausen flipped the legal pad to a
new page and scratched a number of lines with her
Sharpie as they all waited. "Maggie, you mentioned that
Bobby hasn't been requesting his pain medication?"

"That's correct."

Oberhausen pivoted deftly and snatched her leather
attaché case from the worn tiles in the conference room.
She set it on the desk and extracted a large stack of
photocopies, which she had organized into thin piles held
together with clips. She flipped through the top pile,
making a few more notes. "And yet the nurses, when they
do their assessments, all rate Bobby's pain at least 2/7,
and often document a pain as much as 4/7. Were you
aware of this?"

Maggie nodded.

"Then why didn't you do anything about it?" Oberhausen
asked.

"IV Dilaudid is ordered, but he refuses it."

"He refuses his pain medication?"

"Yes."

"Why?"

Maggie decided she didn't like the chief executive
officer. It wasn't so much the questions she asked—they
were, after all, appropriate—but the way she asked them,
in a tone dripping with derision and condescension.

"It sedates him," Maggie said.

Oberhausen made a few notes; the Sharpie squeaked
as it rode over the paper. "Did you try something else?"

Maggie sat back up in her seat; she hadn't been
expecting this. A number of replies flitted through her
head. '*Of course, I did; can't you read?*' or '*Look at the
damn chart*,' but she refused to utter them. She was being
baited, and she wasn't going to take the bait.

"We tried a number of pain medications; he hasn't

tolerated any of them. The Dilaudid seems to work the best, but he rarely takes it," Maggie said.

"By rarely you mean no doses in the last two weeks?" Oberhausen handed her a sheet of paper. It was a photocopy of the Medex on which the nurses documented their administration of all medication. No Dilaudid had been administered for the last two weeks.

"Yes, that's correct."

The Sharpie went back to work on the legal pad. Maggie sipped her coffee. "Can you summarize what *actual treatments* the patient is getting?"

"He's being administered oxygen."

Maggie held her breath for a second—Bobby never wore the nasal cannula because it irritated his nose—but her inquisitor didn't object.

"What for?" Oberhausen asked.

"One of the chemo drugs he was administered at an outside hospital caused scarring in his lungs, and he can't oxygenate well without it."

"Anything else?"

"He gets a cocktail of vitamins by intravenous infusion every day."

"Vitamins?"

Maggie nodded.

"Why don't you just buy a bottle of Flintstones and hand him one?" Oberhausen asked.

Maggie glanced over at Dr. Foster He was staring at her with his spruce green eyes; his face was expressionless. "We tried that actually; he can't swallow them."

Oberhausen went back to her notes. "So, vitamins and pain medication that sits in a drawer. That's it?"

"He gets physical and occupational therapy."

Oberhausen glanced up from her legal pad to look askance at Maggie. "How often does that happen?"

It was ordered for three times per week, Maggie knew, but consequent to cutbacks in the Rehabilitation

Services Department—cutbacks that Oberhausen had made—she doubted that either OT or PT got there more than weekly, and Bobby usually threw them out when they arrived.

"Infrequently," Maggie said.

"Anything else?"

"No."

Oberhausen straightened the collar of her Veronica Beard blazer, which was the same dark grey color as her eyes. "When you say no, Dr. Johnson, you mean that you are doing nothing to address either his pain or the underlying problem causing his pain. Is that correct?"

"That's unfair, Greta." It was Foster. *Finally.*

"What's unfair, Dr. Foster?"

"As Dr. Johnson mentioned, Bobby has already received two bone marrow transplants at an outside hospital. Both failed. A subsequent trial of an experimental chemo agent resulted in the loss of his arm." Foster tried to soften the CEO up with a smile but she just stared at her legal pad, scratching some notes as he spoke. "Yes, Greta, we're not doing anything about the underlying problem because there is *nothing* to do about the underlying problem. He would have stayed at Columbia if there were anything more to do for him. He was transferred here for palliative care."

"A bag of vitamins and a weekly massage? That's what you call palliative care?" Oberhausen asked.

Foster said nothing.

"Why did he have to come here for palliative care, anyway? Couldn't they do that at Columbia?"

"We're a charity hospital, Greta. It's one of the things we do. Are you suggesting we should have turned the poor kid away?" Foster asked.

"Not at all, Dr. Foster. I'm suggesting we do a better job of it."

Swiftly, Oberhausen handed her another photocopy,

this time of the nursing assessments, with the 3/7 and 4/7 circled in red ink. Her full lips—Maggie suspected they were colloid injected—warped into a sneer. "We have only one job to do. These scores indicate we're failing miserably at it."

"I disagree. Bobby chooses to decline the pain medication of his own free will," Maggie said.

"Let me ask you a different question. Why are you letting a thirteen-year-old boy call all the shots?" she asked.

"It's his life."

"You do realize he has a guardian?"

Maggie nodded, now realizing why Melendez referred to Oberhausen as 'the Wicked Witch of the East River.'

Oberhausen turned to Bobby's guardian. "Miss Mills, when is the last time you spoke to Dr. Johnson?"

"I've never spoken to her."

"Never?"

The OSG downed another swallow of her soda and shook her head.

"Is this true, Dr. Johnson?"

"Yes," Maggie said.

"How is it that you have never spoken to the legal guardian, Dr. Johnson, when you have a thirteen-year-old boy in pain and refusing medication?" Oberhausen asked.

Maggie sipped her coffee and collected herself. She was treading water in a maelstrom, and she had both Bobby and her herself to protect. She pointed to the large pile of paper: "This is the entire chart?"

Oberhausen nodded.

"May I?"

Another nod.

Maggie flipped over the stack of paper and started leafing through the sheets. The section of the chart in which telephone calls were documented came last, and Maggie was hoping her adversary hadn't seen it. She found what she was looking for and used her own pen to circle five entries, all telephone calls to the OSG, all unanswered. She set the paper down on the table in front of the lawyer.

"You will see, Miss Oberhausen, that I attempted to reach Ms. Mills on five occasions to discuss Bobby's care. Five messages were left, and I received no calls in return."

Maggie glanced up at Oberhausen, who was regarding the OSG with a look that could have withered flies. The OSG mumbled something, rubbed her bloodshot eyes, and shrank farther in her chair.

"The point remains, Dr. Johnson, that we're doing nothing for this unfortunate patient, other than providing him with meals he doesn't eat and a bed to sleep on. Is there even a discharge plan?" Oberhausen asked.

The medical social worker sat up in her chair, puffing out her enormous chest. "Of course, there's a discharge plan. But it's a difficult case. He has no family, and he hasn't spent one night outside of a hospital or rehabilitation center since he was diagnosed at age seven. Prior to that, he was shuffled in between foster care and a variety of orphanages, including the House of Perpetual Mercy. And no one, *including* the House of Perpetual Mercy, is comfortable with the idea of taking him back."

The old clock on the wall ticked away—no one seemed to notice it was an hour late—and the coffee maker sputtered, filling the air with the aroma of Green Mountain Breakfast Blend.

"So, the patient lays there in Room 12, with no supervision—legal or otherwise—in moderate to severe pain without a drop of pain medication, no nutrition other than a bag of intravenous vitamins, and no treatment or discharge plan?" the CEO asked.

Father McDaniel cleared his throat. "That's quite enough, Miss Oberhausen. We're here to help Bobby's guardian to make a determination regarding his Do Not

Resuscitate status. All this squabbling is counterproductive. We're all on the same team."

Oberhausen glared back at the priest, as if to say "you're not on *my* team," but she set her Sharpie down on the legal pad and lapsed into silence.

"Miss Mills, Dr. Johnson tells us that a Do Not Resuscitate order was drawn up months ago, but it was never signed," the priest continued.

"That's correct. The patient is a ward of New York State, and, as such, there needs to be a court order to change his status to a no code," Mills answered.

"Have you petitioned the court to do that?" he asked.

She shook her head.

"Why haven't you?"

The OSG folded her thick arms across her chest. Her wide face was devoid of expression. "Because I don't have the time it takes to fill out all the paperwork; that's why. And besides that, every time I'm in there to visit him, he seems fine to me."

"Have you ever asked the patient what he thinks?" Father McDaniel asked.

"What he thinks about what?" the guardian replied.

"His code status?" Father McDaniel asked.

The OSG didn't say, but she didn't need to. Oberhausen sat forward. "The patient is a thirteen-year-old boy, which is the reason he has a legal guardian in the first place."

"Just because it isn't his decision to make does not mean we shouldn't consider his opinion," Father McDaniel said, addressing Oberhausen.

Various heads nodded their assents. Miss Oberhausen scowled her dissent.

"Miss Mills, the committee is adjourned until you've had time to speak with the patient," Father McDaniel said with finality.

Oberhausen tried to make a rebuttal, but McDaniel

silenced her with an upturned hand. She gathered her things and stomped out of the room. The rest of the committee members filed out the door, leaving Maggie alone in the conference room with Foster.

"What the hell is this all about, Jack? I feel like I'm being ambushed."

"You are being ambushed—I got the same treatment earlier this morning."

"You could have given me a heads-up."

"I tried. I called your cell a few times after she cut off my head this morning; you didn't call back."

Maggie looked at her iPhone; there were three missed calls. She had seen them earlier but didn't return them. "What's going on? This woman has some kind of agenda, I'm sure of it."

"I'll tell you, but tell me why you didn't return my calls first."

Maggie walked underneath the large crucifix that hung on the far wall and ran her finger over the nail fixing Christ's feet to the wood. "I was busy, Jack."

"You were busy the last three days? I called last night and the night before as well."

"This isn't a good time..."

"I don't get it, Maggie. We had a beautiful evening and a wonderful goodnight kiss, and then you act like I'm some kind of stranger," he said.

"Can we discuss it later?"

"Over dinner?" Jack asked.

"Yes, over dinner, as soon as I rotate off Pediatrics. Now tell me what's going on."

Foster opened the door to the conference room and peered out. Satisfied there was no one listening, he shut the door, and walked over closer to Maggie, close enough for her to smell his aftershave. "Oberhausen was furious with the OSG when she found out you had resuscitated Bobby."

"Why?"

"Because she allowed Bobby to be transferred here from Columbia only on the condition he would be a DNR, and the OSG just never got around to filing the paperwork. Bobby's insurance company denied his admission four years ago, claiming it was only for respite care, which they don't pay for. Golden Arches didn't fight it because no one expected him to live for more than a few weeks. More than four years later, he's still here, and his bills are mounting…"

"So, let me get this straight…are you telling me this bitch wants Bobby to die?"

Chapter Ten

Maggie stopped short of the door to Room 12, listening for the reassuring beat of the cardiac monitor. When she was certain Bobby's heart was thumping along in rhythm, she nodded to the OSG standing behind her and pushed open the door and passed inside. Bobby was curled up in bed, making him appear even smaller than he was, reading his new book. As usual, he neither looked up nor acknowledged her at all when she came in—a habit he had picked up from spending more than half his life in the hospital.

"How was the big meeting?" he asked

"Bobby, there's somebody here to see you," Maggie told him.

He didn't reply. His thumb flicked, and the page turned.

"Did you hear me?"

"Yeah."

The OSG sat down in Maggie's chair. Bobby rolled over and looked her up and down, then rolled back over to his original position with his back to her.

"I'm Saundra Mills, your state-appointed guardian."

"I know who you are," Bobby said.

"I'm here..."

"I know why you're here."

The cardiac monitor beeped on. Oxygen hissed from the nasal cannula the nurses had taped into place so he wouldn't continue to take it off.

"You're here to pull the plug on me," Bobby said.

"There's no plug to pull."

Bobby let go of his comic book and used his arm to indicate all the equipment in the room: the cardiac monitor, the temporary pacer, and the crash cart, stuffed with everything an intern could want to restart a stopped heart: adrenaline, lidocaine, the defibrillator, and even a syringe with a spinal needle in the event the lining around Bobby's heart started filling with fluid and needed to be drained. "What's all this, then?"

Maggie knelt down next to him and answered for her. "You're breathing on your own, Bobby. All this stuff is here in case you don't."

"Like when I went into ventricular fibrillation last week?" Bobby asked.

"Yes. How do know about v-fib?" Maggie was surprised he pronounced it correctly. Maggie had been the one to tell Bobby what had happened to him once he was stable, but she had explained ventricular fibrillation all in layman's terms, *The heart beats so fast that it can't fill, and blood pressure drops to nothing.*"

"The same thing happened to one of the X-Men. Storm had to hit Wolverine with a lightning bolt to save him."

It was the fate of the intern to reduce life and death into a series of equations and formulas—choose wisely and life persevered, choose poorly and the grim reaper started hacking away with his long scythe—and she started the process of calculating the number of joules in a lightning strike. One billion volts in the average strike, according to a program she had seen on the history channel, multiplied by the number of... amps? (Physics had been such a long time ago and never her forte.) Coulombs, perhaps? Yes, that was it, coulombs. But she had no idea how many coulombs there were in lightning, and she couldn't generate enough enthusiasm to look it up on her phone.

The OSG picked a comic book from the stack on his bed. It was the most recent *Uncanny X-Men*, Bobby's favorite. "Why do you like the X-Men so much?" she asked.

Bobby shrugged his shoulder. "The X-Men are mutants, like me. Take Storm, for instance; her mutation allows her to control the weather. That's how she saved Wolverine."

"What about Wolverine? What's so special about him?" the guardian asked.

"Honestly? You never heard of Wolverine?"

The OSG shook her head. "No, I haven't."

The *beep beep* of his heart monitor grew faster, and Maggie's eyes strayed to the monitor, which displayed Bobby's heart rate, respirations, blood pressure and oxygenation—the human condition reduced to a series of green lights on a screen. She had tried to mute the audio a dozen times, but Bobby always turned it on: *"I like the beeping."*

"Wolverine heals at an accelerated rate."

Maggie moved over to the control panel to let the OSG interview Bobby without interference, pretending to fiddle with the dials.

"What about you?" she asked him.

"What about me?"

"You said you were a mutant. What's your special power?"

Bobby raised a narrow eyebrow—one of the chemo agents he had received had trashed his hair follicles, and only a few shaggy hairs remained. "I'm unkillable."

"Unkillable?"

"When I was diagnosed at age seven, the doctor told me I wouldn't make it a year. After my first bone marrow transplant failed, another doctor told me I wouldn't live a month. When the surgeon hacked my arm off, she said I wouldn't make it a week. I'm still here."

Some invisible person stabbed Maggie in the heart

with an ice pick. She glanced at the OSG to gauge her reaction, but her wide face was inscrutable.

"Bobby, there's something we need to talk about," the OSG said.

Bobby rolled his small brown eyes. "What now?"

"When your heart went into v-fib last week, Dr. Johnson preformed something we call a resuscitation."

Bobby flipped the pages. "We already discussed this."

"Yes, I know. But we have never discussed *not* doing it," she said.

"Not doing it? What are you talking about, lady?"

The cardiac monitor droned on and on, thumping along with the steady beat of Bobby's enlarged heart.

"I can ask the court to change your resuscitation status to a Do Not Resuscitate, so that if you go into v-fib again, the doctors and nurses won't intervene."

Bobby looked over at Maggie with his eyes wide and then back at the OSG. "But if they don't hit me with the juice again, I might die."

Beep. Beep. Beep.

"You might, yes. I just want to make sure you know your options."

"Options...really? Get shocked or die? You call those options?" Bobby asked.

The OSG didn't reply. She tried to reach out and hold his hand, but he smacked it away.

"You people are all the same—it never occurs to you that even people like me value their life," Bobby said.

"Bobby, that's not what I meant."

"Sure you did; you just don't want to admit it." He rolled over and looked at Maggie. A single tear dripped down his face. "Maggie, get this wackadoodle outta here, she's trying to kill me."

***

If the Emergency Department was the *asshole of the hospital*—and it was, Yoda said so, that made it so—then the Crisis Room was the foul-smelling, irritated hemorrhoid protruding from that asshole. Constructed in the days when Golden Arches was contractually obligated to provide emergency care for the prisoners at the Lincoln Correctional Facility in the Bronx, it had been designed to prevent dangerous criminals from escaping and was the ideal place, according to Yoda, to "*precipitate a real, honest-to-goodness psychiatric shitshow, because if reinforced concrete and rebar don't make someone bat-shit crazy, nothing will.*"

Maggie identified herself to the uniform guarding the door and he stepped aside, pulling the heavy steel open for her. The crisis room was lit by a trio of sodium vapor lights—representing the cutting edge of 1920's technology—which threw the cavernous space into a gaudy yellow relief. A man wearing an Elmer Fudd cap over a mass of strawberry blond hair paced back and forth in front of the door. She waited until he turned and strode away from her, and she sat down in the chair at the far end of a rickety wooden table.

"Hello, John."

The man didn't respond. The pacing continued.

"It's been a while. How have you been?"

He didn't say. In usual circumstances, she would have opened his chart on her laptop and reviewed his history, but John suffered from many delusions, one of which was that he was an android and could be controlled by computers. She left it on her lap, out of sight.

She looked him over, something Yoda called "*the first glance exam.*" He was thin to the point of emaciation; his fish-belly white skin appeared jaundiced in the yellow wash of the lamps; and dark circles occupied the southern border of his eye sockets.

"Have you been eating?" she asked.

This stopped him mid-stride. He turned his back to her—so that she couldn't reprogram him with her laser vision—and pulled his cap down farther over his ears.

"I don't care about food, Maggie."

"You need to eat, John."

John had been a student at Harvard Divinity School in Cambridge. The night before his first final exam of the spring semester he had come to the realization he could fly, and he ended up in a dumpster at the base of his dormitory. He had spent the next five years in and out of psychiatry wards and mental hospitals, and had ultimately ended up here, in the Crisis Room of Our Lady of the Golden Arches Hospital, where Maggie had first met him during her psychiatry rotation last fall.

"Why are you so worried about food?" John asked.

"Food sustains the body, John."

"Incorrect, Maggie. The soul sustains the body."

"Yes, I remember."

And she did remember, in detail, his incredible history. His previous body had died the night he fell into the dumpster; all that was left of it was the scar that adorned his right temple. His mortal remains had been transformed into an android, into which the soul of a long dead prophet had been reborn, sent back to warn the inhabitants of the new Gomorrah that the end was nigh.

"No one is listening, Maggie."

She didn't doubt it. If his body odor didn't drive people away—he smelled worse than her brother's hockey bag—then the festering wounds on his arms surely would. (During his first admission, the Infectious Disease people had tested him for leprosy. Maggie could remember the palpable feel of their disappointment when it had been negative.)

"I've been having the visions again, Maggie."

Hallucinations were part and parcel of schizophrenia, usually engendered by the distorted perception of a visual stimulus—at least according the *Diagnostic and Statistical Manual of Mental Disorders, Fifth Edition*, the bible of all things psychiatric.

"What do you see?" Maggie asked.

"The fires."

He got up and began pacing again, walking back and forth at right angles to her so that she could see the jagged scar on his right forehead as he walked in one direction and the large bald spot in the beard covering his left chin in the other. Maggie had once considered working him up for mange until she had witnessed him twisting his hair until he pulled it out.

"Do you understand, Maggie? Do you see what it means?"

"Why don't you tell me, John?"

He licked his lips, which were chapped and swollen. Maggie had bought a stick of lip balm for him the last time she had seen him, but it was either used up or discarded long ago.

"I don't have long for the world, Maggie."

Judging by the bloodshot state of his sclera and the congested veins in his extremities, Maggie was inclined to agree with him. She remembered the protein bar she kept in the pocket of her lab coat, and she fished it out and offered it to him.

"I don't need food."

She knew his liver was of a different opinion. "Please."

John accepted it from her, sniffed it over—to make sure it wasn't poisoned—and started eating the bar, swallowing it down almost without chewing it, a consequence of great hunger and poor dentition.

"The nurse said you wanted to see me?"

John didn't reply. The pacing resumed.

"Is there a problem, John? Can I do something for you?"

Maggie's psychiatry rotation had ended months ago, but she'd continued to provide care for John on account of the fact he refused to meet with anyone else. Over the holidays, he had spent three days on the inpatient psychiatry ward without saying a word, only breaking his silence when Maggie returned—early—from her Christmas vacation.

"It's not *you* who can do something for me; it is *I* who can do something for you."

His proper speech and unique inflection fascinated Maggie and betrayed his formal education and upbringing. John was the oldest son of a prominent Manhattan physician, and had graduated from the Trinity School before moving on to Harvard as a theology student.

"Something for me? I didn't realize I needed anything."

"The end is coming."

The apocalypse was his favorite subject, and he spoke of its imminence at all times.

"I know. You've mentioned this to me before."

"I mean *your* end, Maggie. The end is coming for you." He turned around and risked looking at her. There was a penetrating intensity about his green eyes that unnerved her. "It's you I see in the fires..."

***

Maggie had almost escaped from the Emergency Department when she heard Rachel call her name. Her tired body wanted to keep going up the stairs and out the door to her apartment, but she turned around and managed a smile on her face. "What's up, Rach?"

Rachel was a friend of Maggie's from her high school days at the Country Day School in Westchester, a private preparatory school for girls.

"Your dad's looking for you."

"What's my father doing here?"

"Little girl with a broken elbow in twelve."

Roger Johnson had established a reputation as a leading international authority on supracondylar fractures, and he was often asked to do the job even when he wasn't on call.

"Can't you just tell him I already left?"

Rachel cocked her head and put her hands on her hips. "You want me to lie to your father?"

Maggie was about to nod in the affirmative when her father popped out of the room and spied Maggie. He walked over and stood between the two of them. "Thanks for finding her Rachel."

"You're welcome, Dr. Johnson." She winked at Maggie and went back to the nurses' station.

"She tell you the good news?"

"Yes."

"Good, come on in the room, I want to show you something."

A young girl of eight or nine lay on the bed in Room 12, with her right arm immobilized in a fiberglass splint. An IV bag hung from a metal pole, dripping salt solution into her other arm. Her father went directly to the X-ray viewer; Maggie knelt down by the head of the bed and whispered a greeting into her ear. The patient made no response.

"She's already been given the pre-op sedation, Maggie. You won't get anything out of her now."

Maggie checked her pulse, which was fast and thready. Respirations were slow—an effect of the sedative she'd been administered—but she was satting well according to the monitor, and her blood pressure was stable. She yanked her stethoscope out of her lab coat and listened to her heart and palpated her abdomen.

"Come on, Maggie, I want you to see these X-rays."

"Just a minute, Dad."

The patient was lying supine, but at a slight angle so that her right arm wouldn't be stressed. Maggie lifted her left side up enough to slide her stethoscope underneath her and auscult her lungs, which were clear. She was pulling the scope out when she saw something just above the girl's buttocks, which she mistook as a smudge of dirt in the dim light.

"Maggie, we don't have all day."

"Hang on, will you?"

She grabbed a flashlight from the counter and used it to illuminate the girl's backside. Just visible in the naked beam on the flash, a series of faint bruises lanced across her buttocks.

"Maggie…"

The thin veneer of her father's patience was effacing, but Maggie ignored him. "Dad, come here."

Roger Johnson continued to examine the viewer, using the magnifying glass to enlarge the fracture site. A large fragment was displaced and angulated from the bone.

"Dad!"

"What, Maggie?"

"Just come here."

He blew out his breath in exasperation but abandoned the viewer and knelt down next to her. She played the beam over her left buttock. The bruises washed out in the naked light, but she still thought she could see a hint of purple beneath the girl's light brown skin.

"You see anything on her buttock?" Maggie asked.

"Not really."

She switched off the flashlight. "How about now?"

"There might be some bruising there; it's hard to tell."

"It doesn't look to you like she was lashed by a belt?"

"For Christ's sake, Maggie; you can't say things like that."

"Why not?" Maggie asked.

He tilted his head toward the door, and they left the room, conferring in a recess across the hall. "The Emergency Room doctor didn't say anything about suspicious bruising, and there's no history of abuse in her record. And even if those are bruises, she probably got them when she fell down the stairs, which is how she sustained her elbow fracture."

"There's a linear pattern to the bruising, Dad. You didn't see that?"

He shook his head, but Maggie wasn't convinced he was being truthful.

"Maybe she was pushed down the stairs? The Emergency Room doctor probably didn't talk to her alone or examine anything besides her elbow—if he even did that—and the lack of abuse history means nothing."

"Don't let your imagination get the better of you. Medicine is a scientific discipline, Maggie; we rely on the review of facts, *not* the overachievement of your imagination." He stopped to let a nurse walk past, escorting an uncooperative patient to Diagnostic Imaging. "Don't go off all half-cocked, Margaret…" He paused for a minute to examine the floor with his eyes. "Why don't you find some actual evidence to corroborate your theory before you go making accusations that might ruin someone's life… or your own."

Chapter Eleven

It was five p.m., and Maggie was already exhausted, not the best way to start a night of call. She knew the other interns would be looking for her to sign out, but she headed neither for the residency lounge nor the cafeteria—the two places sign out occurred—slipping away to the call room instead. She threw her satchel on the desk, hung her lab coat on the back of the door, and collapsed onto the stiff mattress. In a few minutes, she was asleep, but it was the restless, agitated slumber of an intern. Bobby appeared to her as she slept, choking and hungering for air as she watched from the chair. She tried to help, but her arms were tied behind her back, and all she could do was look on as he turned from pink to blue to white.

She woke up gasping for breath, as if an unseen hand had drawn a cord about her neck. A *knock* came from the door. Her pounding heart accelerated, threatening to explode out of her chest.

"Maggie?" It was Garcia; Maggie recognized her squeaky voice. "You asleep?"

"Just a minute."

She pushed her herself into a sitting position and poured the contents of a plastic water bottle into the towel housekeeping had left on the desk, using it to wipe her face.

"Maggie? Trying to sign out."

"Coming."

Maggie stood up, waited for the waves of dizziness to clear, and moved over to the door. Some previous intern had fixed a shard of broken mirror glass to the inside of the door; she glanced at it, taking in the pale hue of her skin and the dark circles under her eyes.

"Maggie?"

She pushed open the door, and Garcia poker her head around the corner. "You okay? You don't look good."

"Just tired, that's all." Maggie waived her in. "Come on, whatdy'a got?"

Maggie propped several pillows against the head of the bed and sat back against them; Garcia sat down on the chair and sorted through a pile of index cards she used to make notes on her patients.

"Where do you want to start, Maggie, most-straightforward, or most complicated?"

Sign out from Garcia, as Maggie had learned on the four previous call nights she'd had this month, was a long and tortured process.

"Most straightforward."

Garcia shuffled her deck accordingly and started into a dissertation on her first patient, a twelve-year-old with a skin infection caused by scratching at fleabites. The patient was fully recovered and off all medicines but was unable to be discharged because her home had been condemned since her admission. Social services had found over thirty cats inside, not all living, and she simply had nowhere to go. It should have required five seconds to go over, but Garcia insisted on starting from day one of her admission and moving forward day-by-day. Normally, it would have irritated Maggie to have to listen to the whole spiel, but today she smiled and nodded, glad for the extra time to allow her panic attack to dissipate.

It was near enough seven o'clock when Maggie escaped the call room and made it down to the cafeteria, where the rest of the interns rotating though Pediatrics this month were assembled.

"Where you been Maggie, I've got a date tonight."

"Who's the lucky girl, Caid? The Dominican?"

"Why do want to know? You jealous?"

"I won't be able to sleep tonight knowing you're with another woman."

"Just say the word, and I'll dump them all for you." Melendez stared at her with his big brown eyes and, for a second, she couldn't tell if he were being serious. He handed her an oversized index card filled with hen scratching. "Here's my list... Nothing too exciting. See you at six bells."

Maggie sat down across from Williams. Like Garcia, Williams was in the pediatric residency program and would be staying at Golden Arches for two more years, whereas Melendez—assuming he graduated—would be beginning an ophthalmology residency at nearby Rutgers University.

Williams tapped his watch. "I see Natalie already signed out."

"Sorry about that, Mike. I hated to keep you guys waiting."

"There's nothing you can do, Maggie. Shit knows I have tried."

There was something about Williams that Maggie liked; something that, growing up in Westchester as she had, she saw little enough of. In the swirling shit that clouded the air at Golden Arches, it had taken her several months to put her finger on, but it had come to her one night at sign-out. Williams never put spin on anything: when a night of call wasn't that bad, he didn't say it was; when a procedure went smoothly, he didn't confabulate a complication for the sake of a story; when his service was light; he told you as much and offered to help.

"You gotta date tonight too, Mike?"

He nodded. "A hot one. With Harriet Lane."

The *Harriet Lane Handbook* was the quintessential bible of the pediatric intern for the last eighty years.

"I hear she's easy. How's your list?"

"Seven patients, most stable."

"Anyone you're worried about?"

Williams tapped the sheet with a long brown finger. "Yeah, this kid. I admitted him this afternoon from clinic. He came in with shortness of breath. His lungs were okay, and a cardiogram looked good in the office, but I couldn't send him home because he was working too much to breathe."

"He satting okay?"

"Ninety-seven per cent. But you remember what Yoda says about oxygen saturation, right?"

"*I don't give a shit what the oxygen saturation is, Interns, watch the patient breathe. If the patient is working hard to breathe, a good oxygen sat doesn't mean shit. Got that?*"

"His chest film looks okay by me, but the radiologists went home already, and the night shift is swamped. It may be a few hours before it gets read. Can you make sure they didn't see anything?"

Maggie made a To-Do note on her iPhone—she wasn't sure how her father had made it through internship without one—and set an alarm to remind her in case she forgot. Williams finished his sign-out, which left only Schwartz, the second-year resident.

"What are you still doing here, Aaron?" Maggie asked.

"I've got a favor to ask."

"Sure. What's up?"

"You mind if Mary Kate takes call with you tonight?"

Mary Kate was a fourth-year student at Cornell Medical School, doing an acting internship in Pediatrics at Golden Arches this month.

"No problem. Where is she?"

"Putting scrubs on. I told her to meet you here."

Schwartz left, and Maggie assembled a plate from the salad bar for dinner. There was a method to eating at the hospital cafeteria, and it involved ignoring everything but the salad bar, the lesser of many evils. Years ago—the older attendings used to claim—the cafeteria had had some of the best food in all of the city and it wasn't uncommon for the staff to bring their families in to eat on Sunday evenings.

East Harlem had a long tradition of diversity, beginning with the country's first "Little Italy." Dr. Haverford, the longest serving physician on the staff, still reminisced about the lasagna, which, along with everything else, was made at home by the Italian born cooks. By the sixties, waves of Latino immigrants from Puerto Rico, the Dominican Republic and El Salvador had replaced the Italians and East Harlem became known as *El Barrio*. In the cafeteria of Golden Arches, Chiccharons displaced Fusilli, rice and beans pushed out Farfalle, and the Cuban sandwich made everyone forget about the Panini. In 1990, however, the administration got rid of the entire kitchen staff, and farmed out the operation to a faceless—and tasteless, the residents complained— national food corporation.

"Hey Maggie."

Maggie looked up from the stack of greens she had piled on the side of her dish. "Hey, Mary Kate. Ready for a night of adventure?"

Mary Kate nodded and started piling books on the table. First came the *Harriet Lane Manual*; on top of that she stacked *The Pediatric Resident's Guide to On-Call,* which Maggie had never heard of; third came *A Glossary of Medical Terms*; and topping off the stack came a leather-bound journal with "Pearls" stenciled on the cover.

"I've saved several pages for your Pearls, Maggie."

Mary Kate was the kind of person you couldn't help

but like. She was polite, funny in an unintentional sort of way, and hard working. In short, the perfect acting intern with the exception of one thing, that one thing being the fawning respect she had for the residents in general and Maggie in particular.

"Several pages of Pearls? I don't think so, MK."

"Come on, Maggie; everyone knows how smart you are."

"You're delusional. Why don't you grab some dinner?"

"Sure. Need anything?"

Maggie shook her head. "We'll come back later if we have a chance and get some frozen yogurt."

After dinner they went up to the resident's lounge and watched an episode of *Seinfeld*. Maggie supposed she should be doing some medical reading or reviewing X-Rays or looking up lab results, but after twelve hours of work, she needed a break, and the resident's lounge was just what the doctor ordered. The place to let down for all four of Golden Arches' residency programs, pediatrics, general surgery, internal medicine and transitional, there was always someone in the lounge to goof around with— on any day of the week, and at any hour of the night. Tonight was no exception. Felix Cortez, a transitional intern rotating through internal medicine this month, convinced Maggie to watch a second episode of *Seinfeld*, and Nupur Subramanian, an IM intern doing her pulmonology rotation, fed her a steady stream of Peanut M&Ms, of which there was a never-ending supply. No surgical interns were there, an absence attributed to the existence of their own private lounge on the back side of the Operating Room locker room, as well as the fact that most surgical interns never had a free minute to eat, much less watch TV.

"How's your night looking, Maggie?"

"Blue skies and white clouds so far, Nupur."

Cortez almost dropped the ice cream cup he was holding. "You're out of your mind, sayin' shit like that,

Maggie. I know you're a high-falluting white chick and don't believe in *fuku* and all, but you are bat-shit crazy tempting *fuku* like that."

"Do you honestly think anything I say affects the kind of night I am going to have, Felix?"

Interns were notoriously superstitious, none more so than Felix, a second-generation Dominican from East Harlem who kept a chicken foot in his lab coat.

"Hell, yeah." He held out the chicken foot for Maggie to touch. "Here, there's still time to reverse the hex you just screwed yourself with. Rub the foot and say *zafa*."

Maggie laughed, and Felix slid his charm back into its special pocket he had sewed in the lining of his lab coat—where the attendings would not see it. No sooner than Felix had stopped muttering about the "*fuku*" than Maggie's beeper sounded, and Felix fished the talisman out of its hiding place and started rubbing it again, saying *zafa* again and again. "You got no idea what you messing with, Maggie. I'm going to try and reverse it for you."

"You don't have to do that, Felix."

"Sure, I do, Maggie. I still owe you that night of call you took for me last month and I got no time to pay you back."

"Reverse the *fuku* for me and we'll call it even then."

Maggie checked the number, saw it was the Emergency Department, and waved for Mary Kate—who was reading the *Harriet Lane Journal*—to follow. The nurses' station was, as usual about this time of day, a cacophony of sound and fury: drunks bellowed, babies wailed, and the nurses shouted to make themselves heard over the din. Maggie was happy to see her friend Rachel manning the ship.

"You rang?" Maggie asked her.

"Hey, Magpie."

"What's going on?"

Rachel grabbed her arm and led her over to one of the soundproof bays the doc used to make phone calls and dictate charts. The corkboard wall was covered with the limericks that the night shift nurses wrote about the interns. Maggie was especially fond of the rhyme about her:

"There once was a fair maiden from Rye,
Who was said never to lie,
Said she I tell it like it is,
That's how I do my biz,
Now shut up and get me some pie."

"Greenfield wanted me to page you. There's a psychiatric patient here with hyperthermia and he thinks it would be an 'interesting' case for you to see straight off," Rachel said.

"What's the problem; I love fresh meat. It's the only way to learn."

"I know that, but he's just being a lazy turd. He didn't call the pediatrics night float because he knows he would get shut down, so he had me call you directly."

"What should I do?" Maggie asked

"I just saw Yoda wandering around; ask her."

They paged Yoda, and she appeared a moment later, clutching, as always, a can of Diet Coke in her small hand. She regarded them from underneath the heavy rims of her thick spectacles, around which her brown bangs fell. "What?"

Yoda could be, when she had time, the most loquacious of people, and, when she didn't, the tersest. Maggie explained the situation; Yoda turned her head to the left so that the ear with the hearing aid was close to Maggie. No one knew if Yoda had been born hearing impaired or if some childhood malady had made her that way, and no one had ever asked.

"Can I ask you something, Intern?"

"Sure."

"Where are you?"

Looking around, Maggie took in the maelstrom of darting bodies; the yellow glare of florescent lighting; and the blur of ambulance beacons reflecting off the wall.

"The Emergency Department."

"What are you doing here?"

Maggie had just told her what she was doing here, but Yoda had a point to make, and there was no rushing her. "I'm on call for pediatrics."

"And the purpose of taking call is?"

A variety of responses occurred to her: *Cheap Labor? Because the attendings did call when they were residents and now we have to? Because that's the way it's done and why would you want to change a broken, antiquated system?*

"You're here to learn, Intern. Remember?"

That answer hadn't been in her top five, but she nodded anyway.

"So, go ahead and learn."

Yoda turned and went back to wherever she had come from; they watched her walk away, using the wall to compensate for the weakness in her left leg.

"What's the deal with Yoda?" Mary Kate asked.

Maggie watched her turn a corner and disappear into a dark corridor leading into the bowels of the hospital. "She's the chief resident."

"Yes, but *who* is she?"

"She's just Yoda."

"Melendez said she lives somewhere in the hospital," Mary Kate said.

In the entire time she had been at Golden Arches, there were no reports of Yoda ever being seen outside the hospital, and it was generally assumed she lived within its premises. For many years, it had been one of the principal goals of the interns to locate Yoda's lair, but to date it was a goal unfulfilled.

"Never listen to anything Melendez says," Maggie told her.

"Why not?"

"Just don't."

"He's kind of sexy, don't you think?" Rachel asked.

"Melendez?"

"Yeah, Melendez."

"If you're smart, you'll stay away from him," she told her friend.

"What's that supposed to mean?"

Maggie didn't explain, starting off toward the old side of the Emergency Department, which had constituted the entirety of the department before a renovation a decade ago. Maggie waived at Mary Kate to follow, and they darted in and around the stream of traffic: orderlies carrying bedpans; X-ray techs wheeling patients to and from Diagnostic Imaging; and nurses carrying IV bags, cups full of pills, and dinner trays.

The patient in Room 15 was a tall girl in a pink spandex running suit, with pale skin splotched with freckles and a long shock of fire red hair. She was lying on the stretcher, trussed up like a turkey, mumbling incoherently. Maggie's eyed found the monitor; the patient's core temperature was 104°.

"Shit, Mary Kate. Get the nurse now. Tell her to bring the Bair Hugger."

Mary Kate went out, and Maggie examined the patient: heart sounds were normal; respirations rapid but clear; abdomen soft and benign; pupils reactive and equal, and neck supple. Respiratory rate was in the 40s but, Maggie expected that, the body attempting to cool itself by panting. The pulse was likewise high, but regular and strong, and the blood pressure was acceptable.

Mary Kate returned with the nurse, but no Bair Hugger.

"What have you given the patient already?" Maggie asked the nurse.

"Nothing Maggie. The IV isn't even ordered yet. I've got it at 40cc/hour just to keep the vein open."

"Hang a liter of iced saline, wide open. Labs?"

"Nothing's ordered yet."

Maggie opened her laptop and began ordering labs as quickly as she could think of them, tagging them all STAT. "Mary Kate, go grab an enema kit."

"Where are they?"

"I don't know... ask if you have to. And fill two basins with ice water.'

A phlebotomist came in and started the blood draw as the nurse returned with the intravenous fluids. Mary Kate came back with the enema kit.

"Fill the bag with the cold water, and let her have it," Maggie instructed.

"Why is her temperature so high?"

"It was very hot today, and she's wearing running clothes. Looks like she went for a run in this heat. She must be on an antipsychotic of some sort. They're prone to throwing off thermoregulation. Check the meds once you get the enema in."

The nurse was nowhere to be found—off getting that Bair Hugger hopefully—so Maggie stripped the patient down and covered her with a Johnnie. To her dismay, the temperature on the monitor had risen, to 104.8°. An orderly passed by, and Maggie grabbed his arm, shouting Yoda's pager number into his ear. "Tell her I need some help."

Maggie returned to her computer and called up the patient's history, which was highlighted by depression and anorexia nervosa, but no evidence of schizophrenia. There were no more co-morbid medical conditions and no history of drug use, alcohol dependence or sexual activity—although Maggie had ordered a urine pregnancy test anyway. As Yoda had mentioned: *Eight to eighty, blind, drunk or crazy, get a pregnancy test.*

"The Bair Hugger isn't working, Maggie."

"Call Bioengineering and have somebody fix it,"

Maggie replied.

"I already did. They're waiting for a part and it won't be here until tomorrow."

Fuku. "Ice bags on her neck, and get a fan and a spray bottle from Housekeeping."

Twenty minutes later, the patient was covered in ice bags, and an industrial fan propelled a sheet of mist over the patient, but the temperature hadn't budged.

"Why isn't she cooling down, Maggie?"

"She takes olanzapine; it's on her med history. It's an atypical antipsychotic used as an adjuvant drug for depression. It's messed up her thermoregulation."

"Is there any way we can reverse it?"

Rubbing Felix's chicken bone and saying *zafa* were the only things that came to mind. Maybe there was something to this *fuku.*

"Not that I know of, but do a literature search on your computer," Maggie said.

Yoda still hadn't surfaced, and Maggie commissioned another orderly to go and not return until she found her. She buzzed the nurses' station on the intercom and asked if any family or friends had come with the patient, and she was told no: the patient had been found in Central Park, collapsed on the running path near the zoo. The nurse returned with a paper printout of the labs, and they reviewed them together

The good news was that her complete blood count seemed to be okay; the bad news was that her kidney function had been compromised, probably consequent to dehydration. The best way to rehydrate someone was not, as every July 1st intern assumed, intravenous fluids. Even a rate of 250 cc/hour wasn't all that much when you thought about it, not even a can of Keystone Light, which Maggie's college boyfriend could guzzle in less than ten seconds. No, it was always best to use the gut—in a conscious person, that is. She considered dropping a nasogastric tube and pouring in cold water that way but didn't want the patient to end up inhaling the liquid into her lungs.

"Mary Kate, start a second IV, biggest damn needle you can find," Maggie shouted.

Mary Kate's wide mouth pursed, and her sculpted eyebrows narrowed. "I really haven't had that much experience starting IV's Maggie."

"Now's your chance to get some, then. Sixteen gauge at least."

Maggie's beeper vibrated again; this time, it was back line at the Pediatrics nurses' station, the call-back-right-now-dammit number.

Shit.

She picked up the phone in the hall as Mary Kate laid out all the stuff she needed to start an IV and dialed the number. "Maggie Johnson."

"Maggie, did Mike talk to you about that patient he admitted from the clinic?"

"Yeah, what about him?"

"The aide just retrieved his dinner tray, and he didn't touch it. She says he's too short of breath to eat."

"Okay."

"You want to come take a look?"

Mary Kate cursed under her breath—a rolling vein, Maggie would bet.

"What did you think, Olga?" Maggie asked.

"I haven't had the chance to assess him yet. That's why I am calling you."

Maggie remembered a time a few months ago when Melendez had called an attending—Andrews, no less—at midnight without first seeing the patient himself. Andrews had ripped Melendez a new asshole so big that he was diapered to this day.

"Go assess the patient yourself, and then call me back," Maggie said.

"Can't you just come do it? One of the nurses called in sick, and we're way short-staffed."

"I'm really busy down here."

"This is Golden Arches...we're all really busy."

Mary Kate blew another vein; she fumbled with a pack of compresses to staunch the bleeding.

"Don't turn into Melendez, Maggie. The staff all likes you because you're not all obnoxious like him."

"Melendez isn't obnoxious; he just stands up for himself," Maggie said.

The fan droned on. The temperature display blinked on and off.

"Can you just come up and see him for me, please?"

"Okay, I'll be right up."

Chapter Twelve

The teenage boy leaned forward in his chair, mouth wide open as he gasped for breath. His nostrils flared, and his stomach bellowed in and out as his brainstem recruited his abdominal muscles in a desperate attempt to suck air into his lungs.

Shit. Shit. Shit.

Maggie lurched in to the room, sending a bouquet of withered flowers sprawling. She grabbed an oxygen mask from the cupboard, slipped it over his tightly cut dark hair, and jammed the oxygen tube in place. Mary Kate twisted the regulator, and the hiss of flowing gas filled the room.

"Put up his chest X-Ray on the viewer," Maggie instructed.

Maggie introduced herself to the patient as she placed her stethoscope on his back, but she didn't hear the welcome sound of air exchanging in his air sacs. The high-resolution X-Ray viewer above the bedside showed why. Both of his lungs were surrounded by fluid that pressed in on them from the space around them, preventing them from expanding and drawing in air.

"He's got a huge pleural effusion, Mary Kate."

Mary Kate gawked at the black and white image, narrowing her thin eyebrows. "Where did the fluid come from?"

"Let's find out. Get Olga in here with the procedure wagon, make sure she gets his mom to sign the consent form, and call Aaron and ask him to help."

Her beeper vibrated again: this time it was Bobby. She knew she didn't have the time to talk—he usually called about this time because he was bored and couldn't sleep—but she needed to make sure he was okay.

"Where have you been Maggie? I've been waiting for you all night," Bobby told her.

"I'll try to get up there soon, Bobby. Are you alright?"

There was no response. Maggie could hear the reassuring drone of the monitor over the static in the line. "I'm okay, Maggie. Just a little chest pain, that's all."

"Are you really having chest pain, Bobby?"

"You think I would make that up just to get you to come up?"

"You've done it before."

"One little lie and now you don't believe me."

"It's not that I don't believe you. I just don't have the time right now."

Another call came in—from the Emergency Department, again—and she put Bobby on hold.

"Hey, Maggie."

"Hey, Rach. How's your night going?" Maggie asked.

"Like a big turd that won't flush. And I signed up for a double so I'm going to be in this clusterfuck until 7am. Yours?"

"Likewise."

"In that case, you're not going to be very happy about this," Rachel said.

Maggie didn't reply, having used up her supply of clever retorts many call nights ago.

"The surgery resident wanted to ask if you'd admit one of the kids from the gang fight?" Rachel said in more of a question than a statement.

"Why can't he do it?"

"He's got two cases that have to go the OR right now, and one more after that. But there's a fourth kid as well.

He's been beat up pretty good, but he doesn't have any wounds that require urgent surgery. Surgery said that if you'd admit him, he'd consult on him as soon as he gets out of the OR. What should I tell him?"

"Being on call is a crap shoot, Interns. Some nights you're going to be bored out of your skull, and on others you're going to feel like the only whore in the damn brothel. Don't bother complaining; by the time you're done running your mouth about the work you could have most of it done. Just shut up and get 'er done. Got it?"

"Alright. I'll be down when I get a minute." Maggie hung up with Rachel and returned to her call with Bobby. "You still there?"

"Of course, I'm still here—and I'm still having chest pain."

"I'll send Mary Kate up."

"Mary Kate? Who's that?"

"You know, the acting intern on pediatrics this month."

"The girl that tweezes her eyebrows. Don't bother. She gives me the creeps."

Mary Kate ran back into the room, almond-shaped eyes wide, pushing the procedure cart. Maggie grabbed the portable Ultrasound unit and showed Mary Kate how to position the U/S probe—which used radio waves to image the chest similar to the way sonar worked—and how to use the gain to clarify the image. In contrast to the X-ray images, fluid appeared dark on Ultrasound. Maggie handed the probe to Mary Kate, pointing out the large area of fluid extending from the base of the left lung superiorly to the left mid-lung on the monitor.

"Did you get a hold of Aaron?" Maggie asked.

"No. Olga said he's placing an arterial line in PICU."

Fuku. "What about Yoda?"

"She's in the Emergency Department tending to the girl with hyperthermia. She started seizing after we left."

Shit. Shit. Shit.

"And Olga is stuck over in Room 4," Mary Kate said.

Room 4 was occupied by a set of identical twins, both with severe Cystic Fibrosis, a hereditary disease that made it difficult to clear their pulmonary secretions. Pneumonia and other lung infections were common for CF patients; as a result, the twins were frequent flyers on the pediatric ward.

"She's administering a hypertonic saline treatment; she'll be over as soon as she can."

Hypertonic saline was aerosolized and pumped it into the patient's lungs, where it broke apart secretions and cleared plugged airways. The respiratory therapist usually administered the treatment with a nebulizer, but only one respiratory therapist was on duty at night and was rarely ever able to leave the Emergency Department where her services were always in high demand.

Maggie used a marking pencil to draw an X on the patient's back. "I've got to make a call. Prep the area with Betadine so he's ready when I get back."

Maggie stepped into the hallway and called Foster's cell phone. He answered on the third ring. "I hope this is a social call."

"I'm afraid not." Maggie told him about her predicament.

"How big is the pleural effusion?"

"Big. He's in respiratory distress even with ten liters of O2 via mask. I'm prepping for an Ultrasound-guided lung tap. You want to come give me a hand?"

"I can't right now. I'm upstairs in the Birthing Center; there's a delivery going bad, and Obstetrics called me in."

"How come I didn't hear about it?"

"It's a private insurance patient. She requested no residents."

In an effort to buff up its birthing unit, Golden Arches had instituted a policy whereby patients could ask that no house staff or medical students be a part of the delivery.

The pediatric interns hated the policy, of course, because they needed the experience doing neonatal resuscitations, but it was popular among the women living in the gentrified neighborhoods near the hospital. And a hospital, like any other business, had bills to pay.

"How many pleural taps have you done?" Foster asked.

"Two. I assisted on one in surgery and did another on internal medicine with Gene Dursely supervising."

"Alright, go ahead and get started. I'll come looking for you when I'm finished in the Birthing Room. We can get a cup of coffee and talk over the cases."

A pleural tap was done for two reasons, diagnosis and treatment, and oftentimes both. Taking the fluid off from around the lung allowed it to expand and move air, the purpose for what it was designed. In addition, the removed fluid was subject to a battery of tests in order to determine the nature of the underlying problem. Maggie had seen pleural effusions several times before, but never in a child, and a differential diagnosis, the list of things it might be, began to form in her head without asking. Congenital heart problems, neoplastic disease, especially lymphoma, and pneumonia were all on the short list.

Maggie grabbed a set of sterile gloves and tossed them to Mary Kate. "Open 'em up and put 'em on."

Mary Kate slipped them on, staring at her. "Why?"

"Because you're going to do it."

Listen, interns, don't let me catch you hogging all the procedures. You know the rule: see one...do one...teach one...Got that, assholes?

Maggie opened her computer, found the consent form, and made sure it was signed. Turning to the patient and his mother, who sat next to her son, squeezing his hand, Maggie explained the procedure again and notified them that 'the student doctor' would be performing it under her supervision. The mother nodded, her face grim.

"Okay, Mary Kate, you ready?"

Mary Kate didn't say. An army of emotions battled to control her face: anxiety; excitement; curiosity; and fear. Fear won the battle, stiffening her facial muscles into a blank mask.

"Feel the rib with your finger. All the things you want to avoid—arteries, veins and nerves—run underneath, so place the needle above the rib."

Mary Kate did as she was told.

"Now, advance the catheter slowly until you feel a pop."

Like so many first timers, Mary Kate advanced the needle too slowly.

"A little firmer. Nice and steady."

It was a difficult thing, the business of sticking a needle or a knife into someone, and until you did it, you could not appreciate the difficulty. Mary Kate gave the needle a little more pressure, and a clear fluid tinged with blood started dropping out of the back. Maggie provided a running commentary of the proceedings, both for Mary Kate's benefit and to reassure the patient and his mother, who sat next to her son with her eyes closed.

"Okay, good. Now hold the needle steady and advance the plastic catheter, then withdraw the needle when the catheter is in position."

Mary Kate complied and handed the needle to Maggie who dropped it on the waste table. When the fluid cleared, Maggie attached a tube to the back of the catheter, channeling the pleural fluid into a liter jug, saving it for measurement and analysis. One jug after another was filled and then replaced, until a total of nearly five liters was drawn off, at which time the patient was breathing normally.

When the procedure was done, Maggie showed Mary Kate what tests to order on the fluid and reminded her to get a post-procedure chest film.

"One in every four pleural taps results in a collapsed lung. Sometimes it's not that easy to see air in the chest cavity, and when the radiologist is busy, it's easy to overlook an early pneumothorax. We'll look at the film ourselves when we have a minute."

Maggie's beeper vibrated. She pressed a button, and Bobby's number appeared. It vibrated again and the OR number showed.

What did they want?

She used the phone outside the room as Mary Kate typed up a procedure note. "Maggie Johnson. Someone paged?"

"You're the intern covering pediatrics?"

She admitted she was.

"Dr. Murray wants you to see a patient in the Post Anesthesia Care Unit. He just finished pinning his elbow fracture, and his asthma is flaring up."

"Is he in the PACU now?"

As Yoda had told them long ago, the Operating Room was '*the black hole of time,*' over which no one seemed to have jurisdiction—not even the surgeons. Time simply disappeared into the void: when a patient was scheduled to go to the Operating Room, it was often an hour or more before the patient arrived. In a similar fashion, patients never left on time either, and Maggie had been summoned like a truant child to the PACU several times before only to find the patient hadn't arrived.

"Not yet, no."

"Please call me back when the patient actually gets there."

Maggie heard a burst of stuttering—the charge nurse in the Operating Room was not accustomed to being spoken to like this, and Maggie hung up the receiver. A pang of guilt made her pick the receiver up again, but her fingers punched in Bobby's number instead of the Operating Room. There was no answer.

"What now?" Mary Kate asked.

"I have to go check on someone in pediatrics."

"Want me to come?"

The girl who tweezes her eyebrows? Don't bother. She gives me the creeps. "No, go down to the Emergency Department and help Yoda with the hyperthermia patient. If she's awake, she might be able to tell us something valuable."

Classical medical teaching preached that a great majority of cases were solved by the taking of a thorough and meticulous history, a teaching with which Maggie was inclined to agree after her eight months at Golden Arches. The way Yoda put it, *"Making diagnoses is about asking the right questions, Interns...In most cases the physical exam doesn't give you a pot to piss in. Hear me, assholes? Ask the right questions and stop talking long enough to hear the answers."* In the past week, however, Maggie hadn't taken enough history to fill up a business card, a disturbing trend.

"And be on the lookout for Dr. Foster," Maggie said.

"I always am."

"Am what?"

"On the lookout for Dr. Foster. Pure eye-candy, don't you think, Maggie?"

Maggie shrugged. "He's in the Birthing Room doing a private Neonatal Resuscitation. He wants to talk over some cases with us he's done."

Maggie exited the back staircase and hit the annex running. What if Bobby had indeed been having chest pain? His heart was certainly weak enough to give out without much warning. And she had just dismissed him as if he were just faking it to get her to come visit. A picture of his dead body formed in her brain, and she redoubled her pace and burst through the door to Room 12.

Her fears weren't realized: Bobby was, as always, curled up on his right side, holding a comic book with his outstretched right arm. "What took you so long?"

"Why didn't you answer your phone?"

She plopped down in the chair, kicked off her clogs, and rested her feet on Bobby's bed.

"I knew it was you."

And, being the smart kid he was, he knew that if he didn't answer, she would come right up. She swatted his comic book, which tumbled down to the floor. He picked it up and smacked it across her knee.

"Can't sleep?"

"I was waiting for you."

"I have sleeping pills ordered for you. Why don't you take one?"

"Those things are addictive. You think I want to end up like the woman who gave birth to me?"

Bobby didn't admit to having parents. He never referred to his mother as anything other than "*the woman who gave birth to me*" and did not mention his father, ever. If Maggie brought the subject up, he changed it as quickly. As far as he was concerned, he was a boy without parents, which meshed nicely with his world of mutant superheroes and deranged villains.

"You still having chest pain?"

He rubbed his chest. "A little."

"I'll have the nurses do an EKG."

"It's getting better."

Bobby looked at her expectantly, and she realized he was waiting for his gift. For the last two weeks, regardless of the occasion, professional or personal, Maggie had brought something for Bobby. Sometimes it was as little as a package of crackers, and sometimes it was as big as the authentic Wolverine costume, complete with mask and gloves with retractable claws, that she'd ordered for him on Amazon, but it was always something. Lately, she'd taken to bringing him treats from the Italian bakery up the street: large squares of rich tiramisu, creamy pistachio cannolis, and almond-flavored biscotti, which were his favorite.

She tossed him a Snickers bar she'd grabbed from the resident's lounge. Bobby ripped the wrapper off, let it fall to the floor, and made the treat disappear in one bite. "You got anything else?"

"Not for boys who don't show their appreciation."

"Thanks, Maggie."

Her beeper vibrated; the OR was calling back. She used Bobby's phone to call back. The post-op elbow fracture had arrived in the PACU—and he was in full-on status asthmaticus, a potentially lethal condition in which the patient was gasping for air and yet unable to oxygenate his own blood. She lobbed another candy bar at him and hit the stairs in the direction of the Operating Room, silently wishing she had rubbed that damn chicken foot.

Chapter Thirteen

Maggie sat in the hospital cafeteria in her usual post-call funk. Her work was unfinished, sign out had been hasty and incomplete, and she was too wired from adrenaline and caffeine to contemplate sleep. She sat in the back, in the section by the windows that overlooked the faceless street, sending texts to Melendez, Garcia, and Williams regarding all the important medical information she'd neglected to tell them. Texting protected medical information was a gross violation of HIPAA, the Health Insurance Portability and Accountability Act of 1996, the by-laws of Golden Arches, and the rules of Yoda, but all the interns did it for the sole reason that it had to be done.

Melendez appeared, munching on a pastry he'd likely pilfered from the Attending Physician's lounge, and sat down next to her. "Hey, Maggie, you still want to talk to that kid with the supracondylar fracture?"

Maggie had been trying to get some history from the girl she'd helped operate on, but the girl's father had been stuck to her since she had woken up from anesthesia.

"I just sent the dad down to the Cashier's Office to fix some problem with her paperwork. You've got twenty minutes with her if you get going. You need me to do anything for you?" Melendez said.

"No, I'm supposed to be off."

In 1984, Libby Zion, an eighteen-year-old New York University student, died under the medical care of an intern who hadn't slept in two days, and the medical world was changed forever. The most notable of these changes was Section 405 of the New York State Department of Health Code, which limited a medical intern or resident to a maximum of eighty work hours per week, not more than twenty-four hours in one stint.

"For once that stupid law isn't biting us in the ass."

The Libby Zion Law had revolutionized medical education, but neither in the way it had been intended, nor for the good. While it was true that an intern was exhausted after a night of call, it was also true that legally obligating the doctor who knew the patient best to leave the hospital by seven a.m. caused rounds to become chaotic, miscommunication to become epidemic, and patient care to suffer. As a consequence, many interns just ignored the law and continued to attend to patients, a practice to which understaffed hospitals, like Golden Arches, often turned a blind eye.

"I gave one of the clerk's your cell; she's going to text you when he leaves so you can get outta there before he gets back. I don't like the look of this guy."

They took the back stairs up to pediatrics. Maggie knocked on the door and passed inside; Melendez remained outside. The patient was sitting up in bed. Her split long arm cast was resting in a sling. A stuffed bear someone had purchased from the gift shop rested on her lap.

"Hello Grace, I'm Maggie Johnson, one of the pediatric doctors."

The little girl stared at Maggie wide eyes, but said nothing. Maggie sat down next to the bed and picked up her hand, holding it.

"I just wanted to ask you a few questions. Is that okay?"

Grace's big brown eyes became even bigger, and her lips pursed, sealing her mouth. She grabbed the bear with her left hand and pressed it against her chest.

"Your arm is feeling better?"

A slight nod of the head caused her corn rows to sway; the beads at the bottom knocked together, making a soft clicking sound.

"Does anything else hurt?"

Her head shook.

"Are you sure?"

A nod. Maggie fished out her stethoscope and stood up.

"I'm going to examine you now, Grace. Is that okay?"

Grace clutched her stuffed bear but said nothing, which Maggie took as tacit permission to proceed.

"I'm going to examine your eyes."

Lifting the ophthalmoscope from its charger on the counter, she aimed the beam at Grace's iris and focused it on the back of her eye; there were no retinal hemorrhages.

"I'm going to listen to your lungs, okay?"

Grace remained quiet, and for a second, Maggie wondered if she were mute. Maggie untied her johnnie and inspected her back; her caramel-colored skin wasn't bespattered by bruising, and there was no other evidence of injury. Her lungs were clear.

"I want you to lie on your left side, Grace. Do you think you can do that?"

Grace complied. Maggie switched on her flashlight and dimmed it, probing Grace's backside with the light. A few bruises blossomed in the glow, but there was no pattern to any of them, no marks made by a cord or belt buckle or imprints from a hand or ruler. The linear pattern to the bruising was no longer in evidence; perhaps she had imagined it after all.

"I see some bruises on your bottom, Grace."

Grace said nothing.

"How did you get them?"

Grace rolled over and sat up, a maneuver she performed deftly despite the cast on her arm. Maggie returned to her chair.

"You can tell me; I'm just trying to help you."

The young girl reached out and grabbed Maggie's hand. A single tear fell down her face.

"How did you get those bruises, Grace?"

"I fell down the stairs," Grace finally said.

It was the same story Maggie had read in the chart, repeated several times without variation. "Are you sure?"

"Uh-huh."

"Why did you fall on the stairs? Did you trip?"

Her mouth fell open slightly as she shook her head; Maggie noticed that one of her front teeth was chipped. "Your front tooth is chipped. How did that happen?"

"I fell."

"You seem to fall a lot."

"Daddy says I'm clumsy."

"What else does daddy say?" Maggie asked.

"Not to talk to strangers."

Melendez' voice boomed in the hallway. Grace tried to pull her hand away, but Maggie didn't let go. "Can you do me a favor, Grace?"

She heard Melendez again, talking to someone outside the door.

"What?" Grace asked.

"Can you tell how you really got these bruises on your bottom?"

"I already told you."

The door handle turned; her time was running out. "How did you break your arm?" Maggie stroked her arm, encouraging her. "You won't get in trouble, Grace. I'm just trying to help."

Grace opened her mouth to speak, but the words were drowned out in the bang of the door against the wall and the flurry of footsteps. A tall, powerfully-built man strode into the room, followed closely by Melendez. He spied Maggie sitting there. "Who are you?"

Maggie stood up, offering her hand. He looked her over

with disdainful eyes and accepted her offer at length. His tan fingers closed over hers, threatening to crush them.

"I'm Maggie Johnson, one of the pediatric interns."

A sneer crossed his lean, athletic face. "What are you doing here?"

A variety of responses arrived unbidden in her head; she uttered none of them, reiterating she was a pediatric intern.

"You said that already."

"I just asked her to help me out, Mr. Jones, I'm behind on my rounds."

Mr. Jones leered at Melendez, who grabbed Maggie by the arm and started pulling her out of the room.

"Well, don't ask her again. I don't want her in here."

Melendez nodded as he backed up, pulling the door open with his other arm and pushing Maggie out into the hall. He followed her out; the door slammed shut behind him.

"What happened to the warning?" Maggie asked.

"She didn't text you?"

Maggie scrolled through her texts; there was nothing recent. They hit the back staircase and ascended to the resident's lounge, which was empty other than an anonymous intern lying prone on the couch, snoring softly.

"Was that her dad?" Maggie asked.

Melendez nodded.

"I can see why you don't like him."

"The dude is a serious asshole."

They sat on the other couch. His leg fell against hers, and she let it lay where it fell.

"Thanks for coming back to get me, Caid," Maggie said.

"I saw that dude bust back onto Peds on a mission. I knew he wasn't going to be happy 'bout you being in there."

"Why not?"

"Don't know, but you could ask your father. I was in the room when your dad made his post-op check. They were pretty chummy."

124

Chapter Fourteen

The conference room was the same as it had been several days earlier—*Two? Three? Four? The endless days just melded into one another*—the tardy clock ticked, marking out each second with an audible *thunk*, and tension hung like fog in the stale air. Maggie was late, and she slunk into the chair next to Attorney Oberhausen as Father McDaniel finished the opening prayer and looked around the room, counting heads. The chair intended for the OSG was unoccupied.

"Does anyone know if Miss Mills is coming?" Father McDaniel asked.

Foster shrugged. Bobby's social worker continued the text she has been working on. Greta Oberhausen depleted her Sharpie of its ink.

"Why don't we get started without her? We can fill her in on the discussion when we she gets here."

No one objected, least of all Maggie, who had been in the building for nearly thirty hours. Since the ethics committee meeting didn't involve direct patient care, the Libby Zion Law didn't apply, not that this made any difference to Maggie's state of mind. She was sick and tired of the building, the people milling about inside its confines, and its smell—something Yoda called *l'odeur de l'hopital* in a nasally French accent—the nose-wrinkling combination of burnt coffee, stale urine and harsh antiseptic.

Maggie told them about the interview with Bobby, in which he'd clearly told the OSG he wanted no part of changing his code status to Do Not Resuscitate.

"You people are all the same—it never occurs to you that even people like me value their life."

The door swung open, and the OSG walked in, carrying a manila envelope. She slid into her chair, dropped the envelope onto the table, and cracked open a Diet Coke.

"Dr. Johnson was just telling us about your interview with Bobby," Father McDaniel said.

Miss Mills took a large sip of her Diet Coke.

"Did you want to add anything?"

She shook her head.

"Okay, it's pretty cut and dry, then. It seems like we're all of the same mind."

The OSG looked up, locking eyes with Miss Oberhausen who had given her Sharpie a rest for a minute, and slid the envelope in Father McDaniel's direction.

"What's this?"

The OSG didn't say, and he opened the envelope. Maggie's stomach turned a bit when she saw the Great Seal of the State of New York adorning the top page. The priest flipped through the pages for a minute and put everything back in place before sliding it in front of Foster. He glanced at it and passed it to the social worker who passed it to Maggie. She opened it, confirmed her fears, and passed it to Oberhausen who slid it across to the OSG without looking at it.

No one said anything. Maggie glanced at Foster, her eyes pleading him to do something, anything, to help save Bobby. He cleared his throat, starting to mouth words, but nothing audible emanated from in between his whitened teeth. The administrator started caching her belongings into her attaché case.

Father McDaniel stared at the OSG. "You petitioned the court for a change of Bobby's code status?"

"Isn't that what you asked me to do?"

McDaniel's cheeks reddened. "No, it isn't. I requested that you ask the patient what he thought about it."

She shrugged.

"Tell us about your interview with the patient," Father McDaniel said.

"There's not much to tell."

"Dr. Johnson says otherwise."

Thunk. Thunk. Thunk.

"He's a thirteen-year-old boy. You have to take what he says with a grain of salt." She finished her Diet Coke, and another one appeared to take its place.

"I don't understand the change of heart."

Oberhausen shouldered her bag and stood. She tried to slip past Maggie, but Maggie's chair was in the way, and Maggie made no effort to move.

Father McDaniel regarded the CEO. "Do you have somewhere to go?"

"I assumed the meeting was over."

"Please sit down, Miss Oberhausen. The meeting isn't adjourned yet."

She remained standing. "So, adjourn it then. This committee was formed to resolve the patient's code status. We now have a court order that does exactly that." She tried to slip out again, but Maggie extended her legs and used the strength Pilates had lent to her body to prevent her from leaving.

"Miss Oberhausen, let me remind you that you are not in charge of this committee," Father McDaniel said.

"And let me remind *you*, Father McDaniel, that you are. We have fulfilled our obligation. Any further discussion would be pointless...unless you have some kind of agenda you're not telling us about."

"That's rich coming from you."

"How's that?"

"Because I was just going to ask you the same question. What's your agenda, Greta?"

She smiled sweetly at the priest. "You're right, I do have an agenda; my agenda is to look after this hospital. I'm it's chief executive officer. That's my job."

"I'm aware what your job is. What I'm not aware of is how Bobby's code status affects this hospital."

Thunk. Thunk. Thunk.

The chief executive officer sat down in her chair and poured herself another cup of coffee. "Dr. Johnson, would you pass me the artificial sweetener?'

Maggie slid a Styrofoam cup filled with blue and yellow packets in front of her. She dumped the contents of two blue packets into her coffee and used her Sharpie to mix it in.

"Let's start from the beginning. Bobby was admitted... four years ago? Dr. Johnson, isn't that about right?"

Maggie called up the original History and Physical on her computer. "Four years, eight months."

"And what was the plan for Bobby when he first came?"

Maggie reviewed the History & Physical, which, even by intern's standards, was brief and uninformative. "It doesn't really say."

"That's right, Dr. Johnson. It doesn't say because there was no plan. We accepted Bobby as a favor to Columbia, who'd been trying to discharge him for weeks without success because no one wanted him. I personally authorized that acceptance because, allow me to quote Dr. Foster, 'We're a charity hospital; that's what we do.'"

Foster rubbed his pronounced chin. His green eyes were quiet.

"And so, almost five years later, here we are. Bobby remains in a joyless limbo, not dead yet but not really alive either, at least by any criteria I would consider. And Our Lady of Perpetual Mercy continues to pay for his care."

Maggie hadn't heard that name in so long it took her a minute to realize Oberhausen was referring to Golden Arches.

"Want to guess how much his care has cost us?"

No one wanted to guess. The social worker— who should have known better—stammered something about insurance benefits.

"Bobby's insurance stopped paying for his care after a few weeks." She extracted a few sheets of paper from her leather satchel, glancing at them. "And as a consequence, we have been footing the bill to the tune of over a million dollars...and counting."

She returned the papers to her bag and took her time fastening the leather straps securing them in place.

"Before you call me a cold-hearted bean counter, remember that all of our recent initiatives to provide affordable care to the impoverished neighborhoods surrounding the hospital cost money. A lot of money."

She stood up and stepped back from the table.

"I feel for Bobby as much as the next person, but keep something in mind. If we spend another million dollars keeping him in limbo, it's a million dollars that will never be used to fund an outpatient clinic in *El Barrio*, or our women's shelter, or our methadone program. We're not going to save Bobby...but we'll save a lot of other kids if we have the resources."

Oberhausen stared at the head of the table. McDaniel looked back at her, his face impassive. Foster stared into his coffee, stirring it absentmindedly. Oberhausen nodded with satisfaction and started walking out the door.

"This is bullshit," Maggie said.

Oberhausen stopped in her tracks. "What was that, Dr. Johnson?"

"I said, 'This is bullshit.'"

"You're out of line, Dr. Johnson. You were asked to be a part of this committee to present the patient's case. If we want your opinion on something else, we'll ask for it," Oberhausen said.

"Ms. Mills?" Maggie looked at the OSG, who did not meet her gaze. "You asked Bobby what he wanted. You heard what he said..."

Ms. Mills lowered her head further; she said nothing.

"Bobby wants to be a full code. You know that's what he wants," Maggie said.

"That's enough, Dr. Johnson," Oberhausen said.

Maggie continued to stare at the OSG. "Why are you letting her bully you like this. Stand up for Bobby. That's your job."

The clock plodded onward. *Thunk. Thunk. Thunk.*

"Not another word, Dr. Johnson."

Maggie's intestines roiled. Blood rushed to her head, flushing her face. The fragments of a hundred thoughts flitted through her head, but she was too angry to piece them together into a coherent sentence. Her frustration built, coalescing with her post-call fatigue and the exhaustion she had won from eight months of internship. If Oberhausen were closer, she might have lashed out at her, but the woman was out of arm's reach, glaring at her with a smug smile Maggie dearly wanted to knock off her face.

She snatched her satchel from the floor and walked out, brushing past Oberhausen as she stomped to the door.

***

In a hospital as old as Golden Arches, a woman could always find a place to get off the grid: a vacant classroom, an unused janitorial closet deep in the bowels of the basement, or even the stacks inside the rarely used medical library. Maggie had considered all of these as a place to take a nap but settled on the last on account of a rat sighting in the janitorial closet and a recent Melendez hook-up in the classroom—or at least a purported Melendez hook-up, which was not necessarily the same thing.

Maggie found the burnt orange chair in between the last two stacks on the side of the library opposite the window and settled into the overstuffed cushions. There was no one else in the library, which wasn't surprising because virtually all the medical information contained therein was also available with an internet connection and a subscription to PubMed, which was free to all the physicians and house staff. And since the medical librarian, a fussy and ill-dispositioned sexagenarian who still had her job for the sole reason no one had the courage to let her go, was in position at her desk, Maggie doubted the situation was going to change.

She flopped her legs over an arm, rested her head back against the head, and closed her irritated eyes. Fatigue overcame her, and she dropped off to sleep without delay, not waking until a firm hand shook her shoulder sometime later.

"Maggie, wake up."

She recognized her father's voice. "Dad?"

"Yes, it's me."

Prying open her eyes, she saw her father standing there in the light of the fluorescent bulbs. He was wearing his surgical scrubs and hat; the magnifying loops with which he used to operate were propped on his head

"What are you doing here?" she asked.

"Yoda told me you were here."

She scooched over to make room for him, and he sat down next to her. "What's up?"

"We need to talk."

Maggie had heard her father say this only a few times in her life, but enough to know it didn't bode well.

"I got an angry phone call this afternoon."

"Oh? Who from?"

"Brock Jones," her father said.

"Do I know him?"

"You know him alright. In fact, you just met him today."

Neurons synapsed in her tired mind, creating the image of the man who had fathered Grace Jones. She looked him over in her mind's eye, admiring his lean but powerful figure and his erect bearing. Brock Jones was a jerk, but he was a handsome one.

"What'd he want?" Maggie asked.

"He wanted to complain about you."

"For what? Doing my job?"

"His daughter isn't your patient, Maggie."

"Sure, she is. She's on the pediatric floor; I'm a pediatric intern. And not only that, I assisted on her surgery. That creep had no right to complain about me."

"That creep was the starting safety on the New York Giants the last time they won the Super Bowl, Maggie."

"Is that supposed to mean something to me?"

"It means he can cause you a lot of problems if you piss him off."

She snorted, a habit she had picked up from Yoda, who used the snort to communicate derision, disagreement and—most commonly—disgust.

"What are you trying to do, Maggie?"

"You told me to get some actual evidence before I went off half-cocked. So, that's what I'm trying to do."

"Evidence of what?" her father asked.

"Child abuse."

"Brock Jones is not a child abuser."

Another snort. It was possible Melendez was right about her turning in to Yoda. It was possible Melendez was right about a great many things.

"And you know this, how?" Maggie asked him.

"I just know."

"Have you ever met him before?"

"A while back, at the annual team dinner the last year I was on staff for the Giants."

"A handshake at a cocktail party is not a window into the soul."

The librarian cleared her throat at her desk, indicating that they were disturbing the other patrons. The fact that there were no other patrons didn't seem to matter to her.

"Okay, so maybe I don't know him all that well, but I do know him well enough to realize he's the kind of guy you don't want to cross."

He checked his watch and stood up to leave.

"He called me first out of deference for me...the next call will be to your residency director."

Maggie snorted a third time; her evolution into Yoda was progressing. "Big fucking deal." Maggie never cursed, but Melendez did all the time.

"It *is* a big deal; it's your future."

"For one thing, he'd just applaud me for having the balls to stand up for my patient; for another, I could give two shits about my future...it's your future anyway."

Roger Johnson narrowed his eyes and pursed his lips. "I'm warning you, Maggie. Stay away from her."

Chapter Fifteen

Bobby was in his customary position when Maggie slid into Room 12 with a bagful of biscotti and two lattes from the Italian bakery up the street from Golden Arches. Where the cardiac monitor had been, someone—Miss Oberhausen, Maggie would bet—had situated a large vase of flowers, giving the room a funereal atmosphere and a faint organic odor. The crash cart was gone, replaced by a VCR machine, which didn't work, and a lopsided stack of tapes no one watched.

"We're never going to heal those wounds on your hip if you don't change position once in a while," Maggie said.

"So, I'll die with an unhealed wound... what's the big deal?"

"Bobby..."

"This is the only way I can read. I've only got one arm, remember?"

Maggie sat down on the hard-plastic chair next to his bed, and the two of them ate almond biscotti and sipped lattes. She was aware she shouldn't be giving a thirteen-year-old boy so much caffeine, but he did love them, and she couldn't bear the whining when she showed up without them.

"Don't you have somewhere else to be?" he asked her.

"Am I disturbing you?"

Bobby dropped his comic book, the most recent edition of the *All New X-Men* she had just brought him.

"Is something bothering you, Bobby?"

He didn't say, but it was clear from the scowl on his narrow, pinched face that something was. From experience, Maggie knew there was no point in pestering him; he would either come out with it, or he wouldn't.

"What happened to the all the cardiac monitoring equipment?" Bobby asked.

"Didn't the OSG explain that to you?"

"I wasn't paying attention. You're the only person I listen to."

"The OSG asked the court to change your resuscitation status to a no code, and the judge signed the order."

"That's not what I wanted. She knew that."

The first tear caught her by surprise. She wiped it away with the sleeve of her lab coat before Bobby could see it, but the second and the third followed, and then the fourth.

"It doesn't matter, Maggie. As long as I've got you, I'll be okay."

She snatched an emaciated tissue from the box on the tray, trying to stem the flow of tears. "That's something else we should talk about."

"What?"

She grabbed a whole handful of tissues, blotting her face dry, and then stuffed the lot into her pocket. "Today's my last day on pediatrics."

It was something she had been thinking about—a lot—recently, the change of guard that took place on the first day of every month in teaching hospitals across the country.

"I'll be going off service."

There was no response; the biscotti lay in pieces on his stained sheets, and the latte was tipped over on the table.

"Where are you going?" he asked.

"Radiology."

"Radiology is stupid."

Maggie was inclined to agree with him, but she kept her opinion to herself.

"So that's it... I'm never going to see you again?"

"Of course, you're going to see me again. I'll come visit you all the time."

Bobby gathered up a piece of biscotti and chomped down on it with his carious teeth. He picked up the latte—ignoring the spilled liquid—and took a sip. "You promise?"

"Yes, I promise."

He reached for her with his tiny arm and set his hand down on her forearm, stroking her skin with his emaciated fingers. Maggie nibbled a biscotti, sipped her beverage, and wished for time to stand still—a wish she knew would never be granted.

***

Maggie finished stitching up a knee laceration—a seven-year-old had decided to try flying off the swing set—and headed back to her office. Bertie was standing in the middle of the room, swinging her aluminum softball bat and staring into the mirror on the far wall trying to keep her hips level.

"I just finished stitching the laceration in Room 7. Can you put a dressing on the wound and put her on my schedule in a week to take out the sutures?"

Bertie nodded, leaning the bat against the wall. "I just put an add-on your schedule, Maggie."

"Who is it?"

"Carla. She just walked in. I figured you'd want to see her."

"Put her in Room 4."

It was the end of the day, and only a few patients were left at the clinic. Maggie walked by the GYN room where she heard one of the other interns talking to a patient about options for birth control and slipped past the pediatric room where a 2-month-old was getting shots—and screaming bloody murder.

Carla was sitting on the exam table, sobbing with her head down. On the floor next to her, Diego was strapped into a car seat, crying inconsolably. A medium-sized suitcase and two diaper bags lay next to the baby. Maggie shut the door, sat next to Carla, and put her arm around her.

"I shoulda listened to you, Maggie."

Yes, you should have, Maggie thought, but just mumbled, "Let's not worry about that," instead.

"I never thought he would hurt Diego. I swear to you, Maggie."

Maggie had known all along he would hurt Diego, but there was no point in saying so. She pulled her phone out and texted Bertie to call the social worker to come get them as Carla intermittently apologized and sobbed. When she could pry herself loose, she knelt on the floor and examined the baby. A cursory exam yielded two cigarette burns and a probable mid-forearm fracture. She reached for the ophthalmoscope and realized it was in the pediatric room.

"I'll be right back," Maggie said.

She set Diego back in the seat and passed into the hall in time to see the door to the waiting room kicked open from the other side, shattering the glass as it recoiled against the wall. Reggie waltzed in through the empty frame. The secretary stood up to stop him, but he shoved her backwards, and she tripped over her chair and fell to the floor.

Carla came out of Room 4 and ran down the hall towards Reggie. "What the fuck are you doing here, Reggie?"

Reggie smiled, revealing nicotine-stained teeth and thin, bloodless lips. "What kind of greeting is that?"

Chapter Sixteen

Maggie pushed open the door and went outside. The observation deck was empty, despite a sunny and pleasant spring evening. She moved to her favorite spot on the rail overlooking the east side of the hospital. The observation deck had been 'officially' closed for a decade because a distressed intern threw himself over the edge after failing the boards. The interns paid no heed to the official status, however, and it remained the getaway for interns trying not to be found by attendings, fellows, and residents looking to pawn off scutwork.

She leaned against the rail and breathed in the first deep breath she'd had in two weeks, consequent to the bruised ribs she'd suffered in the fight with Reggie, who hadn't been as fortunate, requiring transfer to Columbia for an emergency thoracotomy.

"Want some company?"

Maggie turned to see Father McDaniel approaching, dressed, as always, in a black suit and white collar. In truth, she wanted nothing more than to sit alone in the sun, but she always enjoyed a conversation with the Jesuit.

"Sure."

Father McDaniel sat down on an old exam table— complete with stirrups—some of the past interns had lugged up the stairs, and pulled out a corncob pipe.

"I didn't know you smoked."

He lit up the pipe, filling the air with earthy smoke. "I don't."

They sat quietly, enjoying each other's company and the armada of sailboats on the East River. Underneath them, Spanish Harlem wooed them with its usual serenade: car horns, barking dogs, and the drone of tires on asphalt.

"How are you feeling?" he asked.

"Fine."

He looked at her askance, but didn't say anything. "How's Bobby doing?"

The last time she'd been to see him—a full three days previous—he'd been wearing his oxygen of his accord, and he hadn't been able to muster the strength to berate her for the decreasing frequency of her visits.

"Okay, I guess."

An empty pan had been pushed against the railing, and Maggie opened the carton she had carried up the stairs and filled the pan with whole milk. One of the other interns had told her the stray cat living outside of the pediatric ward had moved to the roof—with her new litter of kittens. There was no sight of her, but a handful of grey hairballs stuck to the tarpaper and a pile of cat droppings in the corner betrayed her presence.

"On the bright side, your internship is almost done," Father McDaniel said.

She shrugged.

"I would have thought you would be overjoyed at the mere prospect of it. Every other intern I've met here in the last ten years certainly was. Why the uncertainty?"

"I'm thinking about staying."

He blew out a long stream of smoke and watched it disperse in the breeze. "Staying here? I thought the transitional residency was a one-year program?"

"It is, but there's a second-year pediatrics spot opening up."

McDaniel digested this by chomping on his pipe stem. "Aren't you supposed to be going over to Columbia soon?"

"July 1st. Six weeks from now."

"Why the change of heart?"

The breeze kicked up, bringing with it the fetid smell of the East River. A flock of pigeons rode down on the wind, settling onto the tar floor at the other end of the deck.

"I like it here," Maggie said.

"Does something make you think you won't like it at Columbia? It's a fantastic hospital."

"I know that, Father, and I think that's where the problem lies."

Maggie felt something brush up against her leg; Whiskers had returned. She picked her up, noting the two rows of swollen teats on her belly, and stroked her behind her right ear, the left having been lost in a territory dispute with another cat or a fight with a feral dog or some other calamity.

"The hospital is fantastic, you're right. The doctors are fantastic, and so are the nurses. The patients are fantastic, too... Everything about the place is fantastic, down to the food court."

"You don't think you're fantastic enough to fit in?"

She set Whiskers down, and she lapped up the milk Maggie had brought for her. "I don't think it's that, exactly, but I'm comfortable here, with this one-eared cat and the other misfits."

The priest attempted to re-light his pipe in the wind. A chorus of purring came from the other side of the heating ducts and Whiskers was gone.

"I'm drawn to people who struggle," Maggie said.

"People struggle at Columbia, too, you know."

"They do, with their health, but they wouldn't be at Columbia unless they had every other resource going for them. Golden Arches isn't like that; we're like the swamp that forms at the bottom of the mountain. Anyone that doesn't have the strength to make it up the mountain ends up in the muck."

Father McDaniel succeeded in re-lighting his pipe and blew a series of smoke rings that were whisked away by the breeze. "To be honest with you, I feel the same way, but I'm a priest. I'm supposed to."

"And you're wondering why an upstate girl like me prefers the swamp of Golden Arches to Columbia's ivory tower?"

"The thought had occurred to me."

"Don't be fooled by what you see on the outside. I look a lot different on the inside," Maggie told him.

Tires screeched, and sirens wailed as an unseen ambulance made its approach into the bay next to the Emergency Department, where a stretcher pushed by one of the other interns would be waiting for it. She imagined the intern standing there—nervous but excited—waiting for the back doors of the ambulance to open.

"What do you look like on the inside?" Father McDaniel asked.

"A thirteen-year-old boy with incurable cancer, a man who thinks he's an android, a little girl with a chipped tooth and bruises on her butt…that's what I look like on the inside."

"Welcome home, Maggie."

***

Maggie swirled the Riesling around in its glass, creating thin streams of wine on the side of the glass. "This really isn't a good idea."

"What's wrong with it?" Foster asked.

"You're an attending, for one thing."

Foster shrugged. "You're a transitional intern. In a few months, you'll be at Columbia doing radiology. No one is going to care if we're seeing each other."

"No one besides Bobby, you mean?"

"What's Bobby got against me?" Foster asked.

"Foster is a dog with fleas! He's just trying to get down your pants."

"Not sure, but I know he doesn't like you," Maggie replied.

"He's probably just jealous."

"I'm jealous of people who buy green tomatoes. Stop changing the subject."

"I don't think that's it."

"Look, Maggie, I think it's great how close you and Bobby have become. It's ill advised, surely, and against all common sense—but it's great. The kid needs somebody, and you're there for him. But he's a thirteen-year-old boy with a crush on you. That's the kind of behavior you're going to get."

The waiter came back and set a couple glasses of cognac on the table, sweeping the table clean with a file.

"Are you trying to get me drunk?" Maggie asked.

"Will it help my chances?"

She didn't say, which Foster took as a yes, lifting up his glass to signal the waiter to keep the cognac coming.

"The other thing is…I'm still considering switching my residency," Maggie told him.

"You mean to pediatrics?"

"Yes, don't you remember we discussed it at the boathouse?"

He sipped his cognac, nodding. "I guess I didn't realize you were still thinking about doing that. You haven't said anything."

"You don't sound very enthusiastic."

He stroked his cowlick with his fingers—something he always did when he wasn't sure what to say—twisting the curl of hair in his index finger.

"Don't you want me to stay at Golden Arches?" Maggie asked.

"It's one thing for us to date with you being a transitional intern, Maggie, but it's another if you accept the 2nd year spot in the pediatrics residency. I would need to report that to Dr. Clarke, and I doubt she's going to be thrilled with the idea."

"So, I'm supposed to do a residency I have no interest in because it would make it easier for you?" Maggie said a little louder than she intended.

"I didn't say that."

"You implied it," Maggie said, her voice lower.

He leaned back in his chair, splaying his manicured hands. The wattage from his smile lit up the darkly lit restaurant. "We've only had a few dates, Maggie. You'd feel differently if we'd started seeing each other a few months ago."

"I don't see what difference that makes."

He shrugged. Maggie excused herself to use the bathroom. Foster had paid the bill when she returned, and they exited out the back door. It was a cool night. Foster slipped his arm over shoulder, and they walked back to her apartment on Murray Hill, in front of which Foster had left his black Audi A8. As they stood next to the car, she wished him a good night.

"Good night? I was hoping you were going to invite me in a for a night cap," Foster said with a smile.

"Sorry, Jack, not tonight. I just want to go to bed."

He flashed another smile at her. "That's what I had in mind as well."

"By myself."

She gave him a peck on the cheek and passed inside her building with him still standing in front of his car, mouth crooked open in surprise.

Chapter Seventeen

Maggie clicked on the next image, a lateral view of the forearm. Somewhere in the recesses of her brain, she remembered Yoda warning her about how easy it was to miss an occult elbow fracture, but she couldn't generate enough enthusiasm to go over it a second time. It was the middle of her third week as night float in the Radiology department, and she still hadn't—as her father assured her she would—developed an interest in sitting alone in the dark and staring at a screen in search of disease. She found herself nodding off on frequent occasion, lulled to sleep by the darkness, the monotony, and her lack of zeal for the work.

She smelled Dr. Edwards, the radiology attending on duty, before she heard him, catching whiff of the mung bean sprouts on his breath prior to hearing his shuffling, almost Parkinsonian footfalls on the carpet. He sat down next to her without preamble, pointing out the many findings she had missed on the dozen films at which she had been staring. He left with as little warning as he came, plodding off toward the gastrointestinal suite where the radiology tech was prepped and ready to fill some poor patient's colon with gastrograffin, a nasty solution which induced a violent and explosive diarrhea.

"Hey, Maggie." Melendez appeared next to her.

"Hey, Caid. What are you doing here?"

He showed her a handful of sugary snacks. "Are you kiddin' me? Diagnostic Imaging has the best candy jar in this dump. And the white pants the techs wear? I swear to God they're see-through." He grabbed a chair and plopped down next to her. "How can you stand staring at these screens all day?"

She couldn't, but she didn't say so. "I thought you wanted me to be a radiologist?"

He nibbled on a cow's tail, which he left sticking out of his mouth. "Never said that. I said I wanted you to go to Columbia so you can get outta this freak show."

"I like this freak show better."

And she did. When she walked through the door of Columbia-Presbyterian and into its stately lobby, she looked for the charm Golden Arches had in spades and found it lacking. The stainless-steel doors glistened—and came together without a gap through which the January wind blew—but had no character. The *avant-garde* artwork was expensive and in vogue but left her cold. The potted plants were exotic and many, but she preferred the lone rubber plant in the lobby of Golden Arches in dire need of water.

"I swear to God you're a moron. I know everybody thinks you're a genius and all, but shit, Maggie... sometimes I don't know if you could find your way out of a paper fuckin' bag."

She would never understand why she liked Melendez so much, and for once, her over-analytical mind let something go.

"But I didn't come down here to harsh on you again," Melendez continued. He looked around, searching the murk for someone who might be listening. There was no else in the reading room. "We have to talk."

Something about the tone of his voice told her he wasn't going to hit on her for the she-had-lost-count-how-many-times.

"I just came from pediatrics..." he said.

"Pediatrics? What were you doing there? I thought you were doing Ophthalmology this month."

He finished his cow's-tail, sucking it in his mouth like a strand of spaghetti. "I am doing optho...but I'm still seeing that agency nurse from Argentina. You know the one I'm talking about?"

"Yes, I know who she is." Maggie could still see her parading around the ward, heavily made-up, wearing skin-tight clothes over her voluptuous figure. "What do we have to talk about?"

She knew what was on his mind, but she couldn't bring herself to say it.

"Bobby... he's not doing well," Melendez said.

"I know he's not."

"When the last time you saw him?"

Maggie admitted it had been a few days.

"You gotta get up there...pronto. I don't think he's got long."

Melendez was a terrible diagnostician, and his prognostication was even worse, but she didn't doubt him. Even a doctor who was paying as little attention as Melendez couldn't fail to see what Yoda referred to as the death signs: the mottling of the skin, the glaze in the eyes, and the fetid odor of the rotting body.

"That jerk-off Cushing is completely ignoring him. I don't think he's even been in the room in days," Melendez admitted with a frown.

Maggie had glanced at Bobby's file earlier, when the tedium of yet another ankle X-ray had been too much to take. If anyone—intern, resident or attending—had been making visits to his room, it wasn't evident from a review of his chart.

"Why are you telling me this, Caid?" Maggie asked.

A hole had opened in her heart, a hole no package of gauze was big enough to fill.

"Besides the fact that the agency nurse gets crazy horny when I act like a decent person?"

"Yes, besides that."

"Because he's going to die Maggie, probably soon...and even a callous asshole like myself would hate it if you didn't get to say goodbye."

***

Maggie switched her viewer off and passed into the locker room, which, due to the non-linear geometry of Golden Arches, was behind the reading room. Maggie collapsed into an overstuffed chair in the corner, which some nameless intern had stolen from the boardroom years ago.

Yoda appeared, clumping into the room from the entrance to the interventional suite. "Hey, Maggie."

Maggie grunted a greeting.

Yoda grabbed a set of scrubs from her pile—they were youth mediums and had to be special ordered—and began changing into them, a process made difficult by the weakness of her left side. "We're putting a stent into a femoral artery. Get your scrubs on."

Scrubbing in on an interventional radiology procedure was the last thing she wanted to do. If given her choice—not that internship was rife with a lot of choices—she would have preferred cleaning the bathrooms in the Emergency Department, which was the punishment Yoda assigned to the first intern who called in sick.

Yoda wiggled into the scrub bottoms, and stared at her through her thick-framed glasses. "What's eating you?"

"Just tired, that's all."

"Tired from what? An exhausting shift sitting in an ergonomically perfect chair reading X-rays?"

In addition to her physical problems, Yoda had her fair share of emotional ones, such as the inability to read social clues, and she didn't seem to notice Maggie's crossed arms and discouraging countenance.

"Yes, must be that," Maggie said.

Yoda wore the same pair of blue slacks every day, pairing them with one of the seven monochromatic blouses she wore on such a scheduled basis that the interns used her shirt color to determine the day of the week. She struggled out of her sunflower yellow blouse—meaning today was Thursday—and pulled on her scrub top.

"You know something, Maggie, I don't think you are tired. I think you're feeling sorry for yourself," Yoda said. She slipped back into her orange plastic clogs, which were the only footwear Maggie had ever seen her wear. "You can imagine how I feel about a girl like you feeling sorry for herself?"

If Maggie wasn't careful, she was going to get a full-on Yoda tsunami, a term which Melendez had coined, having been on the receiving end of many.

But she wasn't in a careful mood. "A girl like myself? What's that supposed to mean?"

"Tall, for one thing." Yoda tucked in her scrub top, drew the waist cord tight, and knotted the remainder into a double bow tie. "Beautiful, for another." She donned one of the blue cloth caps, maneuvered her bangs underneath, and secured the back. "The kind of girl I spent most of my life wanting to be..."

The overhead crackled to life, warning visitors that their hours were nearly over.

"But then one day I just stopped wanting to be someone else," Yoda said as she sat down next to Maggie and scrolled through the dozen or so text messages on her phone. She put the phone in her pocket without responding to any of them. "Okay, so now that I've bared my soul, I'm going to ask again: What's eating you?"

"Aren't we supposed to be assisting on that case?"

Yoda chuckled at this. Her laugh was a cross between a high-pitch giggle and a raspy hiccough, which Melendez said sounded like an ostrich fart. "I know you all think I don't get social clues, but the truth is I do... I just don't care. There's a difference between those two things. Do you understand that?"

"Of course, I understand that."

"No, you don't," Yoda said.

"Are you trying to make me feel better or worse?"

"I don't do either of those things. I just say the things that need to be said." Yoda rocked back and forth on her chair, something Maggie had seen her do frequently.

"Anything else that needs to be said?" Maggie asked, with an edge to her voice.

Yoda stopped rocking and tried to lock eyes with Maggie, although the best she could do was stare at the side of Maggie's face. "Every time I walk through the reading room, you're either asleep, bored to death, or miserable."

Maggie said nothing.

"You're going to be a terrible radiologist. You know that, don't you?"

Maggie nodded as the tears started flowing. It pained her to cry in front of Yoda, but there was no stopping the crying. "Yes, I know that."

"And yet off you go to Columbia to become just that, when it's plain as day you want to be a pediatrician."

"Who told you that?" Maggie asked.

"No one told me that. No one had to...I can see it for myself, and so can everybody else. It's because you care what other people think. That's what I meant when I said you don't get it."

More tears spilled, dripping into her mouth, where they fell onto her tongue, tasting salty and wet.

"You really want to be miserable your whole life?" Yoda took off her hat and handed it to Maggie, who used it to sop up the moisture on her face.

"It's not just that...I can't even deal with the *idea* of Bobby dying, and yet he's heading downhill fast, and I haven't seen him in three days."

"Why not? It's not like you don't have time...you're doing radiology."

The tears streamed in earnest. She tried to use the hat to clear them away, but it was already saturated and just smeared them over her face. "I don't know. That's just it."

Yoda reached over and patted Maggie on the knee, which was the first-time Maggie had ever seen her touch another human being not in the setting of a procedure. "Go see him, Maggie. Go now."

"What about the stent insertion?"

"I'll make an excuse for you." And with that last comment, she grabbed another hat from the box and disappeared into the interventional suite.

Chapter Eighteen

Almost nothing had changed in Room 12 when Maggie passed inside and sat on the plastic chair next to Bobby's bed: the clock on the wall was stuck on three, the window to the outside world was hopelessly clouded up, and Bobby was in his usual position, lying on his side with his one arm extended, the latest edition of the *All New X-Men* folded up in his small hand. There was one difference, however, and Maggie's nose wrinkled with the noxious odor of imminent demise as soon as she stepped inside the door.

"Where ya been?" Bobby asked.

Maggie had no good answer for this, and she wasn't going to start fabricating excuses now. She leaned over and kissed him on the forehead. His pallid skin tasted like cold liver. "What's going on?"

Awkwardness filled the air like a fog. He rolled over to give her the stink eye, an exertion that cost him most of his pulmonary reserve. When he caught his breath, he rolled back over and resumed reading. "I'm lying around waiting to die; that's what."

The hole in her heart opened up so big she had to look down and make sure blood wasn't oozing out of her chest, saturating her shirt.

"Or had you forgotten because you don't come to see me anymore," Bobby said.

Shame.

"You said you'd come visit me all the time..."

She didn't think she had any tears left, but she was wrong about that as well.

"I thought we had something, Maggie..."

The box of tissues on Bobby's tray was empty, but there was a crumpled napkin lying there—a remnant of a trip to the café a century ago—that she used to wipe her face.

"We do, Bobby," Maggie told him. She moved her hand to his neck and used her fingers to massage the knots out of the wasted bulk of his musculature. "I'm sorry."

She was sorry, too, truly sorry. The words reminded her of the time she had broken up with the only boyfriend she'd ever had, but the feeling of profound sorrow was new.

"You're the only one I have, Maggie. Don't leave me..."

She lay down next to him. His body felt hard and cold. "I won't Bobby."

She could feel his chest heaving; he was crying. They were facing in opposite directions, so she couldn't see his face, but she could picture his red and irritated eyes, a consequence of his shriveled-up tear glands.

"Why haven't you been coming to see me?"

The answer to his question came out before she could stop it. "Because I'm having a hard time watching you die..."

Oxygen hissed, mixing with the wail of a distressed infant down the hall.

"Doing the actual dying ain't much fun either."

She gathered him in her arms. It had been years since she had lain in a bed with another person, and it prompted the memory of the night she had said goodbye to her boyfriend. Their yearlong relationship was dead, a victim of failed intimacy.

"Maggie, what's going to happen to me when I die?" Bobby asked.

"What are you talking about?"

A squabble erupted from the adjacent room; something about what video was going to be played. The smell of blood and stool floated in through the open doorway, a sure sign the pandemic of Norwalk virus gripping the Big Apple hadn't played itself out yet.

"I'm almost done here, Maggie. I need to know to what's going to happen to me," Bobby said.

The computer screen appeared in Maggie's head again, and she scrolled down to the Comparative Religion class she had taken at Brown. Every race, every creed, every religion had a creation myth, a way to explain how we got here, and every culture had in turn an afterlife belief, an explanation of what happened to the soul after death. Maggie clicked on several and reported them to Bobby, sounding as dry and dull as her professor had. The Buddhists, Hindus, and others were reincarnated; the Ancient Greeks were ferried across the river Styx; Norse warriors who died in Battle joined Odin in Valhalla; Christians either ascended into heaven or descended into hell, depending upon their actions and beliefs.

"I don't care about any of those people, Maggie, I want to know what *you* believe." His tiny hand clamped around her fingers, pleading for the truth with her. The firm grip spoke, saying 'I deserve the truth.'

Maggie had been raised Methodist, but her family had attended services only on Easter and Christmas, and she'd drifted away from formalized religion at Brown, where the human intellect was worshipped on an exclusive basis.

"I don't believe in anything, Bobby."

"Huh? What kind of crappy answer is that?"

"My answer."

He let go of her hand. "You mean to tell me I'm just going to rot in the ground? Thirteen years of this crummy existence and then nothing? How is that fair?"

She tried to hold his hand again, but he slapped hers

had just gotten engaged—but never had any news about herself. As a rule, to which there were no exceptions, Mary Johnson never spoke about herself.

"How's radiology going?"

"Okay."

It wasn't true. An hour in the reading room seemed like a day, and a night like an eternity. The only thing she didn't mind about the rotation was the interventional procedures, during which she had the opportunity to interact with the actual patient. Reading films for the rest of her career was a prospect too dismal even to consider.

"I'm not your father, Maggie. You can tell me the truth."

"You won't say anything to Dad?"

"Girl Scout's honor."

Mary Johnson had been Maggie's troop leader and the only thing Maggie had liked about scouting. It had taken Maggie four years to tell her mother she didn't want to continue, only to find that her mother felt the same way.

"I don't like it," Maggie said. She listed off a litany of complaints, the last of which was her current attending's body odor. "I don't think the man has showered in weeks."

"Have you done anything about it?"

Maggie shook her head.

"Why not?"

"You didn't raise me to be a quitter."

"I didn't raise you to be a fool, either, and spending three more years training to do something you don't want to do is a fool's choice."

Maggie never took offense from her mother's words; there was no rancor in her voice, no malice in her pale blue eyes, and no acrimony beneath her high cheekbones.

"The chief resident told me the same thing."

"Maybe you should listen…"

"The chief resident doesn't have to deal with Dad."

"You let me deal with your father."

"Easier said than done."

She didn't reply, but her square shoulders and erect posture reminded Maggie that her mother had stood her ground with her father before and promised she could do it again. There was a quiet strength about the woman—and God knew she had needed it—from which Maggie had always taken inspiration.

"If I call the radiology residency director at Columbia, the first thing he's going to do is call Dad," Maggie said.

Her mother's spine remained straight; her strong chin stayed high.

"I'll call him this week."

***

Ray Cushing was the embodiment of everything Maggie hated about medicine.

He was smart, no doubt about that, but he was also arrogant and self-important, and the arrogance was more evident than the intelligence. His white coat was starched to perfection, and it had remained white, a result of weekly dry cleanings. The latest issue of *The New England Journal of Medicine* was always in his hand or rolled up in the pocket of his coat, and the most important of its conclusions were always rolling off his silver tongue. His hair was clipped short—but not too short—and his wire-framed glasses gave him the superior air he had intended them to give.

Maggie caught up to him near the coffee pot, a few minutes before pediatric rounds were set to begin. "Hey Ray, can I talk to you for a minute?"

Cushing looked suspiciously at her. Even though they were both transitional interns—he would be starting his neurology residency at Yale in another month—Maggie didn't know him well. He had pursued Maggie with persistence last summer, in an I-won't-take-no-for-an-answer way, and things had been awkward when he finally took no for an answer.

"What's up?" he asked.

"You're taking care of Bobby, right?"

Recognition didn't flash in his eyes.

"The thirteen-year-old with leukemia...the boy in Room 12," Maggie said.

"Oh, yeah, him. Sure."

In some cases, four words spoke more than four hundred. Cushing never forgot anything, even the smallest detail, *if* he considered it to be important. The converse of this was also true; he had the ability to ignore anything he didn't deem worthwhile, which, in this case, was Bobby. He had written him off for dead and was focusing his energies on the living.

"How's he doing?" Maggie asked.

"Alright, I guess."

"Alright? What does that mean?"

"It means he's still alive."

He was right about that, she knew, having just visited him this morning. Bobby was cold and pale, but alive.

"He's not doing well, Ray. You need to treat him," Maggie said.

"His status had been changed, Maggie. He's DNR now. You know that."

"DNR means do not resuscitate, not do not treat."

"You don't think I know that?"

Maggie thought she was going to get the 'I'm the great-grandson of Harvey Cushing, the greatest doctor of all time' speech he so loved to give, but he disappointed her.

"Apparently, you don't," Maggie said. "The patient is failing, and you're doing nothing about it."

"The attending told me to go easy, so I'm going easy."

"The most important rule of internship, know what it

is? Treat the patient, not the attending. The attending isn't the fuckin' patient, got that assholes?"

"The attending isn't your patient; Bobby is."

"Bobby isn't going to be writing my recommendation; the attending is."

She stepped toward him, and for a brief second, she thought she was going to lunge at him and choke him with her stethoscope. "Look, I didn't come to argue with you." She tried to manage a smile. "Can't you just order a chest film? I'm doing radiology this month. I'll look at it and let you know what I see."

Indecision overcame his face, and she thought he might give in, until his resting smug face returned. "Absolutely not. I was told not to do anything unless I cleared it with the attending or the senior resident. I'm not risking it."

"He's dying, Ray."

"People die, Maggie. I'm not letting my career die with him—and you wouldn't either. We've worked too hard for too long to let that happen."

"You're a coward, you know that? You think you're so smart, and maybe you are, but you don't have any balls."

He looked at her with the supercilious look he reserved for the nurses and adjuvant staff. "Was there anything else?"

She shook her head, and he turned away to join the other interns for the start of rounds.

Chapter Twenty

It was two a.m., and Maggie was alone in the viewing room, other than the attending physician who was trying to ignore her. She was staring at yet another chest film, and she wondered how many she had reviewed in the three hours since she began her first night shift in the viewing room of the Radiology Department. *Nine? Ten? Perhaps eleven.* She wasn't sure, and she wasn't interested enough to count properly.

"Anything interesting, Maggie?"

"Nope, Dr. Edwards, just another negative chest X-ray."

Dr. Edwards tried to cover a burp, but his efforts were unsuccessful and the putrid odor of garlic and onions spewed into the air.

"Any questions for me?" he asked.

"None," she replied. He nodded and shuffled off to some dark corner of the viewing room from which the foul smell of the remnants of his dinner was emanating.

Sometime around three a.m., Dave, the radiology tech, informed her that the portable digital X-ray machine was down, an occurrence that happened far more than it should. As a consequence of that, the old portable machine had staved off mothballs, and the techs had all been taught how to develop film.

"Hey, Dave, wait a second," Maggie said.

He paused, halfway through the door with his equipment in tow.

"Can you do me a favor?" she asked.

"Sure, what's up?"

"Can you take a chest film for me on pediatrics?"

"On pediatrics? What room? I didn't see the order," Dave said.

"There isn't an order. I'm just curious."

"You know we can't do a study without an order."

Maggie had been trying to get one of the techs to do an unauthorized chest X-ray on Bobby ever since Cushing had refused her request, but they had all said no because there was no order to do so. In a hospital, orders were sacrosanct; nothing happened without them. A patient got Tylenol only if an order existed, even though it was available over the counter at pharmacies, grocery stores, and most conveniences. Meals were not distributed without the appropriate order specifying what kind of diet: clear liquids; ground; full; the choices were many. A patient couldn't even get out of bed without an order saying so.

"Take an extra film cartridge with you, and shoot a chest on the kid in Room 12," Maggie said firmly.

"The nurses will see me."

"Room 12 is on the annex; you can take the back elevator and not have to go anywhere near the nurses' station."

"But I still have to scan the films in after I develop them, so they'll go in the system."

"Don't scan it in. Give it to me after you develop it, and I'll shred it after I read it." She could see his resistance was breaking down. "Come on, Dave. If anything goes wrong, I'll take the fall for it."

"Alright."

The door closed behind him, and she tried to focus on a CT Brain of a nursing home patient with altered mental status, but Bobby's cadaverous form hung in front of her like a specter. Before she had even gone through the coronal images and moved on the axial, the door to the darkroom opened, and Dave's arm came out, holding a rectangle of film. She jumped out of her chair and grabbed it, throwing it up on the old-fashioned viewer.

There could be no mistake that it was Bobby's chest that glowed at her; the fragile, underdeveloped rib cage attached to only one arm could belong to no one else. It was a testimony to her inexperience that she needed a minute to spot the abnormality. The pale globe sitting in the middle of his lungs could not be ignored forever, however, and she drew in her breath as her eyes settled upon it, round and white and deadly in the middle of his chest.

Taking one last look one at the film, she fed it into the shredder and found the back staircase. She opened the door to Bobby's annex carefully, looking out. The security guard was still posted outside the room across from Bobby's, keeping watch over a gang member with an infected knife wound. Several years ago, a gang fight had broken out within the pediatric ward, when a member of Air It Out had discovered that a member of the hated 18th Street gang was convalescing just down the hall. Since that time, all gang members received around the clock guards, a policy with which Maggie had never had the occasion to be unhappy. Until now, that is, having to walk right past him to get to the supply cabinet.

She ran back to Radiology, grabbed her backpack from her locker, and found the interventional suite. Owing to the great variety of procedures done within its confines—and to its profitability—the suite's supply cabinet had everything an intern needed to drain the fluid from around the heart of a dying boy, which was exactly what she intended to do, regardless of the consequences.

"Promise me you won't let me die."

"I can't do that."

"You have to…"

It was possible that a small part of her brain was warning her against such a course of action, but, if that were the case, she was paying it no mind. She wasn't concerned about the remainder of her internship, her upcoming residency training, or her future as a doctor. Her only concern was the boy in Room 12 who was going to die if she didn't do something without delay. She ran around the suite, filling her backpack with all the needed supplies, a twenty-two-gauge spinal needle, a one-hundred-cc syringe, Betadine swabs, and a wound kit, and hit the stairs.

Yoda was in the stairwell. "Hey Maggie, where're you going? I was just coming to see what was going on in radiology."

Shit. Shit. Shit.

"Taking a break in the cafeteria," Maggie lied.

Yoda peered at her though her thick spectacles. Maggie could feel her gaze penetrate her like an X-ray. "You know something, I'm kinda hungry. Mind if I join you?"

Maggie shrugged. "I've gotta do a few things first."

"I'm not in any hurry."

They hoofed it up the stairs. Yoda monopolized the left side of the staircase, leaning heavily on the railing. Taking the stairs was an effort for her, as evidenced by the flaring of her nostrils and the heave of her narrow chest—but one she must have deemed worthwhile since she always took them.

"How's night float going?" Yoda asked.

All she could think about was the fluid accumulating within Bobby's pericardium, the lining around his heart, which prevented the heart from being able to pump effectively. Small wonder he'd looked so bad when she had visited him prior to the start of her shift. His skin had been cool and sweaty, and his breath had reeked like death, something that happened when the kidneys stopped excreting toxins and the lungs tried to exhale them in the kidneys' stead.

"Alright, I guess," Maggie replied.

Maggie got a frozen yogurt from the dairy bar, even though she wasn't hungry and had no intention to eat it. Yoda got a cupful of chickpeas, her favorite snack, which she ate at almost every meal, including breakfast. The interns claimed, with some justification, they gave her gas.

"How come you're not eating your yogurt?" Yoda asked.

Maggie shrugged. The frozen yogurt was melting in the Styrofoam bowl. "I'm not that hungry."

"I thought you needed to do a few things?"

"I'll do them later."

Yoda stared at Maggie's backpack. "Like what kind of things?"

"Just stuff. Nothing big."

Yoda resumed eating her chickpeas, which she did by spearing them individually with the outside tine of her fork. "How's Bobby?"

She could see his pericardium, swollen like a balloon, ready to pop. "Okay, I guess."

"You're a terrible liar. Do you know that, Maggie?"

Maggie played with her food, twirling the spoon around in the bowl in an effort to separate the imitation strawberries away from the imitation strawberry-flavored yogurt.

"Bobby isn't okay, and you had no intention of coming to the cafeteria." Yoda used her fork to point at Maggie's backpack. "My guess is, you saw something on that chest film you bullied Dave into taking, and you're planning on doing something about it."

Maggie should have guessed Dave would have called Yoda. The entire ancillary staff worshipped her like a deity—calling her Dr. Yoda with the utmost reverence.

Yoda grabbed the backpack and sorted through it. "Let me see. One-hundred-cc-syringe, Betadine, spinal needle..." She finished her inspection, closed the zipper back up, and returned the backpack to the tabletop. "Pericardial effusion, huh? I should have suspected that."

The intern in her couldn't help but be curious. "Why?"

"It can be a complication of doxorubicin treatment."

Doxorubicin was the chemotherapy agent that had enlarged Bobby's heart. Maggie had read somewhere that it could also cause a pericardial effusion, but she had never put that together with his worsening cardiovascular status.

"Have you ever done a pericardial tap before?" Yoda asked.

A pericardial tap was an intern's wet dream, for the simple reason that pericardial effusions didn't happen that often. When they did, the interns were the last people to get to attempt to drain them, having to defer to the residents, the fellows, and even the attendings, who had been known to come in from home to join in the fun.

"No, just read about it. Have you?" Maggie asked.

"Dozens."

Maggie stared at Yoda, trying to read her small face, but her features remained expressionless. "Are you going to write me up?"

"You haven't done anything...yet. I came to talk you out of it."

"You can't do that, Yoda; he'll die unless I do the procedure."

Yoda rocked back and forth on the bench. "You realize what will happen if you get caught doing this procedure?"

Maggie shrugged.

Yoda grabbed a napkin and used her Sharpie to draw a diagram of the chest, using an X to mark the spot the needle should be inserted. "Find the xiphoid process with your finger; insert the needle underneath it, and aim at the left shoulder. Keep the angle shallow. Bobby has a thin chest."

Yoda went on, explaining the procedure in detail, making additional notes on the napkin. When she was finished, the napkin looked like a page from the *Washington Manual of Medicine.*

"Why are you helping me?" Maggie asked.

"I'm not. You're on your own from here, Maggie. And if you get caught, this meeting never happened."

Chapter Twenty-One

Bobby lay pale and still on the bed. For a second, Maggie thought he was already dead, but he opened his eyes when she grabbed his arm to check his pulse. He mouthed a hello, but there wasn't enough wind behind the words to create any sound.

"Fluid has accumulated around your heart, Bobby. That's why you feel so poorly. I'm going to drain that fluid to make you feel better."

He nodded.

"I have to ask you something first, though," Maggie said. She faltered for a minute, afraid of what was coming next. "I need your permission to do this."

In the modern-day world of medicine, a doctor didn't do a single procedure without a complete disclosure of the purpose of doing it as well a full listing of all the things that could go wrong. The so-called informed consent, almost always done in writing, was medicine's answer to the epidemic of malpractice suits that had arisen in the last score of years. She started to tell him about the possible complications, but he cut her off.

"Just do it," he said.

His voice was just a raspy whisper, but it made his point. He wanted her to proceed. She cleared everything off the tray at the bedside and set the items from the backpack down in their stead. Ripping open a package of gloves, she thrust them on and attached the spinal needle to a 100cc-syringe. Babe's voice floated down from the nurse's station, but Maggie ignored it. She was in too deep at this point to start worrying about getting caught.

Grabbing a pair of Betadine swabs, she wiped them over the bottom of Bobby's underdeveloped chest. She found the solar plexus with her fingers as Yoda had instructed her and positioned the long needle just underneath and to its left. In a conscious patient, standard protocol dictated she numb up the chest wall, but she had forgotten to grab the lidocaine, and she wasn't sure he was going to live long enough to run back down to radiology and fetch it.

"This is going to hurt a bit."

She inserted the needle. He didn't flinch, and only a few drops of blood spilled out onto his chest, a sure sign his circulation was on the verge of collapse. She advanced the needle, pulling back on the plunger as she went forward, but the needle remained empty.

"You done yet?" Bobby's voice was a coarse whisper.

"Not yet."

Maggie pushed the needle forward and felt a pop as the sharp tip speared through the heart's membranous enclosure. Bloodstained liquid spurted into the syringe. She used her other hand to move the plunger back, creating a vacuum that sucked the effusion into the syringe. When the fluid stopped pouring in, she paused, unsure what to do. In normal circumstances, she would have left a plastic catheter in place to prevent the fluid from re-accumulating, but the circumstances were far from normal; not only had the attending not authorized the procedure, he had no knowledge it was taking place— an ignorance in which Maggie was planning on keeping him.

Not able to think of any other options, she pulled the needle out, assuming the tiny hole in his pericardium would seal itself over, recapped the needle in gross violation of sterile procedure, and returned it to her backpack. Blood sprung from the tiny prick in his chest, and she wadded a bundle of gauze and applied it to the wound, taping it in position. She removed the Betadine with a cloth wetted with sterile saline, and tossed it onto the table along with the other detritus.

"Bobby?"

He opened his eyes. "Yeah?" His voice had returned to him.

"Are you okay?"

"No, I'm not okay. Did you forget I have cancer?"

She planted a kiss on his forehead, which was pink and warm from the flow of blood to his skin.

He wiped his cheek off and tried to assume a disgusted air. "Was that absolutely necessary?"

"Yes, it was."

The door banged open; Babe clomped in. She spied Maggie kneeling by Bobby's bedside. "What in the hellllllllllll are you doing here, Internnnnn?"

Maggie's heart stopped, and her brain locked up like a gear long bereft of oil. Babe took a few steps closer, spying the spinal needle on the bedside stable. Her wide face twisted into a triumphant grin. "So that's what you're doing here, Internnnnnn. I knew you were up to something when I heard that X-Ray machine rolling down the hall." She smiled even wider. "I just knew it."

"Up to something?" Bobby snarled at her. "Yeah, she's up to something, alright... like making me feel better. Maybe you shoulda given it a try, instead of sitting around on your fat ass while I suffocated."

The second hand rattled back and forth, advancing to ten past before being pushed back, advancing and being pushed back, making a lot of fuss but getting nowhere in the end.

"She's not supposed to be treating you, Mr. Bobby, not without the attending's say-so," Babe said.

"I don't give a rat's ass about the attending's say-so. I told her I wanted her to do it, and she did. And now I can breathe," Bobby told Babe.

Babe shrugged, as if, despite her position as charge nurse, she had no concern for Bobby's welfare. She smiled almost gleefully at Maggie. "You're going to be in a mess of trouble, Internnnnnnn, a big mess of trouble."

"No, she's not," Bobby said.

Babe rested her large hands on even larger hips. "How's that?"

"I'll deny anything happened. It will be your word against mine."

"It's not just my word. The monitor across the hall said he saw someone bring the portable X-ray machine into your room."

Bobby scoffed. "The guard across the hall? You mean the guy that just got out of Riker's?"

Patient monitors were difficult to hire—and even harder to keep, owing to the monotony of the job, the dismal pay, and the constant stream of expletives flowing at them from the patients they were watching. As a consequence, the hospital had resorted to making a contract with Riker's prison to use recently discharged inmates who had enrolled in a work-release program. The contract was worded such that violent offenders weren't allowed to participate, but due to the paucity of non-violent felons at Riker's and the lack of program oversight, they did.

"Who they going to believe? The convict that spent a nickel in Riker's for aggravated assault? Or the sweet kid trying so hard to beat cancer?"

"I'm not going to lie about this, Bobby. If they ask me what happened, I'm going to tell them I drained the fluid from around your heart," Maggie said.

Babe's satisfied grin reappeared. Bobby's face pinched and darkened, but the snarl disappeared after a moment, replaced by an expression as close to a smile as he could manage. "On second thought, maybe keeping this quiet isn't the right move. Maybe I'll tell the ombudsman you were withholding treatment from me."

The ombudsman was an independent arbitrator who took complaints from patients about their care in the hospital and attempted to resolve them. Bobby knew the ombudsman well, having filed a litany of complaints in the past, usually about not being able to watch R-rated movies. Babe started stammering, something she did anytime Bobby threatened to call the ombudsman, who Babe and all the other nurses hated with a passion.

"The ombudsman's got nothin' to do with this, nothin' at all. This is about Maggie the intern doing what she had no business doing. Noooooooooooo business."

"You say anything to anyone about what happened tonight, and I'm going to have the ombudsman sue your ass for failure to treat," Bobby said.

Legal thrillers were among Bobby's favorite movie genres, and he'd been binge watching them of late on Melendez's computer, picking up all the proper terminology.

"Not only that, I'm going to make sure he sites you as the primary defendant."

Babe took in a long breath and then blew it out.

"Wait 'til they put me on the witness stand and I tell the jury you hated me and wanted me dead." He sat back in bed, affecting a relaxed posture with his arm behind his head. "By the time I'm done, I wouldn't be surprised if they convene the grand jury to ask for criminal charges against you." He tried to smile again; his face radiated joy and malevolence both at the same time. "How do you like them apples?"

From the pursed lips and the wrinkling of her brow, Babe didn't like them. Glaring one last time at everyone gathered there, she turned and stomped away.

"And stay out," Bobby said.

Chapter Twenty-Two

It was only ten a.m., still two hours to go before Journal Club began. The article of the week was from the *Journal American Medical Association,* a tedious exploration of the soaring costs of hemodialysis. She sighed heavily and started wading into it but dozed off despite the constant stream of interns coming and going from the resident's lounge. Her iPhone beeped at noon, and she grabbed her things and headed out.

Journal Club was held in the conference room at the back of the cafeteria. In order to entice the interns to go, the hospital paid to have it catered by the Middle Eastern restaurant up the street. Maggie sat next to Melendez, who had showed up early to get the best pick of the food.

"Hey Maggie."

Maggie nodded and scooped up some hummus with a piece of pita bread.

"Can you believe how good Bobby is doing?" he asked.

She could believe it, having visited him again this morning after the pediatric night nurses—Babe among them—had left the building. She scooped up more hummus without responding to him.

"I was up in peds yesterday, trying to get a quickie in with the Argentinean nurse, but she wanted no part of it because she thought Bobby was going to die any minute and she wasn't in the mood." Melendez grabbed a chicken kebab from his plate, chomping on it with vigor at the injustice. "And then I go back this morning..."

Melendez stopped for a second as a surgical resident he didn't like went past on his way to grab some baba ghanoush from the buffet table.

"She made me go in his room with her because she's convinced he's some kind of sorcerer." He splayed his hands to indicate the ridiculousness of the notion, showing off his powerful arms. "Anyway, he's sitting up, reading a comic book, looking better than he has in weeks."

The lights dimmed. The *JAMA* article appeared on the large viewing screen at the front of the room.

"You don't happen to know anything about this, do you?" he asked.

The instructor started typing on his computer, highlighting several lines in the Methods section. The Methods section—the one in which all the minutiae of how the study was being performed—was the interns' least favorite; they all groaned collectively.

"Do you?" he asked again.

She denied it, hoping Bobby's threats against Babe had kept her quiet. He grabbed something from his pocket and tossed it onto her lap where no one else could see it except for her. It was the bandage she had applied to his chest.

"You suck at lying, Maggie. You're going to have to work on that."

She put the bandage in her pocket.

"Cushing will never notice that tiny needle prick under his breast bone, but even that total asshole would have noticed a bandage." He took a bite out of a piece of baklava, which bled honey onto his lips. "I gotta hand it to you, though. You're one ballsy chick."

The instructor started speaking, droning on about the drastic increase in the incidence of end-stage renal failure and its consequent strain on health care budgets.

"You got balls the size of eggplants, Maggie, you know that?" He pushed back from the table. "And speaking of eggplants, I'm going to get some more of that baba ghanoush. You want anything?"

She shook her head.

He came back a minute later with another heaping plate. "I gotta keep my energy up, I have another date tonight with the Dominican."

Graphs appeared on the viewer. Several of the interns began making notes. Maggie's pencil didn't move.

"I love a girl with balls the size of eggplants. I swear to God we were meant to be together."

"You and me? What about the Dominican?"

"I think about you when I'm with her."

Maggie busted out laughing, drawing a chorus of looks from the congregation. Melendez grabbed his backpack and eased out of his chair, leaving his plate on the table. "Just be careful, will ya? You're the only person I care about in this dump, and I'll be horribly depressed if they kick your ass out of here."

He stepped away but then came back for a second and knelt down next to her. "Because it's such a lovely ass."

She elbowed him in the chest, driving the point of her ulna into the solid bulk of his pectoral muscles.

"You know that pericardial effusion is just going to come back, right?"

She did know; Yoda had drummed that fact into her head.

"You can't keep sneakin' into his room in the middle of the night to drain it. At some point, these sons-of-bitches will catch you."

She didn't tell him she'd already been caught. (Nor had she mentioned it to Yoda, wanting to leave her out of it.) She closed her eyes, trying not to think about Babe finding her in the act of doing a procedure for which she had neither gotten permission from the attending nor written consent from the patient's guardian.

When she opened them, Melendez was gone.

***

Maggie had only been in Dr. Clarke's office once in the past year, the time she had asked the pediatric residency director about the possibility of joining the program. That had been a happy occasion; she could still remember the wrinkled smile on Dr. Clarke's round face and the twinkle in her brown eyes. Today, the smile was not in evidence: her brown eyes were narrowed with concern, and the tussle of curls that sprang from her head was even more chaotic than usual.

She waved for Maggie to sit down in the chair in front of the desk. "Do you know why you're here?"

Maggie shook her head as a dull foreboding filled her chest.

"Dr. Tucker isn't here today, so this unpleasant task fell to me."

"What unpleasant task?"

The director didn't say. She took a sip from the water bottle poking out from between the nursery of potted orchids weighing down her desk. "One of the nurses filed a complaint against you. A very serious complaint."

Maggie felt the tightening in her throat, the palpitations in her chest. A drop of sweat beaded on her brow, which wasn't surprising because Dr. Clarke kept the office stiflingly hot and humid on account of the orchids.

"Do you know who it was?" Dr. Clarke asked.

She had never suspected that Bobby's threats would keep Babe quiet; the woman was just too spiteful to let a chance to get back at Maggie slip through her fingers. She nodded.

"I would like to hear your side of the story."

Maggie complied, presenting it like she would a case summary at Grand Rounds, in concise fashion, with all the necessary facts but no extraneous details. The only part of the story she left out was Yoda's involvement, which had been minimal in any event and not worth jeopardizing the chief resident's career.

"Let me ask you something." Clarke twirled a lock of her long red hair, something she did when nervous. "Why didn't you call the pediatric resident or the attending when you discovered Bobby's pericardial effusion?"

"Neither one of them would have allowed me to do the procedure."

"That's because there's a judge's order not to resuscitate the patient, Maggie."

"It wasn't a resuscitation. He had a pericardial effusion; it needed to be drained. I explained the situation to the patient. He consented."

"The thirteen-year-old patient consented?"

Maggie nodded.

"You realize that verbal consent from a minor means absolutely nothing?"

"I have to ask you something first, though. I need your permission to do this."

"Just do it."

"It means something to me," Maggie said.

"I meant that it means nothing in a court of law."

"Is this going to be a court case?"

"Let's hope not." She grabbed a mist bottle and began to spray the orchids, adding to the oppressive humidity in the room. "You realize the hospital by-laws require written consent from the patient's parent or legal guardian before any procedure can be done on a pediatric patient."

"There wasn't enough time. His vital signs were too weak. He would have died by the time we could have obtained consent."

"Then why didn't you call a code?"

They were both well aware why Maggie hadn't done this. They stared at each other in silence.

"I met with the administration this morning, Maggie;

there is to be a meeting of the Disciplinary Review Committee next week."

Maggie thought about the warmth of Bobby's face after she'd drained the fluid from around his heart, the pink glow of his skin. She had no regrets.

"There are five members of the committee: Doctors Tucker, Andrews and Arnold, as well as Ms. Oberhausen and myself."

Dr. Arnold was the medical director of the hospital, a dark wraith of a man who the medical staff despised because he sided with the administration at all times. He would vote whichever way Oberhausen told him to vote.

"Ms. Oberhausen wanted you to be suspended until after the meeting, but I wouldn't agree to that. You will continue to perform your duties as a transitional intern until the committee determines what, if any, penalty should be given. You will be allowed to attend the meeting and testify on your behalf, and you can bring an advocate who can make sure the dealings are fair and without bias." Her eyes widened, perhaps with sympathy, and her frown lifted, leaving a neutral expression on her face. "I think you should bring an advocate, Maggie. Ms. Oberhausen…"

She didn't finish the sentence, but she didn't need to. Ms. Oberhausen had no love for Maggie.

"Do you have any comments or questions?" Clarke asked.

Maggie had many comments, but she decided to save them for her trial. It seemed to her Clarke was on her side anyway, and she had no desire to antagonize her.

"The advocate…do you mean I should bring a lawyer?"

"The advocate can be a lawyer, but this isn't a legal trial, so it doesn't have to be. I think you'll be better off if you find someone from the hospital, one of the attending physicians, perhaps?"

Foster was the first person to enter her head, but she

discounted him immediately, in case anyone had seen them together over the past few weeks. And he hadn't been much help—he'd been no help—during the proceedings of the Ethics Committee. She shook her head.

"You could ask your father," Clarke said.

The idea of asking her father had also occurred to her. It pained her to even think about asking him—he was the not the person to whom she wanted to owe a favor—but if there were one person who could stand up to Greta Oberhausen, it was Roger Johnson. She nodded.

"What might the penalty consist of?" Maggie asked.

"As little as a written reprimand on your record, which could be expunged in the absence of any further transgressions…"

Tucker reached into her desk and pulled out the hospital by-laws, a copy of which Maggie had read, signed, and handed in prior to the start of her training. The director opened the pamphlet, flipped through the pages and set it down in front of Maggie, underscoring a paragraph.

"…and as severe as expulsion."

Chapter Twenty-Three

Maggie parked the Zipcar on the side of the road and descended on Shady Cottage from the walking path her grandfather had cut from the slope on the property's northern edge. She had gone back to her apartment on Murray Hill after being dismissed from Dr. Clarke's office, but sleep had eluded her. A call to her father's office had revealed he'd taken the afternoon off, so she had hopped into a Zipcar and driven out to Shady Cottage on the chance he was spending the afternoon there.

She made her way down the path as a light breeze blew from the south, ushering in the warm, moist Mid-Atlantic air. A series of cumulus clouds, like a line of dirigibles, floated past, occasionally obscuring the sun, which blazed summerlike in the spring sky. A single, dark cloud, far away on the edge of horizon, was the only dissenter on an otherwise perfect day. Birds sang in the deciduous trees, mostly oak, chestnut and beech, and a buzzard circled overhead. The smell of honeysuckle drifted in the wind.

The path took a circuitous route to the cottage, one that wound around the shore of the small lake that had been created by the damming of the creek that flowed through the property, up the small hill that Maggie used to love to roll down in the spring—ending up dizzy and nauseated but doing it again and again—and across the open meadow at the top to the cottage.

Her father's Mercedes was parked in the driveway, close enough to the cottage to take advantage of the shade provided by the thick grove of trees in which the cottage had been built. A second car, one she didn't recognize, was parked next to it. She walked over to it and peered inside, but there were no clues to its owner, so she kept going toward the cottage, and entered through the unlocked door.

"Dad?"

The echo of her voice was the only reply; when the echo subsided, she mounted the stairs, which led up from the center hallway, the steps creaking with her weight. Halfway up, she stopped and stood on the stair listening to the light breeze riffling through the canopy of leaves over her head, the babbling of the brook, and the squawking of a murder of crows.

Her old bedroom was at the end of the upstairs hallway. The bed was still made, and she collapsed onto it, wrapping herself inside the quilt her mother had sewn for her thirteenth birthday. She called out her dad's name again, but without any conviction, and even the echo didn't reply. Exhaustion eventually overcame her, and she fell asleep.

Maggie woke several hours later to the sound of her father's voice emanating from her parent's room on the other side of the hallway. She started to call out his name, but the sound of a second voice, one much higher in register, paralyzed her vocal cords.

"...aren't you the naughty little boy?"

She heard the sound of a palm being slapped against bare skin.

"Who's calling who naughty?"

She ran out, crossed the hall, and stopped in front of the door to the master bedroom, which her father hadn't even bothered to close in his haste.

"Dad!"

Her father was lying naked on the bed in the center of his room. Lying next to him was a woman she didn't recognize. Maggie might have had an easier time placing her if she were wearing clothes, but she wasn't.

"Maggie?" her father asked.

The woman rolled out of bed, snatched up her clothes from the floor with practiced efficiency, and disappeared into the bathroom. Her father sat up in bed, covering himself with the sheets. They stared at each other without speaking; the woman emerged half-dressed from the bathroom, brushed past Maggie with her head down, and ran down the stairs. The front door flew open, and then banged shut against the frame.

"What are you doing here?" Her father's voice was soft, even placid. If she hadn't seen his paramour leave, she would have been sure he'd just woken from a pleasant nap. He even managed to smile.

"Who is she?" Maggie asked.

He reached down for his own clothes, but Maggie grabbed them first and balled them under her arm.

"It doesn't matter who she is," he said.

"How long have you been seeing her?"

"Not long. It just started recently."

"How recently?" Maggie asked.

"What difference does it make?"

She was inclined to agree with him, but it was far easier to ask about the details of his affair than focus on the infidelity itself. More questions came; she asked about the woman's name, occupation, where they had met. He deflected them all, giving vague answers or none at all.

"Can I have my clothes, please?"

"How could you, Dad?"

Roger Johnson didn't say. Securing the sheet around his waist, he slid out of bed, removed his clothes from the crook of her arm, and went into the bathroom. When he returned, he looked like the father she was used to seeing:

conservatively dressed in chinos and an Oxford shirt, wearing his usual expression of subdued self-confidence.

"I don't expect you to understand, but sometimes a man needs more out of a relationship than he gets."

"So, you're doing us all a favor by screwing around on Mom, is that it?"

"I didn't say that." He sat on the bed, laced on his wingtips—a gift from Maggie's mother last Christmas—and adjusted his tie.

"How many times have you cheated on her, Dad?"

"This wasn't the first time, if that's what you're getting at. But, honestly, Maggie, none of them meant anything to me."

"So, you were just in it for the sex, Dad? Do you really think saying that is going to make me feel better?"

Roger Johnson didn't say.

"It just makes you sound like a self-absorbed asshole, Dad. Is that who you want to be?"

"I'll just tell her it's over, and we'll never speak of it again. Understood?"

The numbness enveloping her began to wear off; her brow tightened, and her lips disappeared into a thin pink line.

"Neither one of us wants to upset your mother or your brothers and sister. Isn't that right, Maggie?" The smile faded and *the look* took its place—the one he used to tell her how much she had disappointed him. (For instance, when she had missed being *Summa Cum Laude* by two-hundredths of a percent.) "That's not what you want, is it, Maggie? You don't want to break up our family, do *you?*"

"How dare you blame me for this."

She took a step closer and jammed her trembling finger into his chest hard enough to leave a mark. The thin veneer of her self-control effaced, but she didn't try to salvage it. Bobby's voice sparked up inside her, urging her on. She was travelling down the road to somewhere with blinding speed, and she was not going to throttle back, no matter what.

"You will not speak to me like that," he said firmly.

"Like hell I won't."

Roger Johnson took a step backwards—the only time she'd ever seen him give ground in her entire life. "Can you stop shouting, please?"

"Why, because you don't want to hear that you're a lousy *cheat*?"

His face fell when he she said '*cheat*,' partly because she half-screamed the word, and partly because she was sure he never thought of himself that way, as a narcissist wouldn't.

"Roger Johnson is a lousy cheat," she screamed.

"Stop saying that, Maggie."

"I'm not going to do that, Dad, because I am sick and tired of doing what you want me to. I've been doing that for twenty-seven years, and all I have to show for it is a lot of sleepless nights and a residency I don't want."

Anger blossomed inside her, and she wondered if Yoda would approve. It was a moot point anyway because she was powerless to stop its flow. Her brain coursed with it, flavoring her thoughts, her heart filled with it, spawning her emotions, and her body surged with it, causing the index finger she was pointing at him to tremble.

"You're a self-absorbed, lying narcissist, Roger Johnson, and I never want to see you again."

Chapter Twenty-Four

Maggie sat down on the far end of warped wooden table, the only piece of furniture in the Crisis Room. John Doe stood next to the chair on the near end, facing the side wall so that his left cheek stared at her.

"How are you?" Maggie asked.

"I'm fine."

The psychiatrist who had consulted on the case had not been of the same opinion, declaring the patient to have suffered a complete psychotic break consequent to stopping his medication.

"The better question is, Maggie, how are you?" he asked.

"Not very good."

"What's wrong?"

"I might be expelled from the hospital."

John Doe stared at her from behind the yellow glasses he employed to prevent people from re-programming him through his eyes. "I told you it was you I saw in the fires."

She'd never given his warning another thought; perhaps she should have. He stood and paced back and forth, but along the length of the room, such that he strode toward her and then away, toward and away, with his long arms clasped behind his back. The squeak of his worn boots on the cement marked his progress—*squeak squeak squeak*—and then a long *sqeeaaaakkkk* as he pivoted on his heel to turn.

"Why will you be expelled? It's me, isn't it? They want to get to me."

Paranoia and delusions were the hallmarks of schizophrenia, constructs of disordered thinking and exaggerated self-grandeur.

"It has nothing to do with you," Maggie said.

"Don't lie to me, Maggie."

"I'm not lying to you. I did something I wasn't supposed to."

He walked past, filling the air with the rank smell of the sewer, over which he slept to keep warm. "Tell me what it was."

She told him, violating several more rules and regulations in the process. He listened intently as he paced, placing his index finger underneath his chin. "You did the only thing you could do. Letting the boy die was not an option."

Perhaps she would call upon him as a witness in her trial. The thought of John Doe staring down Greta Oberhausen almost made her smile despite her foul mood.

"Why haven't you been taking your medicine?" Maggie asked him.

"You know why."

She did; they had discussed it a dozen times. "Tell me again."

"It stops the visions."

"That's why you take it," Maggie said.

"That's why I can't take it. Don't you understand?"

"No, I don't."

"They're trying to control me. They don't want me to speak the truth."

John used the word *they* all the time to describe the people who opposed him, without ever defining who *they* were. At various times, she took *they* to mean various things: the medical establishment; the government; the whole world; her.

"That's why I can't take it. Someone needs to speak the truth." He sat back in his chair, and took off his hat; his long strawberry blond hair fell about his shoulders in slow curls. "You need to speak the truth as well. Tell them it was you who did the right thing. They are the ones who should be on trial."

John might have been delusional about some things— the subway was the train to hell; the police were robots programmed to kill androids—but she agreed with him on that.

"This isn't about me," Maggie said.

He risked taking his glasses off, and stared at her with his light blue eyes. With a haircut, thirty extra pounds and some attention to hygiene, John Doe would have been very easy on her eye, but with his sunken orbits, hollow cheeks, and greasy locks in a tangled mat, he wasn't.

"I think we both know it is." He burped, not bothering to cover his mouth, belching up a small piece of his last meal onto the table. It looked like a bit of undigested fish; the rancid odor suggested it was an anchovy. "What are you going to do about it?"

"What am I going to do about what?"

"Being unjustly accused."

"Keep it about the patient, Intern. It's always about the patient. I know your mother likes to brag about you in her bridge club, and I have never met a doctor who doesn't like to talk about him or herself, but don't do it. For once in your life keep the focus on someone else."

"Let's talk about you. That's why I'm here," Maggie said.

He put his glasses back on, which came as a relief. "What about me?"

"The doctors want to keep you here for a few days. They told me you didn't agree to stay."

"Why should I stay? They all think I'm crazy. You're the only one who believes me."

"They can *make* you stay, John."

Patients who were considered to be a danger to themselves or others could be kept in the hospital against their will, but it required two separate physicians and a lot of extra time. Maggie had been called in to talk him in to staying of his own accord.

"They never do. There's too much paperwork involved," he said.

"Can't you just stay for a few days?"

"Do you want me to?"

She nodded.

"I'll follow your advice, but you have to follow mine, too."

"Never make any deals with patients, Interns: no deals; no bargains; no conditions; no nuthin'. You make your recommendations and the rest is up to the patient. If they don't listen, too effing bad for them."

"Okay." She picked up the in-house phone, and let the charge nurse know John had agreed to sign his admission form. "Lay it on me."

"Lay what on you?" he asked.

Schizophrenics had a penchant for being concrete. When you asked one to explain the idiom "People in glass houses shouldn't throw stones," he or she talked about shards of flying glass, facial lacerations and lost eyes.

"What's your advice?"

"Tell the truth."

He put his right hand to his temple and began to move it in a winding motion. After three twists, he did the same with his left hand. Powered up, he replaced his cap and tucked his hair inside his collar.

"People don't want to hear the truth when it doesn't fit nicely in with what they already believe..." John began.

She was sure that the Disciplinary Review Committee was certain to be of the same opinion next week when she explained to them that Bobby's desire to be treated to the full extent possible was being ignored by the attending, the residents and the administration.

"But you have to tell them the truth anyway." He took off his glasses again and risked looking directly at her. "Will you do that, Maggie? Will you them the truth even though they don't want to hear it?"

Maggie nodded and left the room. The door swung shut with a heavy thud.

Chapter Twenty-Five

John Doe remained in the hospital, refusing to sign the discharge papers. Maggie rounded on him daily, even though she wasn't officially on the psychiatry service. The visits were lingering, multiple on most days, and unproductive; he continued to forgo taking his medication and insist he'd been recreated to warn the human race that the end of the world was near at hand. The psychiatry nurses, known throughout Golden Arches for their gallows humor, dubbed him the 'Android of the Apocalypse.' John had overheard one of them saying it, started referring to himself by the moniker, and acknowledged no other name.

"Why are you here to see the Android of the Apocalypse?" he asked her.

"I'm your doctor."

"No, that's not it."

She might have said focusing on someone else's problems took her mind off her own, but sometimes the truth was better off left unsaid.

"Are you still anxious about your trial?" he asked.

"No, I'm not."

"You can't lie to the Android of the Apocalypse."

"Yes, I am," she admitted.

The obligatory review period had just ended, during which Father McDaniel—whom she'd chosen to be her advocate—and the members of the Disciplinary Review

Committee had had a chance to read a copy of Bobby's chart as well as written statements from Babe and Maggie. She'd tried to keep her mind off the meeting, which was set to convene at the beginning of the next week and do her job as best she could, but with less than a week to go, it was becoming difficult.

He stood up to leave. "Then there is no other way."

Maggie barred the door. "Where are you going?"

"I return to the fires where I was made."

She made no move to get out of his way. "And what then?"

"Nothing. I will perish in the flames."

She didn't reply.

"It's the only way to save you. If I take your place in the fires, you will be saved."

The next day when Maggie came to round on him, he was gone. He'd been seen last by one of the aides on the graveyard shift who had watched him going through the fire escape—she thought—for a smoke. Maggie went out through the door herself to investigate, wondering if he were still sitting there, but there was no evidence of him, and the fire escape ladder hadn't been extended. She came back daily to see if he'd returned, but no one had seen or heard anything from the Android of the Apocalypse, and after several days, she stopped coming.

Interventional Radiology—which she started on the first day of the month—dragged on; although, she did like some things about the rotation, most of all the extra free time, which she used to spend with Bobby. She'd developed a routine, coming in early to see him before scrubbing in for the first case of the morning at seven a.m. and having coffee with him in Room 12 after the last case of the day around three p.m. On occasion—not often enough as far as Bobby was concerned—she was called in after hours to assist with an emergency intervention, and then, she stayed the rest of the night with him sitting on the plastic chair with her stocking feet next to his on the bed, listening to him talk about Wolverine and the other X-Men.

This morning was such an occasion. Maggie had been yanked out of bed to stent a blocked popliteal artery in a patient with threatened limb loss, and she'd wandered up to Room 12 after the affected leg was warm and pink again. Bobby was awake in bed, wearing his yellow Wolverine mask with the pointy blue ears, reading *X-Men: Worst X-Man Ever #1,* the comic book she had brought him the day before.

"How's the new magazine?" she asked.

"How many times do I have to tell you it's not a magazine?"

Bobby's sarcasm had been given new life as well, often blossoming as brightly as the lilacs Sister Thomasena nurtured outside the convent next to the hospital. With only five Sisters of Perpetual Mercy left, the convent was much bigger than required, and the extra space was being used as a women's shelter. The hospital had tried to move Bobby in to one of the bedrooms, but he'd stubbornly refused, *"What do I want to live with a bunch of crotchety old nuns for?"*

"Comic book, magazine… whatever."

He rolled over without becoming winded, a good sign that the fluid she'd drawn off several weeks ago had not re-accumulated. "It's a comic book. Please get the terminology correct."

"I don't see the difference."

"It's just what we call them. Please keep it straight."

"Yes, sir."

"You getting smart with me?" he asked.

She tickled the underside of his feet with her toes. He tried to pull his feet away, but Maggie used her other leg to trap them in position, and she had strong legs, something Melendez confirmed every time she wore a skirt. When his squealing became loud enough to wake the patient next door, she released him and he curled into a ball to ward off further attacks.

"Why do you that? I hate it when you do that," Bobby said.

"Maybe someone should watch his attitude."

"Someone? You mean me? My attitude's fine. Are you forgetting I have cancer?"

She was not; his diagnosis and prognosis were almost always on her mind. "How could I? You remind me night and day."

"Well, maybe if you tried doing something about it, I wouldn't have to."

"Bobby, we've tried; you know that. Think about all the chemo you've been on."

The Medical History file in her brain clicked on; she saw the names of all the chemotherapy agents that had tried and failed to cure Bobby's cancer, listed in a vertical column like the names of war dead on a memorial.

"Might be you just didn't choose the right stuff," Bobby said.

"I've been through your chart fifty times. You received all the correct treatments."

"You're sure?"

"Yes."

"Are you right all the time?" Bobby asked.

"We're right a lot of the time, yes."

Bobby donned his blue Wolverine glove, extended the retractable PVC claws, and lifted up the bottom of his scrubs with them, revealing his calves. Where his gastrocnemius muscles should have been, there was only skin and bone. "You weren't right about me. Otherwise, I'd be walking instead of being in this stupid bed."

They had been through this before. Maggie had tried to explain to him the difference between diagnosing a patient with an incurable disease and misdiagnosing him—the difference between treatments that didn't work and prescribing the wrong treatments. Bobby always just shrugged, as if to say, 'What's the difference, I'm still going to die.'

"Anyway, that's not what I meant," Bobby said.

"What did you mean?"

He didn't say straight off, setting the comic book down on the bed. "I'm sick of this place."

It was a difficult point to counter; she didn't try.

"Staring at these same four walls is driving me insane."

Maggie looked around, taking in the cinder block walls, the single, opaque window, and the bouquet of flowers wilted down over the vase.

"I want to get out of here," Bobby said.

"Then why do you play dead every time someone comes to evaluate you for placement?"

"Because I don't want to live in some stupid orphanage. And I'm damn sure I don't want to move in with the nuns. Have you ever smelled Sister Antonia?"

The oldest of the Sisters of Perpetual Mercy, Sister Antonia was a firm believer in the health benefits of eating raw garlic with every meal. Maggie thought it was possible she was on to something, being that she was over one hundred years old and still working at the hospital gift shop every day.

"Where do you want to go, then?" Maggie asked.

He retracted the claws but left the glove on. "I thought I could move in with you."

"Me?" Maggie asked.

"Yeah, you. What's the matter with you?"

Maggie didn't volunteer any answers.

"You should think about adopting me," Bobby said.

"Adopting you? I'm not married. I don't even have a boyfriend."

"Sure, you do."

Bobby loved to gossip and had been known to ask the orderlies to load him into the portable wheelchair and transport him down the hall into the alcove where he would sit for hours eavesdropping on the nurses in the breakroom. Perhaps one of the nurses had seen she and Foster together?

"I do?"

He nodded and took off the mask, rubbing his cheeks, which had filled out in the last few weeks with the advent of his appetite.

"You want to tell me who he is?" Maggie asked.

"Honestly, Maggie, no wonder your social life is so pathetic."

"My social life isn't pathetic."

"Then why do you spend most of your free time with me?"

He was a little shit, but he was a perceptive little shit. "Okay, who is it?"

"Melendez," Bobby said.

She let out a breath of relief. "Caid Melendez is not my boyfriend."

"Maybe not now, but you want him to be."

"How can you tell that?" Maggie asked.

"Because I'm like Empath."

"Who's Empath?"

"A mutant who can sense and manipulate the emotions of others."

"You're not a mutant, Bobby."

"I'm not, Maggie? Give a look at me."

She observed his sallow complexion, the empty shirtsleeve where his left arm should have been, his rotting teeth, his wasted muscles. "You have cancer, Bobby; that doesn't mean you have empathic powers."

"Oh no, Maggie? Then how come I know exactly how you're feeling right now?"

"Ok Bobby, I'll play. How am I feeling?"

He lowered his lids over his grey eyes, and touched his 2nd and 3rd fingers against his temple. "You do like Melendez, and you're frustrated with yourself that I picked up on it when you thought you had everybody fooled, and by everybody, I mean everybody, even you. You're confused, too; you can't figure out why you like him when he's obviously dead wrong for you. And now you're embarrassed."

"I'm not embarrassed." Her cheeks flushed. "And I don't like Caid Melendez."

"Yeah you do. I can tell."

"Oh yeah, how?"

"You talk funny when you're around him, all giggly like. And you're always looking at him out of the corner of your eye. And you talk about him all the time. Caid this and Caid that..."

"That doesn't mean anything."

Bobby looked hurt. "C'mon Maggie, this is me. I've seen every Rom/Com made in the last ten years."

Bobby had cajoled Melendez into giving up the password to his Netflix account, which he used to watch not only RomComs but Gangster films, horror movies, and action thrillers to pass the long watch of the night.

"I can't adopt you, Bobby," Maggie said.

"Why not?"

"I work, for one thing."

"So, I'll watch movies during the day, and then we can have dinner when you and Melendez come home."

"I don't live with Melendez."

"That won't be a problem; Melendez likes me okay, and he's wild about you."

"I don't have any...What did you say about Melendez?"

"He's obviously dead wrong for you?"

"No, the other thing."

A triumphant smile appeared on his face, giving Maggie a picture of what he might have looked like had cancer and chemotherapy not ravaged his body. "Nuthin'."

"No, you said he's wild about me or something like that."

"Did I? My tongue must have got all twisted up."

"Bobby..."

"If you don't like him, why do you care how he feels about you?"

It was at times like these that Maggie was most saddened about Bobby's non-future. A person with his intelligence and spunk—not to mention his empathic powers—would go far in this world. But Bobby would not go far, a victim of the malignant cells his bone marrow continued to spit out into his stunted body.

"I'll tell you how he feels about you if you admit you like him," Bobby said.

"We're not in sixth grade."

"That reminds me, no school. I haven't set foot in a classroom for six years, and I don't intend to again."

"I have a career. Did you forget about that?"

"Sitting in front of a screen and looking at pictures all day? You call that a career? All I've ever heard you say about radiology is that you hate it."

It was the same thing that Yoda said, Yoda being the only other person to whom Maggie confided, further evidence that Bobby was right about the pathetic nature of her social life. "It just wouldn't work out."

"It'll work out just fine."

"No, it won't."

"Gimme one good reason..."

"My apartment's too small."

"So, have your sugar daddy get you a bigger one."

"My sugar daddy and I aren't on very good terms right now."

She hadn't spoken to her father since that afternoon at Shady Cottage. Her father had texted her several times a day and had tried calling as well, but she'd returned neither the texts nor the calls. And, owing to the annual two-week vacation he took every year with his wife and her family at her maternal grandparents' lake house on Lake Champlain, he hadn't been in the hospital at all. She knew she had to face him at some point, but that point was still well off.

"So, get your own place. Some place nice, with a view of the skyline and a hot tub on the roof," Bobby said matter-of-factly.

"How am I supposed to pay for this?"

"You're a doctor, aren't you?"

"I'm a resident doctor, yes, who can't even afford the one bedroom flat I'm living in now."

"So, get money the old-fashioned way."

She knew she shouldn't ask, but she was possessed by a morbid curiosity: "What's the old-fashioned way?"

"Hold up a liquor store."

She had no clue if he were kidding or not; his face was resting in its usual scowl, and his small, grey eyes were fixed on the comic book that had returned to his hand.

"Honestly, Maggie, it's like you've never been out on the streets."

"I'm not holding up a liquor store."

"Never had you figured for a yellow-bellied coward."

This was rich, having risked—and perhaps ended—her career to save his life. "It's against the law, Bobby."

He didn't even grace this comment with a response.

"You're aware that there are laws against holding up a liquor store," she said.

"So, what? If it goes bad, you could end up in jail. How cool would that be?"

"What do you know about being in jail?"

"I've seen *The Shawshank Redemption* like twelve times. It's one of my favorite movies."

It had been apparent to her in the past that Bobby's sense of reality wasn't entirely clear, but she had never thought he truly believed that the X-Men were the only thing preventing the world from slipping into chaos or that dinosaurs had been cloned and were roaming the earth as in *Jurassic Park*. He'd enjoyed the movie so much she took him to the American Museum of Natural History soon after, but he hated it, insisting on leaving the Hall of Saurischian Dinosaurs within minutes.

She later reasoned he had imagined the museum to be like *Jurassic World* and not just a place of ancient artifacts, circumstantial evidence, and theories that could never be proven. In an effort to salvage the trip, she diverted to the Butterfly Conservatory, which was a hit. On the verge of extinction himself, Bobby found the world of the extant a lot more appealing.

Her phone bleeped, indicating an incoming text. The message was from Yoda, and, like all messages from Yoda, it was short and to the point.

Meet me in the ED. Now.

Chapter Twenty-Six

The Emergency Department was unusually quiet. The nurses huddled together against the back wall, gripping their coffee mugs like life jackets and whispering in low tones. There were no drunks to bellow, no addicts screamed to ease the pain of withdrawal, and, despite the late epidemic of Influenza running through the city, nary a cough could be heard. Other than the squeak of the morgue cart wheeling across the floor, the silence was total.

There were only two sets of initials on the white board, and since the morgue attendants were headed for LJ in Room 6, Maggie opted for Room 12, where GJ awaited her. The ventilator icon had been drawn in, indicating the patient had respiratory failure, and the **T** next to that told Maggie that the source of the respiratory failure was trauma. The intern in her started piecing the puzzle together. GJ had been in a car accident, suffering two collapsed lungs, hence the need for the ventilator.

Yoda was standing outside the room when Maggie arrived. The door was closed, but Maggie could hear the quiet whoosh of air being sucked into the patient's lungs and the beeping of the cardiac monitor, announcing the patient's condition to all who wanted to listen.

"Do you remember what I told you about this place when you first got here?"

Yoda had told them so many things about Our Lady

of the Golden Arches it was sometimes hard to keep them all straight, but the pinching of her face and the intensity of her dark eyes directed Maggie to the right quote:

"This is Golden Arches, Interns, not some private hospital in the Hamptons. You're going to see some bad shit—real, bad shit—and you're going to see it all the time. Rule number 1? Know what it is? Never get angry. It's easy to give in to anger, interns, but don't ever let me catch you do it. Never once, not even one time. Anger is the enemy of good doctoring. Got that?"

"Yes, I remember."

"You're not going to get angry?"

Maggie assured her she wouldn't.

"You ready?"

Maggie didn't reply. Yoda pushed the door open and they passed inside. Not sure what else to do, Maggie followed her in.

If it weren't for her brown hair in corn rows, Maggie would never have recognized Grace Jones. Her eyes were swollen shut, her face bruised and beaten. An endotracheal tube emerged from her bloodied mouth. Her left arm—her good arm—had been splinted, but not well enough to bring the forearm bones into proper alignment. Several lines hung from the metallic poles above her, dripping blood and saline into her right arm, the same arm her father had repaired less than a month ago.

Maggie stepped forward and lowered the covering sheet. A maze of wires led from her chest to an automatic defibrillator that stood by the bedside, ready to shock her heart back into rhythm if it decided to quit. Several of her ribs were cracked, and her belly was already dotted with bruises, boding ill for her internal organs.

"What happened?" Maggie asked.

"You know what happened."

Maggie replaced the sheet. "LJ? That was Grace's mother?"

Yoda nodded. "Lila Jones. May she rest in peace."

It was the same thing Yoda said every time a patient died, with the same lack of inflection and expressionless face. "Are you okay?"

"No."

Yoda's diminutive hand reached out and grabbed Maggie's. "I'm sorry, Maggie."

The minutes passed slowly, marked by the trickle of tears down both of their faces, the quiet hum of the fluorescent lighting, and the orchestra of Grace's life support.

"How is she?" It was a stupid thing to say, especially for an intern at the end of the year, but Maggie's inner intern had left her body.

"She'll live."

Maggie knelt down by the bedside, laid her head next to Grace, and stroked her arm with her hand, running her finger back and forth over the short stretch of her arm in between the intravenous sites. "I failed her."

"You did not fail her, Maggie. I don't want to hear you say that again."

"But it's true, I failed her. I had a terrible feeling she'd been beaten when she came in the last time, and I didn't tell anyone.

"I wasn't sure…I didn't know what to do."

"What are you talking about?" Yoda asked.

"I helped my father operate on her. When I was examining her before surgery, I saw some bruises on her bottom. I asked her about them one day post op; she said she'd fallen. I didn't believe her, but I couldn't get her to tell me the truth. When I went back a second time to talk to her, she'd already been discharged."

"You tried to help her, Maggie, which is more than anyone else can say."

"Trying isn't enough. You know that."

"Don't try, Interns; Do."

"Sometimes there is no doing," Yoda said.

A nurse came in. She checked to make sure all the lines were running, mumbled something about the imminent arrival of the transfer team from the Pediatric Intensive Care Unit, and left. The door swinging shut behind her sounded like the lid slamming down upon the coffin.

"They need to stabilize her before they take her to the Operating Room. The fractures of her radius and ulna bones need to be reduced openly and internally fixed, and her eye socket needs to be surgically repaired, but we have to re-inflate her lungs and get her kidneys working better first," Yoda told her.

"What's the matter with her kidneys?"

"They're choked with blood from getting punched repeatedly."

Beep. Beep. Beep. Whoooossshh. Beep. Beep. Beep. Whoooossshh.

"How can you do this?" Maggie asked.

"Do what?"

"This…"

Maggie's hand strayed from Grace's arm, and her fingers pointed to the depressed fracture of Grace's orbit, and to the wound in the middle of her forearm where the ends of her arm bones had lanced through the skin, and to her chest, where four displaced rib fractures were hidden from sight by the thin sheet.

"You just deal with it…you have to."

"What if I don't want to?" Maggie asked.

"You're too good of a doctor to walk away."

"I can't do it, Yoda."

"You can. You have to."

A noxious odor wafted through the air, wrinkling Maggie's nose. It was the unmistakable smell of blood being curdled by the acid contained in the gastrointestinal tract.

"I forgot to mention her colon has a small perforation. Should heal over without surgery," Yoda said.

"Anything else?"

"Don't think so. Her head CT was okay, so that's good."

Her brain was intact, so she'd be able to remember her nightmares forever.

"Her liver looked alright," Yoda continued. "There's some blood in her pericardium, but once that resorbs, her heart should be fine."

But this little girl was more than the sum of her parts; Maggie wondered if she'd ever find enough reason to smile again.

"Kids are resilient, Maggie."

"It's not her body I'm worried about."

It was a strange to say about a girl with seven fractured bones, two collapsed lungs, a pair of bruised kidneys and a ruptured colon.

"Me either," Yoda said.

After a while, the PICU team burst onto the scene and transferred her upstairs to the unit. Yoda left with the patient, sitting cross-legged on the end of Grace's stretcher as it was wheeled out. Maggie watched them go, tears streaming down her face.

***

Melendez found her there an hour later, still standing in the same spot. Her tears had dried up, but her eyes were still puffy and red. He grabbed her in his arms and squeezed her against him.

"What are you doing here?" she asked.

"I got called in by the medical examiner."

Maggie had forgotten he was doing an elective in pathology for his last month, normally a cushy gig.

"When I saw who it was, I came straight over to the

Emergency Department. The charge nurse told me you were still in here. How is she?"

Maggie sobbed in reply. When her shoulders stopped heaving enough to speak, she gave him a quick rundown of Grace's condition.

"I should have told someone, Caid," Maggie said.

"She was my patient, Maggie. I didn't tell anyone either. To be honest with you, I didn't put a lot of stock in your theory anyway."

"Why did you help me, then?"

"The usual reasons."

They sat down on the floor, leaning against the wall. She rested her head on his shoulder. "Did you hear anything?" Maggie asked.

"The medical examiner told me Grace called 911 to report her father was beating her mother. When the cops got there, the mother was unconscious, and that crazy fuck was whaling on Grace."

She put her arm across his chest. It didn't help the horrible ache in her heart, but at least she could share it with someone.

"He beat the mom up bad, Maggie, like bus accident bad. The ME even had to look away."

"Where is he?"

"Don't know. The local precinct, I suppose."

The housekeepers came in to clean the room, and they headed out to the big board where the triage nurse was relating what she'd heard from the ambulance driver about the crime scene. The listened for a while, but it became evident she didn't know anything new, so they went out into the lobby of the Emergency Department.

"Where are you going?" Melendez asked.

Maggie looked at her watch, shaking her head. "I don't know. I've got a case in a few hours, so I'll probably just stay in house. I think I'm going to lie on the couch in the residency lounge."

"Want to get something to eat?" he asked.

"No, I'm not hungry." At the moment, she wasn't sure she'd ever want to eat again.

"You alright?" he asked.

"I guess so."

Melendez grabbed her by the hand. "Come on."

"Where we going?"

"Just follow me."

She followed him outside into the physician's parking lot, where Greta Oberhausen's Lexus occupied the spot nearest the door. Melendez walked around to the front of the car, which was pushed so far forward the nose of the car displaced a pair of juniper bushes. He knelt down, examining the front bender, and waived Maggie over.

"Take a look at this," he said.

The fender was smashed in; a large dent besmirched the corner panel on the driver's side.

"One of the janitors told me about this. Looks like the Wicked Witch of the East River was up to her old tricks again."

"Her old tricks?" Maggie asked.

Melendez picked a piece of Twizzler out of the crook between his lateral incisor and medial canine. "The word is she's a bit of a lush and likes to get loaded and then go driving. I heard she's been busted at least three times for DUI, but the charges didn't stick."

"Why not?"

"Oberhausen went to Cornell with Manhattan District Attorney Whittaker. It's rumored she's got some kind of hold over him."

"What kind of hold?"

Melendez shook his head. "Don't know, but it has to be some kind of serious shit because she's bulletproof."

"Who told you this?"

"The cop who works the night shift in the Emergency Department. You know the one who's always trying to hit on your friend Rachel."

He straightened back up and they went back inside and descended the backstairs into the sub-basement. They walked past the boiler room, and Melendez used a key to unlock the door of a small room next to the janitorial locker room.

"Welcome to Chez Melendez."

Chez Melendez was a storeroom—or it had been before Melendez had converted it to a kind of living space. A hospital bed occupied the far wall, next to which a trio of milk crates stacked on top of each other acted as a chest of drawers. On the other side of the room, a small frig was plugged into the wall, and on top of that was a microwave oven. The only other furniture in the room was a bean bag. A variety of dirty laundry—boxers, socks and t-shirts—littered its surface.

"You live here?" Maggie asked.

"Beats paying rent." He tapped the wall abutting the locker room. "And the bathroom is right here. We're right next to the boiler, so I get all the hot water I want." He pointed to his bed, which was turned down neatly. Crisp, white sheets gleamed in the fluorescent glare of the overhead lights. "The maids make my bed every day, too, with fresh sheets. It's awesome."

"Where are your clothes?"

He pointed to the milk crates. A pair of jeans and a few polo shirts were stuffed inside one. Two sweaters were loosely stacked in another. The third crate contained a tangled snarl of charge cords, headphones, and dollar bills.

"I don't really need any. I wear scrubs every day," he explained.

"What about all these hot dates you're going on?" Maggie asked.

His face lost its cocksure countenance for a moment, but it returned as quickly as it had left. "The kind of dates I've been having…let's just say clothes only get in the way."

She sat down on the bed. The mattress was firm and supportive, one of the new ones that had been purchased for the wards but not yet delivered yet. "Hey, where'd you get the new mattress?"

He shrugged. "Make yourself at home. I'm going to get something to eat."

The door swung closed and she lay down on the bed. The lack of sleep caught up with her, and she fell off to sleep.

Chapter Twenty-Seven

Maggie pushed open the door to the chapel and sat down next to Father McDaniel. They sat on the last pew in silence, listening to the whisper of the air conditioning and the murmur of the rosary being prayed over by the woman kneeling at the altar.

"You ready?" Father McDaniel asked.

Maggie nodded. "Are you sure you don't mind being my advocate?"

"I'm honored, Maggie. But you realize I teach ethics at Fordham Law. I'm not a lawyer, right?"

She shrugged. "Anyway, I really appreciate it, Father. It makes me feel better to have you on my side."

They slipped out of the chapel and took the back stairs up to the conference room. The long mahogany table was crowded when they got there. Maggie sat at the far end of the table, on the opposite side of Dr. Tucker, who, as the director of the transitional internship program in which Maggie was enrolled, was running the hearing. Father McDaniel sat to her left, in between Maggie and Medical Director Arnold. Greta Oberhausen sat on the other side of Dr. Arnold, sitting up prim and proper in her chair, dressed in her usual business suit, a navy-blue selection that would have cost Maggie an entire month's salary.

The other side of the table was given over to Dr. Clarke and Dr. Andrews, the head of the general surgery program. Maggie had rotated through General Surgery in

July of last year; she remembered Dr. Andrews well, but not fondly. Two of the things she remembered best about him were his bad breath and his penchant for brushing up against her during surgery.

Dr. Tucker took a sheaf of papers out of his briefcase and set them on the table to begin. "We're all here, so we may as well get started. This is a disciplinary hearing, and, as such, nothing said here is discoverable by statute in any other type of suit, including malpractice or criminal. The stenographer will transcribe what is said, but the transcript is privileged. Are we all clear on that?"

All eyes shot over to the chief counsel of Golden Arches, who nodded without looking up from the yellow legal pad in front of her.

"The sole purpose of this hearing is to determine if Dr. Johnson behaved in such a way as to merit disciplinary measures from this board, and, if so, what measures might be appropriate. Any questions?"

Father McDaniel rubbed his well-trimmed beard. "I have a question."

"Yes, Father McDaniel?"

"Why are we here?"

"I just told you why we're here."

"No, you explained the purpose of a disciplinary hearing. I want to know why the hearing was called in the first place?"

The Jesuit priest regarded Dr. Tucker coolly and lifted up the packet of paper all the members of the committee had been given. "There is nothing in here, Dr. Tucker, unless we want to discipline Dr. Johnson for doing her job."

Maggie resisted the urge to give the priest a hug.

"There's no reason to start off like that, Father McDaniel. We're just trying to discharge our duties as members of the committee."

McDaniel donned a pair of readers and started leafing through the papers in front of him. "The patient had a life-threatening pericardial effusion, correct?"

Tucker nodded, causing the long strands of hair he combed over the bald spot on his head to fall in front of his face.

"Am I also correct in saying that none of the doctors taking care of the patient at the time, including the intern assigned to the patient, the senior resident on service, *and* the attending physician, discovered it?"

Tucker smoothed the strands back onto the top of his head. "I wouldn't put it exactly like that."

"Oh? How, exactly, would you put it?" Father McDaniel asked.

"A pericardial effusion can be quite subtle and is often difficult to diagnose."

"So, tell me, then; how does a doctor diagnose such a condition?"

"Examination of the patient, chest X-Ray, echocardiogram," Tucker said.

McDaniel leafed through the papers, then splayed his hands and regarded the committee chair. "But I don't see any of those things in the patient's chart? Do you?"

Tucker started going through his own stack; from the fallen look on his narrow face, he didn't see any of them either.

"All I see here is a short note written by Dr. Cushing, who was the intern on the case. Do you see the note I am referring to? It's on page thirty-three of the materials provided," Father McDaniel said.

The whisper of shuffling paper filled the conference room.

"Under the Objective heading, I see the acronym LGFD. I'm not familiar with this acronym, so I looked it up in the hospital's handbook of approved acronyms, but

I didn't find it. Would you like to tell me what it means?" Father McDaniel asked.

Oberhausen continued to make notes with her head down. Andrews consulted his watch and grimaced. Arnold was staring off in the distance.

"It means 'Looks Good from Door.' Dr. Cushing is well aware he isn't supposed to writing that," Tucker said.

"Am I to assume, then, that Dr. Cushing will be the next intern to sit in front of this committee?" Father McDaniel asked.

No one responded.

"That's what I thought," Father McDaniel said, addressing Tucker.

Oberhausen looked up from her pad. "You're trying to sidetrack us, Father McDaniel. It won't work. This meeting concerns Dr. Johnson, not anyone else. Serious charges have been made against her."

"Let's get to those, shall we?" Tucker said, trying to maintain order.

Oberhausen ticked off several charges, finishing with Maggie's failure to obtain consent.

"Actually, Dr. Johnson did obtain consent," Father McDaniel said.

"So, she says," Oberhausen retorted.

"The patient corroborates her story,"

"Oral consent isn't allowed."

"Except in the case of emergency, isn't that right?" Father McDaniel asked.

Oberhausen capped her pen, laid it on the pad, and sat upright in her chair. If nothing else, McDaniel had won her undivided attention. "If it was an emergency, she should have called a code…"

"Except that you railroaded the OSG into making the patient a DNR, Ms. Oberhausen. Don't forget I was there when you did that," Father McDaniel said.

"The court issued that order, not me."

"That's because the OSG—under your orders—made no mention of Bobby's wishes when she made an application to the court."

"This isn't the OSG's hearing, Father McDaniel. Let's stick to the charges against Dr. Johnson, for whom we are gathered to determine the proper punishment," Oberhausen said.

"Punishment?" Dr. Clarke lifted a bushy eyebrow. "Don't we need to determine guilt or innocence first?"

"The defendant admitted doing the procedure…there's no doubt about her guilt," Oberhausen said.

The priest slapped the table, giggling the water inside the plastic pitcher on its center. "This is exactly what I'm getting at." He looked around the room, making eye contact with all the members of the committee, save the CEO. "Dr. Johnson's bright future as a physician should not be ruined because someone has an axe to grind against her."

This time the priest glared at Oberhausen, who met his glare with her own.

"I suggest we follow due process and not embark on a witch hunt," Father McDaniel said. "Dr. Johnson hasn't even been allowed to state her case, and yet Ms. Oberhausen has already condemned her. I motion that Ms. Oberhausen be removed from the committee on account of the clear prejudice she has demonstrated."

Tucker removed his Elvis Costello glasses and used a handkerchief to wipe them clean. "You're not a member of the committee, Father McDaniel. You can't make a motion."

Dr. Clarke raised a ring-festooned finger. "I'll make the motion, then."

The fluorescent lights hummed; street noise filtered in through the cracked windows.

"You're not seriously considering this, Dr. Tucker?" Oberhausen asked.

Tucker popped the glasses back on. "No, I am not, Miss Oberhausen, not at this time, but I do understand Father McDaniel's position. You are warned; any further display of prejudice will see you removed from these proceedings. Dr. Johnson, let's hear your testimony."

Maggie wasn't sure where to start; Yoda breathed into her ear: *"Remember your Alice in Wonderland, Interns. When you present a case, begin at the beginning and go on until you get to the end; then stop."*

"The patient is a thirteen-year-old boy, diagnosed with Acute Myeloid Leukemia at age seven…"

The words, having uttered them time and time again, issued from her mouth without hesitancy or inflection, as if she had no other relationship with the Bobby other than the sterile, purely clinical relationship espoused by the intern's handbook.

"Admitted to the Pediatrics Ward four-plus years ago for respite care after two failed bone marrow transplants…"

The hygienic discourse continued, summarizing the care the patient had received at Golden Arches. Her objectivity weakened as she gave account of the patient's successful cardiac resuscitation, and it abandoned her when she reported his response to the OSG's interview about his code status.

"You people are all the same—it never occurs to you that even people like me value their life."

"Bobby, that's not what I meant."

"Sure, you did, you just don't want to admit it."

Oberhausen tried to object, citing irrelevancy, but Tucker allowed it, citing relevancy. Maggie recounted Dr. Cushing's refusal to order a chest X-Ray: *'The attending told me to go easy, so I'm going easy.'*

"So, you're saying that Dr. Cushing did not order the X-Ray?" Tucker asked.

Maggie nodded.

"And yet there was an X-Ray, wasn't there Dr. Johnson?"

"Do Not Resuscitate means just that… it does not mean Do Not Treat. At no point has Bob…the patient…been Comfort Care only," Maggie said.

"That's not the point," Oberhausen said.

"That's exactly the point," Maggie retorted.

Dr. Arnold sighed heavily, but Maggie ignored him. It was clear that he and Oberhausen would oppose her— and equally clear that Tucker and Clarke would support her. Dr. Arnold was the swing vote; she studied him in the yellow wash of the lights. His sturdy face was impassive, and his brown eyes betrayed nothing.

"Are you aware of the hospital's policy regarding verbal orders?" Oberhausen asked.

Verbal orders were verboten, only allowed in the case of emergency and with the caveat that the corresponding written orders needed to be made and signed within twenty-four hours. It was a policy that the busy interns hated and to which the administrators often turned a blind eye.

Except for now.

"I don't see an order for a chest X-Ray here," Tucker said, rifling through the papers.

"I didn't write one."

"You put the hospital in a difficult medical-legal position when you don't document the tests you order, Dr. Johnson," Oberhausen interjected.

"And you, Ms. Oberhausen, put the hospital in a difficult medical-legal position when you…encourage…the medical staff not to treat a patient," Maggie said.

"I don't like what you're implying," Oberhausen said.

"You shouldn't," Maggie told her.

"Do you have any evidence to support this accusation, or is this just a smear campaign?" Oberhausen asked.

"Actually, I *do* have evidence," Maggie said.

Dr. Arnold woke up from his daydreaming; Dr. Andrews stopped consulting his watch.

"We're getting side-tracked again," Oberhausen said.

"No, we're absolutely not." Father McDaniel had a way of speaking that enabled him to emphasize a point without raising his voice. "The crux of this matter is not whether Dr. Johnson failed to write down an order or obtain written consent; the crux of this matter is whether she acted in the best interests of the patient. And I think it's abundantly clear she did."

"Abundantly clear to you, perhaps, but not to me. And you, Father McDaniel, have no vote," Oberhausen said snidely.

The temperature in the room dropped despite the inadequacy of the air-conditioning. Priest and administrator stared each other down.

"Alright, let's settle down here." Tucker put his hands up in request for appeasement. "Before these proceedings go any further, let's see if there's will to continue. Dr. Johnson, Father McDaniel, please excuse yourselves for a few minutes."

Maggie stood to leave, but McDaniel didn't move.

"I'm not going anywhere, Dr. Tucker. Miss Oberhausen has demonstrated that she is anything but impartial with regards to this issue, and I intend to stay to ensure she doesn't bully the vote."

"Why should I be impartial, Father McDaniel? My job is to look out for the interests of this hospital, and, in my opinion, having a resident physician here who acts in complete disregard of its rules and procedures is not in the best interests of this hospital," Oberhausen said, frustration reflecting in her voice.

"You see what I mean? This whole hearing is nothing but a kangaroo court. I move that we drop these charges right away before we do any further damage to Dr. Johnson's reputation and the reputation of this hospital," Father McDaniel said.

Clarke seconded the motion, causing Oberhausen to mutter under her breath. Tucker wiped off his glasses.

"We'll vote now to drop the charges against Dr. Johnson and expunge them from her record. Father McDaniel, you may stay," Tucker said.

Maggie gathered her things and left the room.

***

Only Father McDaniel and Dr. Tucker were in the conference when the door opened to let Maggie in. The looks on both of their faces were enough to tell her that the vote had gone against her.

"I tabled the matter for now, but Oberhausen insisted we convene again shortly. I'll try to stall as much as possible, but with the end of the year coming in a few weeks…" Tucker said.

Residency programs across the country began on July 1st and ended on June 30th of the following year. Given the chaos that ensued every year on the beginning of the month, nothing of import was ever left over from June to be completed in July. Tucker gave her a wry smile and left the room, leaving her alone with Father McDaniel.

"Andrews voted against me?"

The priest nodded. "I hate to say this, but I don't think he ever really considered the evidence."

The inference was clear. For whatever reason—Maggie suspected it was some kind of dirt Oberhausen had on him—he would continue to vote in alignment with the CEO.

"What do we do now?" Maggie asked.

"I don't know."

The door opened, and Foster walked in, which McDaniel took as his cue to leave, patting Maggie on the shoulder as he left.

"Did you hear?" Maggie asked.

He nodded. There was no twinkle in his green eyes, and the smile that made the nurses on pediatrics forget about being overworked and underpaid was in abeyance.

"Oberhausen just called me," Foster said.

"To tell you about the hearing?" Maggie asked.

"No. She screamed at me for telling you she wanted us to go easy on Bobby." He stared at her with his arms folded across his chest. "I told you that in confidence. You shouldn't have repeated that, Maggie."

"It's the truth."

"Doesn't matter." A frown spoiled the rugged features of his face; the cowlick of hair on his forehead spiked up without a hint of curl.

"What was I supposed to do? Just sit there and let her crucify me?" Maggie asked.

"You were supposed to just sit there apologize and tell them you weren't thinking because you were overtired and promise you'd never do it again," Foster said.

"And what was that going to get me?"

"A slap on the wrist, and, in two weeks, your diploma. And then you could be safely over at Columbia."

"I don't want to go to Columbia. We've discussed this."

He walked over to the coffee tray and poured a single cup of coffee and stood there drinking it broodingly. "Now she's going for your jugular."

"She was always going for my jugular," Maggie said.

"You don't know that." He paced back over but stopped short, too short for her to smell the pleasant aroma of his aftershave. "And now she's after my ass, too."

"I'm sorry." She wasn't sorry. "I thought you'd want to stick up for me."

"You're not the only one with a career, Maggie."

He tossed the coffee cup in the garbage, painting the wall with the contents, and left the room without looking back.

Chapter Twenty-Eight

A brisk wind was blowing the last of the clouds away as Maggie escaped through the back door of Golden Arches: sunlight glinted off the broken glass in the parking lot, the squawking of pigeons floated on the breeze, and the smell of freshly mowed grass blunted the more noxious odors leaking out of the subway vents. She weaved her way in between the attendings' cars—a collection of Japanese and German offerings and the occasional Escalade—and slid through the hole in the fence that led to McDonald's.

The restaurant was empty except for the waitress and the usual pair of older men drinking coffee and playing dominoes at a small table by the window.

"Melendez told me you wanted to talk to me?" Maggie said to Cindy.

A patron dared to approach the counter, and Cindy scowled at him, sending him shuffling back to the domino table without a refill. Cindy walked around from behind the counter and waived for Maggie to follow her into the play area, which smelled of urine and anti-septic.

"I got something to tell you," Cindy said. She closed the door to the play area, making it smell even worse. Nausea stirred in Maggie's throat. "I've been dating this cop lately, Kevin...I tell you about him?"

Cindy talked about him all the time, even relating the details of their love life in graphic detail. Maggie nodded.

"Now, mind you, he's no Doctor Delicious, but he's not half-bad lookin' neither and he treats me good. Anyway, he was on patrol on the graveyard shift last week, when he sees this big Lexus jammed into a parked car, driver struggling to get outta the car." She stopped and looked Maggie in the eye. "Guess who the driver was?"

Maggie didn't guess.

"It was your dear friend Greta Oberhausen, that's who."

Maggie remembered the caved in front panel on the Lexus in the physician's parking lot.

A malicious grin spread over Cindy's face. "Drunk as a skunk, she was. And when he opened the door to help her out of the car, the stupid bitch fled the scene. Can you believe that? Kevin chased her down and caught her easy enough, but the damn woman struggled like a rabid cat. Kevin nearly had to taze her to get her to submit."

"I haven't heard a word of this," Maggie said.

"No, you haven't; no one has. That's why I'm telling you. Kevin took her down to the 23rd Precinct. She called the District Attorney, and the next thing you know, she's walking out of the place, and the captain tells Kevin to keep the whole thing quiet."

"Why are you telling me this, Cindy?"

"Because of your hearing."

"You know about my hearing with the Disciplinary Review Board?"

"Honey, everyone knows about your hearing with the Disciplinary Review Board. Whodaya think has been spreading it around?"

"What about it?"

"That damn bitch is the only reason this stupid hearing is taking place."

"How does this have any bearing on my disciplinary case?"

"It doesn't have any bearing on your disciplinary case...as it stands now. But that can change in a heartbeat."

"So, what do you want me to do? Blow the whistle on her?" Maggie asked.

"I don't want you to do anything. I'm just giving you an opportunity."

The idea of ratting out Greta Oberhausen—even as much as she despised her—didn't sit well with her; she admitted as much to Cindy.

"All you gotta do is waltz your pretty ass into that bitch's office and tell her you know about her arrest. In ten minute's time your case will be dismissed—I'd bet my '64 GTO on it," Cindy said.

"Blackmail her, you mean?"

"Hell, yes."

Maggie took a long swallow of coffee, letting the scalding liquid burn its way down her esophagus.

"You can call it blackmail if you want, college girl," Cindy said. "I'd call it justice, but it doesn't really matter what you call it. The important thing is that you do it. Now. That bitch is trying to ruin your life for no other reason than you're prettier than her..."

Maggie said nothing.

"You're not going to do it, are you?"

"I know this sounds funny to you, Cindy—and I do appreciate this—but I want to go to this hearing. I did nothing wrong; what do I have to be afraid of?"

"You think every inmate on death row is guilty, honey? Shit, no. But the innocent ones are going to die all the same because life ain't fair; that's why. Everyone knows that the only thing you're guilty of is being a damn good doctor, but that lousy skank will tie you up into knots all the same. My first divorce...I caught that son-of-a-bitch in bed with so many other women—he'd screw anything, that one, bar bitches, cleaning ladies, fitness freaks from his health club, you name it—but when it came to divorce court, guess who got made out to be the bad girl? You know why, sweetie?"

Maggie had a strong suspicion why, but she allowed Cindy the satisfaction of telling her.

"Because he had money—and he wanted to keep it for himself. His fat wallet bought him a good lawyer, some well-dressed sack of shit with an office on the corner of 5th and 23rd. And do you know what happened? That fancy lawyer screwed me in the ass so hard I couldn't shit for a week. And my ex-husband got off whistle clean. Not because he was whistle clean, Maggie, but because he had a good lawyer. So, that's what I got myself for my second divorce, a good lawyer. Don't you know I hired the same piece of shit that got my first husband off?

"I put my pride aside, lovebird, and I hired that scumbag. My second husband was a bastard, let me tell you, but he was a rich bastard—at least before my new lawyer took him for half of what he was worth."

Cindy stopped the story for a minute, chuckling at the memory.

"Why are you working here if you have so much money?" Maggie asked.

"I like working here, honey. But let's not worry about me. Let's worry about you."

"There's nothing to worry about."

"That's a load of shit, Maggie. There's plenty to worry about. You college girls are all the same. You think that because your daddy is rich and powerful nobody's going to try to screw you in the ass."

"I don't know, Cindy."

"Listen, sweetie, I grew up in the hood right close to here, and because of that, I've been screwed in the ass plenty of times. It don't feel so hot, take it from me. I like you, Maggie. You're a decent person. You stand up for people that need help, and you don't walk around all day telling everyone how smart you are—I like that in a gal. I'm trying to help you because you need the help. That bitch is going to fuck you in the ass."

***

There was something different about Room 12, but try as Maggie might, she couldn't place it: the crack still scarred the far wall, like a fault line between tectonic plates; the window remained clouded, obscuring the view of the drab tenement building across the street; and the faucet in the bathroom continued to drip with irregularity, as if it were a participant in a macabre game of Chinese water torture. The vase of flowers hadn't moved, although the flowers themselves had withered to the point of petrification, the carnation being particularly well preserved. The pile of *X-men* comics hadn't changed either; the bag of new comic books she'd bought last week—featuring different heroes from the Marvel Universe—remained unopened underneath the chair.

"Why don't you at least try something new?" Maggie asked.

Bobby shrugged his shoulders and kept on reading. The nurse came at nine p.m. to let her know that calling hours were long over, but she let Maggie stay after Bobby pleaded with her.

"What's eating you, Maggie?" Bobby asked.

"Nothing."

Bobby set the comic book down. "Sure, there is."

"What makes you so sure?"

"You're just sitting there and letting me read."

"You have a problem with that?"

"Nope, but you normally pester with me questions. The only times you leave me be are when something is bugging you," Bobby said.

He was a perceptive little bugger; Maggie gave him that much.

"Plus, your face is all pinched; it looks like you haven't taken a shit in weeks."

Maggie burst out laughing, in spite of herself. There were so many reasons she loved this little boy, honesty being chief among them. "You're not supposed to say things like that!"

"Says who?"

Maggie considered explaining to him the complicated rules of etiquette she'd learned in the finest girl's school in Westchester County, but she knew Bobby would fail to understand their importance; at the current moment, she failed to understand them as well.

"You going to tell me what's eating you?" Bobby asked. He'd closed the comic book and was regarding her with a look of concern. It moved her—the furrow of his small brow, the purse of his thin lips—this thirteen-year-old kid with all the problems in the world was concerned about her.

"It's nothing."

Bobby rolled his small, bloodshot eyes. "You don't want to burden me, is that it?" He laughed his high-pitched squealing laugh—a consequence of the effect of the mustard gas on his developing vocal cords. "Come on, Maggie. You're the only person in the whole world I care about. You have to tell me."

Maggie told him about the disciplinary hearing that was set to reconvene in a few days and about how the committee had voted 3-2 to continue the hearing. She even told him about the secret she had learned about the general counsel, the woman who was out to get her. When she glanced up from the floor after finishing her story, she saw that the concerned look in Bobby's face had turned into a horrified one.

"Let me get this straight. You found out that the wicked witch committed a crime, and you're just sitting here as she takes a massive dump on you?"

Maggie nodded. When he put it like that, her choice sounded neither noble not proud, just sad and pathetic.

"This is the woman that wants me dead, Maggie. You remember that, right?"

"Yes, I remember."

A noxious odor wrinkled her nose. It was a familiar smell, but she couldn't quite place it, mixed it as it was with the harsh reek of the cleaning agents and the rank scent of East Harlem that leaked in through the fractured window panes.

"Then why aren't you doing something about it?"

"Because I didn't do anything wrong, Bobby, and blackmailing my way out of this situation makes me as rotten as her."

"That is the dumbest thing I have ever heard, Maggie, dumber even than the time some stupid doctor told me he was going to cure my cancer." Bobby rolled over to look at her, a process which took several seconds. When he had gathered his breath, he turned again and resumed reading his comic book. "Please leave, now."

"Bobby, don't be like that..."

"I'm tired, Maggie. Can you please go?"

Maggie started to protest, but the door opened, and the nurse beckoned to her from the hall. She stood up, grabbed her raincoat, and retreated from the room.

Chapter Twenty-Nine

The social work office was on the fifth floor of the hospital, right next to the Psychiatry Ward where the medical social workers spent most of their time. The space had been salvaged from the old Tuberculosis Unit, which had closed in the early 1940s when streptomycin had been discovered by a graduate student at nearby Rutgers University. Most of the furniture dated back to the forties as well—or even earlier—the cause of a great deal of complaining on behalf of the staff. But they were complaints that fell upon deaf ears, consequent to the color of the hospital's budget, which was hopelessly in the red.

Maggie pushed open the door to the office and found the meeting room where Tammy Hunter, the MSW assigned to pediatrics, was waiting for her. Social workers everywhere were overburdened and undercompensated, but nowhere more so than at Golden Arches, where Greta Oberhausen's honed axe had been chopping away at the social work budget for years. As a consequence, the last pediatric MSW to have retired wasn't replaced, and Miss Hunter, of whom the interns had a poor opinion, was the whole show.

Hunter held up her index finger to indicate it would only be another second and then proceeded to talk on the phone for several minutes more, extolling the virtues of some sort of recipe before she set the receiver down and regarded Maggie with a plastic smile on her face. "So nice to see you Maggie."

Maggie doubted the veracity of her comment. The last time she'd been in this office it was to complain that not enough—and by not enough, Maggie meant that nothing—was being done to overturn the court's decision about Bobby's DNR status.

"It's nice to see you too, Tammy."

A survivor of one of the most prestigious girl's schools in Westchester, Maggie could be as fake as the girl if need be. They made small talk for the obligatory minute, before Maggie got down to it. "What's going on with Grace Jones' disposition?"

"Grace Jones?"

Maggie nodded.

"I didn't realize you were on Pediatrics this month?"

Maggie translated in her head as the MSW spoke. *"Grace Jones' disposition isn't any of your damn business."*

"I'm not."

"Why are you concerned about Grace?" Hunter asked.

"Why are you wasting my time?"

"I've taken a personal interest in the case," Maggie said.

Hunter opened up her computer; it was turned the other way so Maggie didn't know if the social worker was opening up Grace's file or looking for other recipes to extoll.

"That seems to be a bit of a thorny area," Hunter said.

"I have no fucking idea what's going on with Grace's disposition."

"Thorny?"

"Both of her parents are dead," she said.

"I'm going to stall for time by stating known facts."

"That's what I read in the papers," Maggie said.

Grace's father, the former NFL star, had been found swinging from the rafters of his prison cell. The story had been front page news for a few days, especially in the tabloids, before becoming old news and then no news at all.

"The father was an only child, and he was estranged from his parents," Hunter said.

"This girl's up Shit's Creek."

"Her mother was raised by her grandmother, who's now dead," Hunter continued.

"No paddle."

"There's a maternal aunt... but she's in prison for at least ten years for dealing crack," she said.

"This tale of woe is depressing even me, and I thought I'd seen everything."

"What about Brock Jones's will? He must have had a will," Maggie said.

Hunter raised an overly manicured eyebrow; in *El Barrio*, no one had a will.

"Brock Jones was a star in the NFL. He must be worth millions," Maggie continued.

"Brock Jones's last year in the NFL was 2012. His first year in prison was 2015: the first of a five-year sentence for dealing narcotics. He got out in less than a year, the Parole Board being Giants fans and all."

"Brock Jones blew all his money on hookers and coke."

"Where does that leave Grace?" Maggie asked.

"In the same spot as thousands of other children in New York," Hunter said.

"Refer back to my comment about being up Shit's Creek without a paddle."

"No parents or family of any kind. No money or resources of any kind. No insurance or medical coverage of any kind. Should I go on?" Hunter asked.

"She's totally fucked."

***

Melendez was there when Maggie got to Grace's room in the Step-Down Unit, the holding area PICU patients went to before transitioning to the general pediatric floor. They were playing rummy on the nightstand, a difficult proposition due to the table's small surface area and Melendez's penchant for cheating—not to mention that Grace only had one usable arm, the other being in a cast held by a sling.

Patients celebrated the move to the SDU; not only did it represent a downgrade in their status, it also meant that many of the rules and protocols mandatory in the PICU no longer applied: vitals were done less frequently; visiting rules were much laxer; and a television was provided.

"How are you feeling, Grace?" Maggie asked.

"Good."

It was the same thing she'd said with the first breath she'd taken since having the endotracheal tube withdrawn from her trachea, the same thing she'd said to the orthopedic and plastic surgeons who had come to evaluate their handiwork, and the same thing she said to the nurse that came in every hour.

Maggie joined the card game, and they played a few more rounds of rummy before the physical therapist kicked them out to work on Grace's ambulation, which still required a rolling walker and a one-person assist. Maggie kissed her goodbye and joined Melendez in the stairway heading down. On the descent, she informed Melendez about what she had learned from the MSW.

"Doesn't surprise me that Brock Jones died penniless. It's a big problem in the league; these guys blow through money as if they're going to get millions every year for the rest of their lives. Within a few years of being out of the league, most of 'em are dead broke."

They were in the sub-basement before Maggie realized it. Melendez turned toward his abode; Maggie followed him.

"That girl I've been seeing in the Cashier's Office..." Melendez said.

"You've been seeing a girl in the Cashier's Office?"

"Yeah. Why, do you care?"

"I don't care," Maggie told him.

"I think you do." He stopped in front of the door to his room and fumbled for the key in the side pocket of his lab coat. "Anyway, as I was saying, that girl told me the Blue Cross account that Brock Jones gave the hospital had been expired for a year."

They passed inside and he started to say something else but Maggie kissed him. "Shut up for a second, will you?" she said.

She kissed him again. They fell onto the bed, entangled in each other's arms, mouths connected. Her hands massaged his strong back, his wide shoulders and his chest. Melendez rolled on top of her, and she wrapped her legs around him, pulling him closer. She could feel his hands on her back, strong and masculine. A peculiar—but pleasurable, definitely pleasurable—feeling overcame her, a mixture of desire and anxiety with a tinge of curiosity. She wanted it to stay.

His hands dropped down, running over her buttocks back and forth, back and forth in a sensual rhythm. She felt his fingers pulling at the drawstring of her scrubs. He untied the bow knot and slipped her pants down.

"Do you know how many times I've dreamed about this?" he asked.

"No, tell me."

He responded by helping her wiggle out of her scrub top, which she tossed on the floor. He took off his scrubs and threw them over hers. The pile grew; first his boxers, then her panties and bra, Melendez assisting on the removal.

They came together again, this time with nothing between them, clothing, uncertainty, or anything else. Maggie would later remember every detail of the event— every kiss, every caress, every sensation—although it would not be the corporal details that stayed with her most. Even more poignant than the warm feel of his body enmeshed deeply within hers was the great emotion she felt, to be scared and vulnerable and, at the same time, joyous and exuberant, moving forward not backwards, forging ahead. There was a line somewhere there, drawn in the air in between their groping hands and writhing bodies; Maggie crossed it, never looking back, not second-guessing, harboring no regrets.

When it was all over, they lay still on the bed, exhausted. Neither spoke; if there was a dimension where words were not necessary, then they were tucked away inside it, content with perception. They drifted off to sleep in each other's arms only to wake and repeat the process again, this time much slower, more deliberate, more rationale.

And then Maggie slept, not the fitful sleep of an intern, but a deep, sound sleep, like that of a brown bear in winter, fat and satisfied from gorging on salmon flesh.

Chapter Thirty

Knock. Knock. Knock.

Maggie stirred in bed and tried to roll over only to get hung up on Melendez, who was lying on his side with his back facing her.

Knock. Knock. Knock.

The raps were louder this time, more persistent. She glanced at her watch; it was five a.m. Nothing good ever happened at five a.m.

Knock. Knock. Knock.

She rolled out of bed, discovering she'd been sleeping naked. Her scrubs were on floor; she slipped into them as the knocking came again, harder. She slipped her feet into her clogs and opened the door a crack. The hallway on the other side was dimly lit; she couldn't see anyone there.

"Who is it?" Maggie asked.

"Maggie? It's me."

"Yoda?"

"We need to talk," Yoda said.

Maggie opened the door, and Yoda walked in, wearing her usual Tuesday attire, navy blue slacks and a red short-sleeved blouse.

"How'd you know I was here?" Maggie asked.

"I know everything."

Only Yoda could pull off a statement like that without sounding boastful or pompous; her small face retained its factual expression, and her voice was uninflected, as if reporting the hour.

"What do you want?" Maggie asked her.

"Your father's been looking for you since last night. He went to your apartment and you weren't there, so he called me, wanting to know if I'd seen you. I told him you were crashed in a call room and that I would give you the message he was looking for you first thing in the morning."

"First thing in the morning isn't for an hour yet."

"Not for a surgeon. He showed up a few minutes ago looking for you," Yoda told her.

"What'd you tell him?"

"I said I'd get you out of bed and send you up to the physician's parking lot. He's waiting for you in his car."

Maggie grabbed a scrunchie out of her lab coat and used it to tie her hair back into a bun.

Yoda went out, but stuck her head back in as Maggie applied some lipstick. "One more thing."

"What is it now, Yoda?"

Yoda pointed the pile of underclothes on the floor. "Don't forget to put your panties on."

***

Maggie opened the passenger door and slid into the seat next to her father, who was using his iPad to go through e-mails.

"Yoda said you wanted to see me?"

He set the tablet down on the dashboard. "I wanted to make sure you're alright. Your mother and I haven't seen or heard from you in weeks."

She shrugged. "I'm okay, you?"

"Okay."

The wind picked up, blowing in through the open window with a mournful sound. The smell of ripe trash emanated from the dumpsters next to the car.

"I came to apologize," he said.

She couldn't remember him ever saying those words, and they struck her as being vaguely insincere as a consequence.

"It's not me you should be apologizing to," Maggie said,

A feral dog appeared. It slinked underneath the fence around the disposal area, flushing a flock of house sparrows and starlings.

"I'm not seeing that woman anymore...I told her it was over."

A swarm of flies buzzed around a partially eaten hamburger that hadn't quite made it into the receptacle.

"I'm embarrassed. I've been behaving badly," he said.

A rat scurried along the top of the fence surrounding the parking lot, carrying a piece of a sandwich in its mouth.

"Aren't you going to say anything?"

"You always do all the talking, Dad. Why should it change now?"

"Don't be like that, Margaret. I'm trying to make things right."

A silver Tesla sedan pulled in to the spot next to them, and her father exchanged pleasantries with the driver, a pathologist who never left the basement. Maggie remembered him from delivering Christmas cookies to his office when she was a teenager.

"You could have at least called your mother. She's been worried about you."

A trio of youths wearing the backwards red baseball caps of the Air It Out gang, whose turf ran straight through the hospital campus, sauntered through the parking lot. The security guards were under strict orders not to let them on the premises, but these strict orders were often ignored in favor of a less confrontational approach.

"I'm sure she'd appreciate a call. I told her about the affair and we're trying to work past it."

"You told mom?" Maggie asked.

"I thought a lot about what you said the last time we saw each other. It hurt to be called a narcissist because I always resented my father for being one, but I decided that the shoe fit. If you can believe this, I'm even seeing a psychologist."

At one point in her undergraduate education at Brown, Maggie had thought about forgoing medical school in favor of pursuing a graduate degree in psychology, a plan which had not found her father's favor. He'd threatened to stop paying her tuition, and she eventually stopped talking about anything other than medical school as a career choice.

"Anyway, she could use the support. And she's worried about you…we both are."

"I'm fine."

The sweet odor of *chocolate con churros* wafted across the parking lot from the bakery across the street, reminding Maggie she hadn't eaten in much too long.

"No, you're not. I just found out about your disciplinary hearing last night in the OR locker room. I tried to get a hold of you as soon as I found out, but you didn't answer my phone calls, and your apartment was empty. I called Yoda, and she said you were sleeping in a call room."

The Number One train rumbled underneath them, accelerating after picking up passengers from the 116th Street Station.

"How come you never told me about this?" her father asked.

"It's not a big deal, Dad."

"Not a big deal?" His voice cracked, and the capillaries in his cheeks swelled with blood, staining his face red. "Do you have any idea what a complete bitch Greta Oberhausen is?"

"Actually, I do."

A cat or some other animal slipped underneath the façade around the disposal area, a shadow in the darkness. For a second, she wondered if it was Whiskers, who she hadn't seen in over a week. The kittens had disappeared as well; the only evidence that they'd ever been there was their dried-up placenta which had been partially eaten by gulls and a pile of scat against the wall.

"Anyway, I've got a call into one of my partners…he went to UVA with Bob Andrews. From what he tells me, they were good buddies in the same fraternity. He should be able to persuade Andrews to let this go with a slap on the wrist."

"I don't want your help, Dad."

"You need my help, Maggie. You're in deep shit. I don't know what you did to piss off Oberhausen, but she's out for your head. Rumor has it she's not going to settle for anything less than expulsion."

A mounted policeman clip clopped past on his rounds, the 23rd Precinct's most recent answer to the increase in gang violence.

"Expulsion will effectively mean the end of your career as a doctor."

"I know what it means."

"No other internship is going to take you with that on your record…"

"I'll do something else, then."

"Something else?" he asked. The mere prospect of his daughter considering a different line of work caused his voice to go an octave higher; the color of his face advanced along the spectrum of visible light, ending up somewhere between indigo and violet.

"Promise me you will not intervene on my behalf."

"It's a phone call," he said.

"It's so much more than that. It's you controlling everything, pulling all the strings, calling all the shots."

"You say that like it's terrible thing, but look at you. Look at the success you've had, Margaret."

A black Escalade pulled to a stop at the light next to them; the ground shook with the reverberations of the bass rhythm driving the song.

"Success, yes, I've been successful. Happiness, now that's a different story."

"Happiness doesn't pay your mortgage or send your children to college."

Two squad cars screamed past, flashers twirling.

"I'll speak to my partner," he said.

It was a statement, not a question. He wasn't asking her permission; he was only making her aware what he intended to do, regardless of her wishes.

"You can't fix this for me," Maggie said.

A collage of memories came to her: the time he had picked her up at a bar when she was too drunk to drive and never mentioned it anyone; the time he had Skyped with her the night before her Biochemistry final and managed to get her to understand the Krebbs cycle when everyone else—the professor, the teaching assistant, her lab partner—had failed. He had always fixed things for her, always endeavored to keep her on the path he'd created for her.

"I have to do this myself."

"What is so important about doing it yourself?"

"Because it won't mean anything to me otherwise."

Sirens wailed, announcing the arrival of another ambulance. Lights twirled, creating a dizzying carousel of shadows against the façade.

"You need to promise me you'll let me do this on my own."

He blew out his breath, which smelled of licorice and peppermint.

"You have to work on rebuilding my trust, Dad. This is how you start."

"I know you think you're doing the right thing, Margaret, but tell me something. Are you still going to feel the same way when they show you to the door?"

"Yes, I am."

It was one of the few things she was sure about.

"Promise me?" she asked.

He nodded.

Chapter Thirty-One

Maggie got out of bed around four a.m. and laced on her sneakers. She left her building through the back door and took to the nearly deserted street. If there was one hour that the Big Apple didn't see, it was four a.m. The partiers were either passed out or buried in the bowels of some dark club, and the early risers were still reading the paper over their first cup of coffee. Only a few delivery vehicles and the occasional taxi fouled the streets, still wet from last night's rain. Maggie plodded along, up 3rd avenue, running like the weight of the world was on her shoulders. She hooked a left on 57th and another left on Lexington, and started back towards Murray Hill.

She showered after her run, put on her scrubs, and sat down on her balcony watching the dawn overwhelm the city. A pile of textbooks lay next to her, but her mind was too cloudy and dim, and her eyes hurt from the lack of sleep. In any event, she might not need them after today anyway—if Greta Oberhausen had her way.

Maggie left for the hospital at six a.m., deciding on the subway. She usually took the bus, but something about being far under the earth seemed fitting on the morning of her last day as a doctor. She knew she shouldn't think that way, but any optimistic spirit she might have had abandoned her. The train doors opened at Times Square, and she filed out with the other New Yorkers, trying to absorb some of their resilience as she climbed the stairs toward the Number One train.

The sun was up when she emerged from the 125th street station, but it did nothing to brighten her mood. She felt like a condemned inmate, walking slowly down death row, innocent but doomed to die anyway. She walked past the McDonald's, desperate for a cup of coffee but not willing to face Cindy, who would be as disappointed with her as Bobby had been. She found the back door and used the staircase to ascend to the top floor, where her doom awaited her.

The conference room was empty when she got there, but it was still early, and her executioners hadn't gathered yet. At 6:45—fifteen minutes before her hour was to be at hand—the door opened and the kitchen staff wheeled in a cart of donuts and bad coffee. She ignored the donuts—not being the slightest bit hungry—and poured herself a large cup of coffee.

At five minutes to seven, she was overcome with a strong urge to run down to the first floor—to the lair of the Wicked Witch of the East River—but she resisted it by sitting on the bench bolted into the far wall and grabbing the seat with all her strength until it passed. These were the kinds of moments when her panic attacks gripped her, and she waited for one to overcome her, but her chest didn't tighten, her breathing remained calm, and 'the cold dread,' the feeling that her soul was being drowned in an ocean of cold water, didn't wash over her. She sat up straight on the bench and held her chin high; she was going to go down in flames today, she just knew it, but at least she would go down with her self-respect intact.

At quarter after the hour, she wondered if the time for the meeting had been changed? (Of course, no one bothered to tell her.) Or, perhaps they'd met without her and concluded her to be unworthy of being a doctor, but just no one had the chutzpah to tell her.

At 7:30 a.m., she sat down on the couch at the back of the room and closed her eyes. It occurred to her it wouldn't look good to the members of the committee to find her sleeping there, but she was past caring. The end of her career had come, a thousand nights of studying until her eyes couldn't focus anymore, a thousand mornings of prying her eyelids open—all come to naught. The door opened just before eight o'clock, and her head snapped up; she had nodded off with the cup of coffee still clutched in her hand.

"Hello Maggie." Dr. Clarke walked to the back of the room and sat next to her on the couch. "I have been trying to text you."

"My phone's dead."

Dr. Clarke nodded and sat down on a chair across from her.

"Where is everybody? Did they reschedule the hearing?" Maggie asked.

Dr. Clarke picked up the clicker from the table next to her and turned on the TV mounted to the wall. She flicked though the stations until she found the one she was looking for and cranked up the volume. A commercial was airing, filling the air with its catchy melody and the promise of the happy consumer. When it ended, the screen filled with cars and people. The buzz of a dozen voices shouting emanated from the speakers BREAKING NEWS scrolled across the bottom of the screen, encased in a red banner.

A pair of police cars pulled up next to the camera, and there was a mad rush to the cars. Whoever was holding the camera was a little slower than the rest, and the backs of several people blocked the lens. Six people got out of the cars, four uniforms and a man and a woman in plain clothes. The crowd parted and let the trio through; they climbed up the steps of some official looking building and disappeared inside. A throng of people tried to follow them, but a line of police officers formed and prevented them. People started shouting questions, but with so many people talking all at once, she couldn't decipher any of it.

The camera retreated from the melee and centered on a reporter, who waited with a solemn face as the producer switched the audio feed. "We're here this morning at the Municipal Courthouse, as District Attorney Robert Whittaker and lawyer Greta Oberhausen have turned themselves in to the police to answer charges that they colluded to obstruct justice to cover up a drunk driving accident..."

Clarke slipped her arm over Maggie's shoulder as they listened.

"A reporter broke the story early this morning, based on an anonymous tip. Allegedly Miss Oberhausen was involved in an accident last week. A policeman tried to assist her, but she fled the scene and resisted arrest once he caught her. The reporter is claiming she called the district attorney, who is an old friend of hers from Cornell University, and he put the kybosh on the whole thing and told the arresting officer to delete the arrest report and forget the entire incident. The officer who arrested her was wearing a body camera, and the video of the arrest has already made it onto YouTube."

A murky video played. The only light came from a few anemic streetlamps and the headlights of a car that had crashed into a line of others parked along the street. A woman stumbled out of the offending car, wearing a silver dress with a stain over the front. She slapped at the officer as he neared her, and then took off down the street as if possessed by a demon.

"The hearing has been postponed?" Maggie asked.

"The hearing has been cancelled, Maggie. That's why I was trying to reach you. The committee had a special meeting early this morning when the news came out, and we came to a decision. All the charges have been dropped, and your record was expunged. You're in the clear."

Maggie couldn't stop herself from hugging her.

"From this moment on, you're a 2nd year pediatrics resident," Clarke said.

Maggie looked her watch; it was still June. "Aren't I still on radiology?"

"I talked it over with your attending this morning. We thought that since you're pediatrics now, you'd want to get started as soon as possible. And we're down a few residents because of vacation...I was hoping you could start right away."

After another commercial break—this time hawking a medicine that had three times more possible side effects than it did benefits—the reporter returned to the screen.

"Local news has just obtained another video feed, this one from the Closed-Circuit television network covering the city."

The reporter moved to a box in the bottom corner of the screen; a blurry video stream started playing.

"This is a camera footage from the 23rd Precinct from this past Sunday morning."

A gold Lexus sedan appeared at the top of the screen, going much faster than the speed limit. As it approached the camera, a tall figure emerged from the unlit side of the street and walked into the path of the oncoming car. The figure was just a shadow in the dim video feed, but there was something about it—the way it moved, perhaps, with a long jaunting gate and an exaggerated swing of the arm—she recognized in a deep corner of her brain.

The Lexus sped forward, oblivious of the person in its path. At the last second, the driver must have seen the man in her way, slamming on the brakes and swerving to the left side of the road. The car had too much momentum to swing clear, and struck the man, who made no effort to get out of the way. The Lexus veered into the line of parked cars, and the man was sent sprawling into the darkness out of the field of view.

"Police are attempting to identify the man who was struck by the car allegedly driven by Miss Oberhausen but report that no one was found on the scene, and a search of local hospitals did not turn up anyone meeting his description."

Maggie grabbed the clicker from Dr. Clarke and rewound the tape, watching the man lope into the street in slow motion. She played it forwards and backwards, pausing it to freeze the man in various positions.

"I know that guy," Maggie said.

Dr. Clarke raised her eyebrow. "It's a pretty bad picture, Maggie. Are you sure?"

They watched it several more times. Maggie became more certain with every rewind.

"Who is it?" Clarke asked.

Maggie told him about John Doe, the engineering student who had thought he could fly. "He lives in a cardboard shelter in a park in the Meatpacking District. Would it be okay if I go down there to make sure he's okay?"

"Of course, Maggie. We can manage without you for a few hours."

Dr. Clarke left the room, and Maggie zigzagged her way to the rear fire escape the interns used to sneak over to the bodega across the street, which featured the best fruit in the Five Burroughs. She took the subway to the Meatpacking District and located the green space where John Doe used to live. The last time she'd been there was over a month ago—to bring him some leftover bagels from a breakfast meeting she had attended—and to her great relief, the cardboard shanty was still there. A pair of worn boots stuck out of the box.

"Rise and shine, John," she said.

The only response was a deep chortle. She knocked on the top of the lean-to, causing it to sway.

"It's me, Maggie. Wake up, I want to talk to you."

The box shook as its occupant rolled over, causing the puddle of water that had accumulated on top to splash over Maggie's feet.

"Come on, wake up. I want to make sure you're okay."

The snoring continued, so she set off the alarm on her iPhone and lowered it into the box. The heavy breathing stopped, replaced by a string of curses foul enough to shame a sailor. A moment later, up popped a dark brown head with large eyes that were trying to explode out of their sockets.

"What the hell are you doing, lady?" the man asked.

Maggie stared at him in horror. "Who are you? You're not John."

The man scratched his hair, which he wore in a voluminous Afro. "No, I ain't John. My name's Fred."

"Where's John?"

Fred closed one eye and regarded her with the other. "John the tall, skinny dude that used to live here?"

Maggie nodded.

"I haven't seen that cat in two weeks."

"I return to the fires where I was made."

"And what then?"

"Nothing. I will perish in the flames."

Fred went on, but Maggie wasn't listening. The CCTV video played over and over in her head; each time the tumbling figure struck by Greta's Lexus looked more like John Doe.

"Do you know where he might be?" Maggie asked.

Fred shrugged. "Why do you want to find him so awful bad? He a relative or summtin'?"

"No, I just need to talk to him."

She thanked him for his trouble and rode the subway to the homeless shelter to which she had discharged him several months ago. He'd stayed there one night—according to the front desk clerk—but hadn't been back since. The director of the shelter gave her a copy of the picture they'd taken upon his admission and suggested she try a few other places. She went to all of them; no one had seen anyone that looked like the man in the picture.

The last shelter was around the corner from Times Square, and she wandered toward it, aimless and unsure. Times Square was, as always, overflowing with people gazing at the giant screens that floated above them. On the largest screen was a headshot of none other than Rex Miller, the reporter who visited Bobby. Underneath his acne-scarred face, Maggie read the subtitle.

Rex Miller: Investigative journalist who broke the story about District Attorney Whittaker and Attorney Oberhausen.

Chapter Thirty-Two

Maggie hailed the first cab she saw and settled into the back seat as her driver weaved his way over to Golden Arches. It was a busy weekday morning in Manhattan, and the traffic was dreadful. In usual circumstances, she had great patience for things she couldn't control—like traffic jams and bad weather—but today was far from usual. She tossed the driver a few twenties when they pulled up at the hospital and ran out of the cab without waiting for her change.

Yoda was waiting for her in the lobby of Golden Arches, but Maggie ran right past her, taking the back stairs two at a time. She burst through the door to the annex, which was dark and quiet, unusual for the hour. She walked down the hall, her footsteps echoing as if she were in a tomb, and stopped in front of Room 12. The door was shut. No light seeped out from underneath it. The handle was cold; she turned it and went inside.

The lights were off, but enough ambient illumination came through the window to see the white sheet covering the bed. She pulled it back and saw Bobby lying there, cold and lifeless on the cot. His face glowed palely in the dimness.

The door opened, and Yoda came in. Maggie didn't realize she was crying until Yoda leaned forward and handed her a box of tissues. Yoda started talking, explaining that one of the nurses had come in take his vitals and found him dead, but Maggie's focus had abandoned her; Yoda's words echoed unheard off the walls. The tears came quicker, and her shoulders started to heave. Pressure built up in her chest; her eyes burned; her throat swelled as if she had vomited up her stomach.

"I'll leave you alone for a while."

The door closed behind her. Maggie pulled the sheet all the way down and laid next to Bobby on the bed, gathering him in her arms. The trickle of tears on her cheek turned into a torrent, and she dabbed at her mouth with the wadded-up ball of Kleenex. She started sobbing, annoyed at herself for being so melodramatic, but she was powerless to stop it: the heaving of her shoulders; the great whoops of air; the uncontrollable shaking.

How long she remained there, crying in the dark, she would never be sure. She was only aware of her sorrow and a strong sense of unfairness. It was unfair, she thought, that anyone would come into the world the way Bobby had, spit out from his dying mother's womb under a bridge. It was unfair he had lived his whole life in a succession of foster homes and charitable institutions, never having experienced the comfort and solace of a real home. It was unfair he had been diagnosed with cancer at age seven, a high-grade leukemia against which all the weapons of modern medicine had proven useless. And it was unfair—terribly, grossly unfair—that he had died alone, without Maggie there to hold his hand as he passed from this world into the next.

The door opened, and someone entered the room, but the lighting was too dark, and Maggie's eyes too blurry with tears to see whom it was.

"It's me."

Yoda had come back. Maggie tried to open her eyes, but the sting of salt was sharp, and she let her eyelids close. Something damp and cold—Yoda's small hand— settled onto her forearm.

"Are you okay?"

Maggie said nothing. What was there to say? At times, words failed people, and this was one of those times.

The injustice, the terrible inequality.

"You should read this."

Maggie felt something light land on her chest.

"It's a letter from Bobby. The nurses found it under his pillow."

Maggie sat up, used the wad of tissues to wipe the salt out of her eyes, and held the letter up to read, but it was too dark. Yoda switched on her flashlight application, throwing the piece of paper she was holding into focus.

Dear Maggie:

If you are reading this, it's because I was wrong about being unkillable. I want to tell you so many things, things I should have said to your face, but never did. I hate writing though, and this pencil is pretty dull, so I will only say one thing.

Thanks.

You are the only person in the whole world I'm going to miss. The only reason I still wanted to live is because you needed me—just as much as I needed you. I will miss your pale blue eyes and the smile that made even the darkest days a little brighter. You are a doctor, Maggie, a real doctor. I say that because you cared about me when no one else did.

Before I met you, I wanted to be forgotten, as if my whole life had never happened. What good had ever come out of my life? You changed that for me because you were the only person I have ever loved. A life without love should be forgotten, like the dead rat I was once found in the sewer behind my foster home. But not a life with love. A life with love is immortal. (I guess I am unkillable after all.)

Please remember me.

Bobby.

Ps. Remember Rex Miller, that reporter that wanted to do the story on LDK369? He gave me his card, and I kept it because I was using it as a bookmark. I called him Maggie, and I told him the story about that awful woman who is trying to ruin you. I know you wanted to fight her on your own, but I didn't want to take the chance you would lose. I couldn't take the chance you would lose, not after everything you've done for me.

He got the whole story from the cop, even a copy of the video from his body camera. She's going down, Maggie, and you are safe. Now I can die. I have saved the woman I love, just like any good X-Man would, and I can die and know that my life had a purpose. It is a terrible thing to live your whole life thinking your life has no purpose, like a stain on the bed sheets, but that is how I have always felt. Until now.

I can die now in peace.

Goodbye.

The sobs returned. Maggie let the letter fall on her lap, and she hugged Yoda as if she were the last person on Earth. When her tears were exhausted and her shoulders stopped heaving, she let go of Yoda and got to her feet. She helped Yoda up, slipped Bobby's letter into pocket, and left the room with Yoda in tow.

The darkness had dispersed when the two of them exited the hospital, revealing the early sun, which smiled down upon them. Maggie couldn't help but think it was Bobby's face that was shining, now that he was free from cancer and pain and the stale air of hospital rooms. It was warm and pleasant, and they decided to take a walk, enjoying the smell of fresh bread, the caress of the wind, and the comfort of the crowd on the street. They got coffee and sat on a bench in the shallow rays of the sun.

"What am I going to do now, Yoda?"

"Finish your coffee and go back to work."

It was a corollary of the sermon on Diet Coke—
Melendez had dubbed it that—she gave every few days.

She continued by saying, "You're going to take everything
you learned from caring for Bobby, and carry it with you
always. That's what we do. We learn from experience."

"I don't think I can do it again."

"You can."

A song played from the open window of a passing car,
Carole King's *Will You Love Me Tomorrow?*

"You will," Yoda said.

A small child, a girl of about nine or ten, skipped
down the street, lugging a backpack almost as big as she
was. She would have skipped right out onto the street
were it not for her mother, who grabbed the backpack with
impeccable timing and didn't let go until the flashing
green man appeared, indicating it was safe to cross.

"You have to."

"Why do I have to? Why can't I just quit?"

"Tell me something…" Yoda's gaze moved from her
left temple— where it always lay—down and to the right,
settling straight into her eyes. "Did Bobby ever quit?"

"Maybe he was tougher than me."

"Tough people decide to be tough; wimps decide to
be wimpy."

They returned to Golden Arches, and she parted ways
with Yoda in the lobby, descending into the sub-
basement. She knocked on the door to Chez Melendez;
there was no answer. The handle didn't turn. A janitor
came out of the locker room, and she waved him over,
asking to be let in. He tried to explain to her in his broken
English that it was just a storeroom for cleaning supplies,
but he unlocked it at her insistence.

She opened the door and went in. The bed was empty;
the bed clothes lay in a tangled heap on the floor. The milk
crates were empty. The small refrigerator and the bean
bag were gone, although the pile of scrubs that had been

on the bean bag was still there, strewn over the floor. The smell of Melendez's cheap aftershave still hung in the air.

Exhaustion overcame her, and she flopped onto the bed. She had no idea what time it was but didn't check her watch, even though it was on her wrist, just inches from her face. She wanted sleep and oblivion, nothing else. In time, sleep prevailed, but it was a restless, dream-filled sleep from which she woke an hour later.

Knock. Knock.

"Go away."

Knock. Knock.

"Maggie?"

Maggie pushed herself off the bed, and trudged over to the door, which she opened a crack. Foster was standing there.

"Yoda told me you were here."

They stared at each other awkwardly.

"Were you sleeping?" he asked.

"Yes."

He walked into the room unbidden, surveying the real estate.

"What do you want, Jack?"

"I need to talk to you."

She shrugged.

"I heard you're a pediatrics resident, now. Congratulations."

"Thanks."

He sat down on the bed and pushed aside the pile of linens to make room for Maggie to sit next to him. She remained standing.

"You okay?" he asked.

"No, I'm not okay."

"What's the matter? I thought you'd be overjoyed."

"Overjoyed? Didn't you hear about Bobby?" Maggie said, her voice rising.

"Oh yeah, well…"

"Well, what?"

"Well, you knew he was terminal."

"So… fucking… what…"

Maggie was glad she didn't have anything in her hand because she was sure she would have thrown it at him.

"Don't you get it?" she asked, her voice even louder now.

"You don't have to shout."

"Yes, I do," she replied.

"What don't I get?"

"Anything, you don't get anything," she said.

She moved over to the opposite wall and slumped back against it. Neither spoke; the hum of the ancient boiler plant was the only sound. The milk crates rattled with the vibration of the hot water pipes.

"I cared about him, Jack; it doesn't matter to me if he was terminal or not."

"I'm sorry about your loss."

She doubted he was, but she let it go, not wanting to prolong the conversation. Instead, she got straight to the point. "What did you want to talk about?"

"I've got good news." The smile returned. "I've taken a position at Columbia."

"Okay?"

He turned up the wattage, creating shadows against the far wall. He continued to speak, explaining how Columbia had been trying to recruit him to their pediatrics faculty for several years, but Maggie was only half listening, unable to exorcise the vision of Bobby's pale and lifeless face.

"Don't you understand?" he asked.

"You got a new job?"

"Yes, at a different hospital. You know what that means."

Maggie did know what that meant; it meant she wouldn't have to see him every day of the week.

"We can still see each other," he said.

"Don't you think that's kind of a moot point now?"

Uncertainty crossed his face. "What are you talking about?"

"I'm talking about the last time we saw each other…"

"I thought you'd want to stick up for me."

"You're not the only one with a career, Maggie."

"You're still mad about that?" Foster asked.

"I wouldn't say I'm mad; I'd say I'm enlightened."

"Enlightened?"

Maggie rose to her feet, walked over, and stood in front of him. "Enlightened as to what kind of person you are."

"What kind of person is that?"

The overhead squawked in the hall, asking for Dr. Maggie Johnson to report to the Emergency Department.

"Not the kind of person for me," she said.

She slipped out of the room without a backward glance, hearing the door close with a soft *thunk*.

Epilogue

It was a beautiful Saturday evening on Central Park Lake: an armada of rowboats navigated the placid water; a raft of goslings squabbled over a crust of bread left over from someone's picnic; and the bright pink blossoms of a thousand water lilies swayed in the breeze. Frogs croaked, sparrows chirped, and the patrons of the boathouse—now on their second or third cocktail—sounded off, filling the air with a pleasant buzz.

Melendez tugged on the oars of the boat, thrusting it forward to avoid colliding with a kayak bearing down on them from the west. He left the port oar in the water, swinging the bow toward less congested waters. Once they were in the clear, he grabbed a pair of *Fat Tire Ales* from the cooler tucked against the stern and handed one to Maggie, who clinked it against the one he held.

It was the middle of August and the first day Maggie had had off in several weeks. It was also the first drink she'd had in weeks, and she took a long swallow of the ale in celebration, which prompted a chorus of exhortations from Melendez. She set the beer down on the seat and scanned the shoreline for her parents, who were meeting them for dinner. After a short search, she located them, standing atop the Bow Bridge, with Grace between them, waiving at her as if she had been lost at sea for weeks. Melendez cranked on the port oar, sending them in the opposite direction.

"What are you doing?" Maggie asked.

"We're going to dinner with them in a little while. I wanted you all to myself for now."

It was a difficult comment with which to find complaint; she sipped her beer instead and let her hand trail in the warm water.

"I see Grace has taken to your parents," Melendez said.

"They've had her all weekend. I'm a little concerned she won't want to come back on Sunday," Maggie said.

"All weekend? Does that mean we'll be alone tonight?"

"Not quite."

The smile fell from his face.

"Have you forgotten about Bobby Jr.?" Maggie asked.

Bobby Jr. was one of Whiskers' kittens. Melendez had rescued the last two from the roof of Golden Arches and taken them to his friend in veterinary school in New Brunswick. Once they'd been quarantined and immunized, he'd given one to Maggie, keeping the other—which he'd named Maggie—for himself.

"How are things at Golden Arches?" Melendez asked.

"We survived the July Phenomenon relatively unscathed."

The July Phenomenon was the name of the perceived increase in medical errors and surgical complications during the first few weeks of July in teaching hospitals across the country. Despite not being confirmed by medical studies, the nurses loved to propagate the myth of morbidity and mortality, referring to it as the 'killing season.'

"Yoda doing okay?" he asked.

"Yoda? I thought you didn't like her?"

"She's alright."

"Yoda is Yoda. Yoda will always be Yoda. It's one of the things I love about her," Maggie said.

Melendez rested the oars on the keel; the boat drifted into a mass of lily pads. "How are you doing?"

Maggie shrugged. "Okay, I guess. I miss Bobby, but I keep trying to tell myself he's better off…"

I can die now in peace.

An angry goose swam at them, wings extended, hissing maliciously, trying to chase them away from its territory. Melendez tried to shoo it away with an oar, but he eventually gave up and moved them back into the middle of the lake.

"Thanks for coming to his funeral," Maggie said.

Father McDaniel had said Bobby's funeral mass at the Chapel of Perpetual Mercy. Other than Maggie and Melendez, only Yoda and Saundra Mills had attended—and the OSG strictly because she'd had paperwork to sign.

"You still got his ashes?"

Maggie nodded. They were in an urn she had made in a ceramics class she'd taken at Brown, sitting atop the table next to her bed.

"That's weird, Maggie."

She shrugged. "Maybe it is, but honestly, I don't care. It makes me feel better to know he's not alone."

Melendez checked his watch and started rowing back to the boathouse, where Grace and Maggie's parents were waiting by the shore. "How much longer are you going to have Grace?" he asked.

"Don't know. Tammy Hunter has been trying to find a permanent home for her, but with all of her issues, it hasn't been easy." Maggie finished her beer and slid the empty into the cooler, taking advantage of the proximity to Melendez to plant a kiss on his lips. "I've been managing okay. Grace has Medicaid now, which pays all her medical bills, and she has a full-time home health aide."

"A full-time aide? Medicaid can't be paying for that."

"Tammy Hunter found some grant money that pays for the aide and helps me with the rent on my new apartment as well."

With Grace living with her, Maggie's old flat on Murray Hill had been too small, so she'd moved into a two-bedroom apartment on the Upper East Side, which, in addition to being a lot roomier, was close enough to Golden Arches to walk.

Maggie continued, "And my mother helps out as often as she can, which is pretty often. So, we're doing okay."

"How about your dad?"

Maggie glanced over at the shoreline; Roger Johnson was standing with his back to them, his phone stuck to his ear. She shrugged.

Melendez rested the oars and let the boat float in the direction of launch area. A gull squawked above them, barely audible over the singing of the cicadas. Several children played soccer on a small plot of ground behind the boatyard, hollering as if it were the finals of the World Cup.

Behind them, a lone boy, ten or eleven by the looks of him, sat against the bole of a tree, staring at a book. He looked up as they coasted in; for a second, Maggie thought he looked familiar. A group of people walked past, obscuring her view, and after they passed by, he was gone. Maggie searched for him among the pines that dotted the shoreline, spotting him shuffling in the other direction. She watched him limp away, growing smaller and smaller, until he turned a corner and was lost to sight.

Made in the USA
Coppell, TX
04 August 2020

32373794R00156